Christmas at The Mysterious Bookshop

Christmas at
The Mysterious
Bookshop

'Tis the Season to be Deadly

Stories of Mistletoe and Mayhem
from 17 Masters of Suspense

Edited by Otto Penzler

Vanguard Press
A Member of the Perseus Books Group

Copyright © 2010 by Otto Penzler

All rights reserved. No part of this publication may be reproduced, stored in a retrieval system, or transmitted, in any form or by any means, electronic, mechanical, photocopying, recording, or otherwise, without the prior written permission of the publisher. Printed in the United States of America. For information, address Vanguard Press, 387 Park Avenue South, 12th Floor, New York, NY 10016, or call (800) 343-4499.

Designed by David Janik

Set in 11 point Excelsior

Cataloging-in-Publication data for this book is available from the Library of Congress.

First Vanguard Press edition 2010

ISBN: 978-1-59315-617-6

Published by Vanguard Press
A Member of the Perseus Books Group
www.vanguardpress.com

Vanguard Press books are available at special discounts for bulk purchases in the U.S. by corporations, institutions, and other organizations. For more information, please contact the Special Markets Department at the Perseus Books Group, 2300 Chestnut Street, Suite 200, Philadelphia, PA, 19103, or call (800) 810-4145, ext. 5000, or e-mail special.markets@perseusbooks.com.

10 9 8 7 6 5 4 3 2 1

For Claiborne Hancock and Jessica Case
Stylish publishers and dear friends

Table of Contents

Introduction

Book stores have been a place of worship and wonderment for me since I was a child and little has changed in the ensuing decades. One of the enduring thrills of my fortunate life is when visitors to my own store have kind things to say about it.

While it is a great source of emotional joy and pride, The Mysterious Bookshop offers little in the way of financial benefits; just ask my valued but underpaid staff! Like most independent bookshops, it engages in a mighty struggle against the chain store behemoths, the 800-pound online gorilla, and the newest attacker of old-fashioned book stores, electronic books. Nonetheless, if we don't quite flourish, we endure, and it is largely due to the friendship of our loyal customers and the generosity of the mystery writing community.

As a way of thanking our customers for their support, I have commissioned an original story from some of the finest mystery writers in America each Christmas season for the past 17 years. These stories are then published in handsome booklets and given to my customers as a Christmas present. The only criteria for the authors to follow were that the stories should be set during the Christmas season, involve a mystery, and have at least some of the action take place at The Mysterious Bookshop.

The resultant stories have ranged from humorous to suspenseful to heartwarming. They have been so loved that customers from whom we rarely hear (alas) make a point of ordering books during the holiday season just to be sure they get a copy of the latest booklet. They have become highly collectable, too, single stories selling (we have heard) for more than the price of this entire collection.

None of it would be possible without the warm friendship shown by the authors of these stories, of course. Trust me when I tell you they didn't do it for the money. Even if *Christmas at The Mysterious Bookshop* hits the best-seller list, it won't change the lives of the contributors. It may, on the other hand, influence the life of the bookshop. My entire share of royalties goes directly to the bookshop's bank account, which will thrill my creditors.

It should be pointed out that The Mysterious Bookshop, which opened on Friday the 13th of April, 1979, was located at 129 West 56th Street for nearly 27 years. It was well-known for its two stories connected by a spiral staircase, with my very elegant office at the back of the second floor. The store moved down to 58 Warren Street in Tribeca in October 2004 to a larger, more modern (if less cozy) space.

It's also worth mentioning that, although I am a real person, the character with my name who appears in several of these stories is fictional.

Have a very merry Christmas!

—Otto Penzler, 2010
The Mysterious Bookshop
58 Warren Street
New York, N.Y. 10007
www.mysteriousbookshop.com

Give Till It Hurts

By Donald E. Westlake

It was hard to run, Dortmunder was discovering, with your pockets full of bronze Roman coins. The long skirt flapping around his ankles didn't help, either. This hotel is either too damn big, he told himself, huffing and puffing and trying to keep his pants up under this bulky white dress, or it's too small.

Okay, the dress isn't really a dress, it's an aba, but it gets in the way of running legs just as much as any dress in the world. How did Lawrence of Arabia do it, in that movie that time? Probably trick photography.

Also, the sheet on his head, called a keffiyeh, held on by this outsize cigar band circlet called an akal, is fine and dandy if you're just walking around looking at things, but when you run it keeps sliding over your eyes, particularly when you have to go around a corner and not run straight into the wall, like now.

Dortmunder turned the corner, and here came a half dozen of his fellow conventioneers, Arabian numismatists jabbering away at each other and kicking their skirts out ahead of them as they walked. How did they *do* that?

Dortmunder braked hard to a walk, to a stroll, and fixed a brotherly smile on his face as he approached the approaching sheiks, or whatever they were. "Sawami," he said, using the one word he'd found that seemed to work. "Sawami, sawami."

They all smiled back, and nodded, and said some stuff, and proceeded on around the corner. With any luck, the cops would arrest one of *them*.

Here's the thing. If you happen to hear that in a big hotel in midtown Manhattan there's going to be a sale of ancient coins, where most of the dealers and most of the customers are going to be rich Arabs, what can you possibly do but dress yourself up like a rich Arab, go to the hotel, mingle a little, and see what falls into your pockets? If the dealer with the heavy beard and the loud voice hadn't also happened to see what was falling into Dortmunder's pocket, everything would have been okay. As it was, he'd eluded pursuit so far, but if he were to try to leave the hotel by any of its known exits he was pretty sure he'd suddenly feel a lot of unfriendly hands clutching at his elbows.

What to do, what to do? Getting out of this OPEC drag wouldn't help much, since his pursuers had no doubt already figured out he was a goof in sheik's clothing. In fact, wearing it helped him blend in with the hotel's regular guests, so long as he didn't have to engage in conversation more complicated than, "Sawami sawami. Sawami? Ho, ho, sawami!"

And at least he wasn't got up in Santa Claus rig. Every year around this time, with shiny toys in the store windows and wet snow inside your shoes, wherever there might happen to be any kind of a robbery in a public setting, the cops *immediately* would nick the nearest Saint Nick, because it is well known that Santa Claus is every second-rate second story guy's idea of a really terrific disguise.

Not Dortmunder. Better a sheet among sheiks than a red suit, a white pillow and handcuffs. Leave your camel at home.

NO ADMISSION. That was what the door said, and that was perfect. That was exactly what you would look for when you're on the run, a door that says *No Admission*, or *Authorized Personnel Only*, or *Keep Out*: any of those synonyms for 'quick-exit.' This particular door was at a turn in the corridor, tucked away mostly out of sight in the corner of an L. Dortmunder looked down both lengths of empty hallways, tried the knob, found it locked, and stepped back to consider just what kind of lock he was expected to go through here.

Oh, that kind. No problem. Hiking up his skirt, reaching into a coin-laden pants pocket, he brought out the little leather bag of narrow metal implements he'd once told an arresting officer was his manicure set. That cop had looked at Dortmunder's fingernails and laughed.

Dortmunder manicured NO ADMISSION, pushed the door open, listened, heard no alarm, saw only darkness within, and stepped through, shutting the door behind him. Feeling around for a lightswitch, his fingers bumped into some sort of shelf, then found the switch, flipped it up, and a linen closet sprang into existence: sheets, towels, tissue boxes, soap, quart-size white plastic coffee pitchers, tiny vials of shampoo. Well, hell, *this* was no way out.

Dortmunder turned and reached for the doorknob and felt a breeze. Yes? He turned back, inspecting the small but deeply crowded room with all his eyes, and there at the rear was a window, an ordinary double hung window, and its bottom half was just slightly open.

What floor am I on? Dortmunder had gone out windows before in his career that had turned out to be maybe a little too high up in the air for comfort and he'd lived to regret it, but at least he'd lived. But where was he now?

The window was behind shelves piled with towels. Dortmunder moved towels out of the way, leaned his head in between two shelves, pushed the window farther open and looked out into December darkness. A kind of jumbled darkness lay in an indefinite number of stories below, maybe three, maybe five. To the right were the backs of tall buildings facing 57th Street and to the left were the backs of shorter buildings facing 56th Street.

Didn't people make rope ladders out of sheets? They did; Dortmunder followed their example, first tying the end of a sheet around the handle of a coffee pitcher and lowering that out the window, then tying sheets together and playing them out until he heard the far-away *clunk* of the pitcher against something hard.

Far away.

Don't look down, Dortmunder reminded himself, as he tied the top sheet to a shelf bracket and stripped at last out of his Middle East finery and switched off the linen closet light, but then he had to figure out how to get this body from this position, standing in the dark linen closet, to hanging on sheets outside the window. How do you get from here to there? To slide between the shelves and out the window head first seemed utter folly; you'd wind up pointing the wrong way, and you wouldn't last long. But to get up on the shelf and through that narrow opening feet first was obviously impossible.

Well, the impossible takes a little longer, particularly in the dark. *Many* parts of himself he hit against the wooden edges of the shelves. Many times he seemed certain to fall backward off a shelf and beat his head against the floor. Many times he had all of himself in position except one arm, on the wrong shelf, or maybe one knee, that had found a way to get into the small of his back. Then there came a moment when all of him was outside the window except his left leg, which wanted to stay. Ultimately, he was reduced to holding onto the sheet with his teeth and right knee while pulling that extra leg out with both hands, then in a panic grabbing the sheet with every molecule in his body just as he started to fall.

The sheets held. His hands, elbows, knees, thighs, feet, teeth, nostrils and ears held. Down he went, the cold city breeze fanning his brow, his descent accompanied by the music of ancient coins clinking in his pocket and tiny threads ripping in the sheets.

The jumbled darkness down below was full of *stuff*, some of it to be climbed over, some to be avoided, none of it friendly. Dortmunder blundered around down there for a while, aware of that white arrow on the side of the hotel in the evening dark, pointing its long finger directly at him, and then he saw, up a metal flight of stairs, a metal grillwork door closed over an open doorway, with warm light from within.

Maybe? Maybe. Dortmunder tiptoed up the stairs, peered through the grill, and saw a long high room completely encased by books. A library of some kind, well lit and totally empty, with a tall Christmas tree halfway along the left side.

Dortmunder manicured the metal door, stepped through, and paused again. At this end of the room was a large desk and chair, at the far end a long marble-topped table, and in between various furniture; sofa, chairs, and a round table. The Christmas tree gave off much bright light and a faint aroma of the north woods. But mostly the room was books, floor to the ceiling, glowing amber in the warmth of large faceted overhead light globes.

At the far end was a dark wooden door, ajar. Dortmunder made for this, and was halfway there when a short gray-haired guy came in, carrying two decks of cards and a bottle of beer. "Oh, hi," the guy said. "I didn't see you come in. You're early."

"I am?"

"Not *very* early," the guy conceded. Putting the cards on the round table and the beer on a side table, he said, "I have this right, don't I? You're the fella Don sent, to take his place, because he's stuck at some Christmas party."

"Right," Dortmunder said.

"Pity he couldn't make it," the guy said. "He always leaves us a few bucks." He stuck his hand out. "I'm Otto, I didn't quite get your ... "

"John," Dortmunder said, fulfilling his truth quota for the day. "Uh, Diddums."

"Diddums?"

"It's Welsh."

"Oh."

Two more guys came into the room, shucking out of topcoats, and Otto said, "Here's Larry and Justin." He told them, "This is John Diddums, he's the guy Don sent."

"Diddums?" Justin said.

"It's Welsh," Otto explained.

"Oh."

Larry grinned at Dortmunder and said, "I hope you're as bad a player as Don."

"Ha ha," Dortmunder said.

Okay; it looks like there's nothing to do but play poker with these people, and hope the real substitute for Don doesn't show up. Anyway, it's probably safer in here, for the moment. So Dortmunder stood around, being friendly, accepting Otto's offer of a beer, and pretty soon Laurel and Hardy came in, Laurel being a skinny guy called Al and Hardy being a non-skinny guy called Henry, and then they sat down to play.

They used chips, a dollar per, and each of them bought twenty bucks worth to begin. Dortmunder, reaching in his heavy pockets, pulled out with some wadded greenbacks and a couple of bronze coins, which bounced on the floor and were picked up by Henry before Dortmunder could get to them. Henry glanced at the coins and said, as he put them on the table and pushed them toward Dortmunder, "We don't take those."

Everybody had a quick look at the coins before Dortmunder could scoop them up and slip them back into his pocket. "I've been traveling," he explained.

"I guess you have," Henry said, and the game began. Dealer's choice, stud or draw, no high-low, no wild cards.

As Dortmunder well knew, the way to handle a game of chance is to remove the element of chance. A card palmed here, a little dealing of seconds there, an ace crimped for future reference, and pretty soon Dortmunder was doing very well indeed. He wasn't winning every hand, nothing that blatant, but by the time the first hour was done and the cops began to yell at the metal grillwork door Dortmunder was about two hundred forty bucks ahead.

This was Otto's place. "Now what?" he said, when all the shouting started out back, and got to his feet, and walked back there to discuss the situation through the locked grill.

Looking as though he didn't believe it, or at least didn't want to believe it, Al said, "They're raiding our poker game?"

"I don't think so," said Henry.

Otto unlocked the door, damn his eyes, and the room filled up with a bunch of overheated uniformed cops, several of them with new scars and scrapes from running around in that jumbled darkness out there. "They say," Otto told the table generally, "there was a burglary at the hotel, and they think the guy came this way."

"He scored some rare coins," one cop, a big guy with sergeant's stripes and Perry on his nameplate, said. "Anybody come through here tonight?"

"Just us," Larry said. Nobody looked at Dortmunder.

"Maybe," one of the cops said, "you should all show ID."

Everybody but Dortmunder reached for wallets, as Otto said, "Officer, we've known each other for years. I own this building and the bookshop out front, and these are writers and an editor and an agent, and this is our regular poker game."

"You all know each other, huh?"

"For years," Otto said, and grabbed a handy book, and showed the cop the picture on the back. "See, that's Larry," he said, and pointed at the guy himself, who sat up straight and beamed a big smile, as though his picture was being taken.

"Oh, yeah?" The cop looked from the book to Larry and back to the book. "I read some of your stuff," he said. "I'm Officer Nekola."

Larry beamed even more broadly. "Is that right?"

"You ever read William J. Caunitz?" the cop asked.

Larry's smile wilted slightly. "He's a friend of mine," he said.

"Of ours," Justin said.

"Now there's a real writer," Nekola said. "He used to be a cop himself, you know."

"We know," Larry said.

While the literary discussion went on, Dortmunder naturally found himself wondering: Why are they covering for me here? I came in the back way, I showed those coins, they don't know me for years, so why don't they all point fingers and shout, "Here's your man, take him away!" What's up? Isn't this carrying the Christmas spirit a little too far?

The symposium had finished. One of the cops had gotten Justin to autograph a paperback book. The cops were all leaving, some through the front toward the book store, the rest returning to the jumbled darkness out back. Otto called after them, "In case anything comes up, how do we get in touch with you people?"

"Don't worry," Sgt. Perry said. "We'll be around for hours yet."

And then Dortmunder got it. If these people were to blow the whistle, the cops would immediately take him away, meaning he would no longer be in the game. *And he had their money.*

You don't do that. You don't let a new guy leave a poker game after one measly hour, not if he has your money, not for *any* excuse. And particularly under these current circumstances. Knowing what they now knew about Dortmunder, his new friends here would be replaying certain recent hands in their minds and seeing them in a rather different light.

Which meant he knew, unfortunately, what was expected of him now. If this is the quid, that must be the quo.

Otto resumed his seat, looking a bit grim, and said, "Whose deal?"

"Mine," Justin said. "Draw, guts to open."

Dortmunder picked up his cards, and they were the three, five and seven of spades, the queen of hearts and the ace of clubs. He opened for the two dollar limit, was raised, and raised back. Everybody was in the hand.

Since it didn't matter what he did, Dortmunder threw away the queen and the ace. Justin dealt him two replacements and he looked at them, and they were the four and six of spades.

Has anybody ever done what before? Dortmunder had just drawn twice to an inside straight in the same hand, and made it. And made a straight flush as well. Lucky, huh? If only he could tell somebody about it.

"Your bet, John," Justin said.

"I busted," Dortmunder said. "Merry Christmas." He tossed in the hand.

It was going to be a long night. Two hundred and forty dollars long.

Schemes and Variations

By George Baxt

Christmas in NewYork. No longer the kind that once inspired Yuletide songs destined for a prominent place on *The Hit Parade*. Yet after sixty-two years, the Rockefeller Center Christmas tree was still a big attraction. It towered over the ice skating rink, facing Fifth Avenue as proud as an aged whore who could still score tricks. A bunch of vendors catered to the holiday tourists, mostly women from all points of the country wearing stretch pants that emphasized their watermelon-sized buttocks. Two-fisted women with a nosh in each hand, clutching a knish, a hot dog, an oversized pretzel, a soft drink, wearing backpacks or sporting oversized handbags stuffed with boxes of cookies, candies and sandwiches wrapped in tin foil, prepared for the famine they thought might overrun the city.

They were unaware that a murderer was threading his way among them, hurrying to a destination six streets further uptown and dreading to let his employer know the mission was unaccomplished. His victim didn't have the manuscript, just as two earlier victims didn't have the manuscript. Damn these victims; did they have to be such disappointments?

Two hours earlier at Kennedy Airport, a young man in an ill-fitting chauffeur's uniform stood at an arrival gate. The

jet from San Francisco was on time — a rarity for this particular airline, noted for its poor service but pretty stew-
ardesses. The chauffeur held high a cardboard on which was
crudely penciled: JONATHAN LAKE. He had seen a snap-
shot of the man standing in front of the Fifth Avenue Library
with a woman who seemed to look impatient. Lake, in his
sixties, looked like a diplomat and carried an attache case
that added to the impression.

Now the chauffeur studied the faces of the men disembark-
ing. They were mostly young or middle-aged, carrying suit bags,
briefcases or department store shopping bags stuffed with gifts.
Most of them looked as though the parade had passed them by,
if there had ever been a parade. There were squeals of delight
as some of the passengers were greeted by friends and relatives
and business associates. The chauffeur heard a strong voice
telling him, "Young man, I am Jonathan Lake." He could have
been announcing the second coming of Christ.

"Oh, good," said the chauffeur, "I was beginning to think I
might have missed you."

"I am rarely missed," said Lake with authority. "I was making a date with a stewardess. Pretty thing. Redhead. I'm par-
tial to redheads — especially when they whisper in my ear,
'what are you doing later, dear?' Terribly brazen, don't you
think?" His eyes twinkled and the chauffeur wasn't sure he
believed him. "She must think I'm disgustingly rich."

You are disgustingly rich, thought the chauffeur, who knew
him to be one of the world's most respected dealers in rare
books and manuscripts. Lake was questioning him.

"Who sent you? I didn't order a limousine."

"I'm from Otto Penzler. The Mysterious Bookshop."

"And on the seventh day he rested. How nice of Otto to be so
considerate. I had no idea he knew I was arriving. Thank God
you're not from that deadly Dora Lester woman." The chauffeur picked up Lake's overnight bag, then reached for his attache case. Lake pulled back. "I'll carry this myself."

"Yes, sir, " said the chauffeur.

Traffic into New York was worse than usual, almost bumper

to bumper. The chauffeur was a careful driver. He had no choice. Although Lake felt as though they were advancing towards the city by inches, they actually were doing about twenty miles an hour.

"I loathe Christmas," said Lake.

The chauffeur said nothing.

"It's a conspiracy between Macy's and K-Mart. The only worthwhile thing the communists ever accomplished was the abolishment of Christmas." He paused and said, "I hate Yom Kippur worse. Christmastime you at least can feast. On Yom Kippur you aren't allowed to eat, which is why Chinese restaurants are always jammed then. Don't tell me we're on the Triboro Bridge!"

"We are, sir."

"Well, you certainly snuck that one up on me." He paused. "Why didn't you take the Fifty-Ninth Street Bridge?"

"Jammed. Bumper to bumper. I used it coming to the airport. I was afraid I'd be late."

"Did I tell you where I'm staying?"

"No, sir. I was about to ask."

"The Plaza. I always stay at The Plaza. If you have to stay someplace in New York that isn't a friend's apartment, stay at The Plaza. Despite Donald Trump, the Oliver North of real estate."

The limousine was leaving the bridge. Jonathan Lake peered out the window. "This is Harlem. What are we doing in Harlem?"

"I'm taking a short cut, sir. This will take us to Second Avenue. At Seventy-Second Street I'll cut over to Fifth Avenue and then down Fifth to the hotel."

Lake was still staring out the window. "Where are we? Why are we on this street? There's nothing here but derelict buildings. There's not a soul in sight. Not even a mugger. Young man! This is dangerous! What the hell are you doing?"

The chauffeur had parked outside a ruined brownstone. He got into the back seat with Lake, pointing a handgun at Lake's head.

"This is crazy," Lake sputtered. "This can't be happening to me."

"It's happening to you. Open your bag and the attache case."

"Take my money. Go ahead. I've got lots of money." He was reaching into his jacket for his wallet.

"Don't, and make believe you did."

Lake was perspiring despite the freezing temperature outside. "I was only reaching for my wallet."

"Open the bag and the attaché case."

Lake said, "The keys are in my coat pocket."

"Which one?"

"This one. The left." The chauffeur patted the pocket. He felt the keys. There was no weapon.

"Okay," said the chauffeur, "now use the keys and be quick about it."

When the bag and the attaché case were open, the chauffeur rummaged about in them.

"I can't imagine what you're looking for!"

"The manuscript, damn you," exploded the chauffeur. "The God damned manuscript!"

"I have no manuscript! I have contracts and agreements, that's all I have. I'm only here for a couple of days to close two deals. That's the truth! I'm telling you the truth! I have no manuscript with me! What is this manuscript I'm supposed to be carrying?"

"The Dashiell Hammett, you idiot! The Dashiell Hammett!"

The bullet smashed into Lake's head, between his eyes, just above the bridge of his nose, no improvement on the cosmetic surgery Lake had endured forty years earlier, thereby miraculously turning a Levitsky into a Lake. The chauffeur stared at his victim with a look of distaste that seemed to suggest that he, the chauffeur, had been the victim. He scattered the contents of the overnight bag across the back seat and floor and then emptied the contents of the attaché case. He carefully moved the body so he could retrieve Lake's wallet without getting blood on his jacket. Lake hadn't lied. There were lots of hundred dollar bills. The chauffeur pocketed them, whistling *Jingle Bells* to honor not only the murder, but the season.

He hurried away from the scene of his crime, wondering whether the *Post* and the *Daily News* would try to surpass each other in lurid reporting. It might even make *The New York Times*. After all, Jonathan Lake was a reputable dealer in rare books and manuscripts, certainly worthy of coverage by them. The chauffeur looked at his wristwatch. There was still time to get back to his dreary fourth floor walk up on 48th Street between Fifth and Madison. Time to change into his Levi's (fashionably torn at the knees) and his thick sweater, time to push his way back to his job through the crowds of tourists on Fifth Avenue.

About twenty minutes later, a little old lady walking her mangy mutt bravely looked into the back seat of the limousine at the body of Jonathan Lake staring sightlessly at the roof inside the limousine. "Oh, my," she said softly, "what lovely brown eyes." She said to the mutt, "Look, Clinton dear, we have another new neighbor."

Detective Pharoah Love sat at his desk in the newly opened Harlem precinct to which he and his partner, Detective Albert West, had been temporarily assigned in order to bring order to the chaos of a newly opened police station. Asked by a detective if they knew what they were doing in Harlem, Pharoah sassily told him, "We're guest stars, sweetheart." There was no sass in Pharoah now. He was groaning.

"Stop groaning," said Albert, "it doesn't help."

"Me it helps. Another dead book dealer. Who needs another one?"

"Who do you think might be killing them?" asked Albert as he unwrapped a ham and cheese on seedless rye.

"Not a bookworm. Oh, God. This is the third book dealer iced in only two months. Do you realize, Albert, do you realize that this is the third murder? Three's not only a crowd, now three means we've got a serial killer." He slapped his hands on his thighs, imitating Jimmy Durante's familiar gesture. He even sounded like Durante. "That's just what New York needs.

Another serial killer." He addressed another detective in the room, adorably named Bill Robinson Anderson by an adoring grandmother who had doted on the late Negro tap dancer, Bill Robinson. "Forensics do a thorough job on the limo?"

"There was little to do. It was rented from an outfit on Second Avenue and 51st Street and paid for with a stolen credit card by a young guy in a chauffeur's uniform."

"Anybody describe his face?"

"Nothing disturbing. Young. Nothing unusual about the face except it seemed washed. He got into the car around two this afternoon. Said it would be back by six or so."

"Jonathan Lake," said Pharoah. "Very big in the rare book world, according to my friend Otto Penzler. Based in San Francisco. You inform his family?"

"They took it very hard. That is, the son I spoke to was all shook up. Lake's lawyer is away for the holidays and it'll be weeks before they can get to his will."

"Heartbreaking," said Pharoah. "Albert, how can you eat when we've got another corpse on our hands!"

"It's not on our hands, it's in the morgue with, I assume, an identifying tag around a big toe. This ham is stringy."

"Bitch, bitch, bitch. That's all you do is bitch. Give me a bite."

Albert obliged and, as Pharoah chewed, he asked Bill Robinson. "You're positive the son said he wasn't carrying a manuscript? A very valuable manuscript?"

"That's what the son said," said Bill Robinson. "He also said he wished he had been carrying it, as it's probably very heavily insured. Except his father didn't own the manuscript. Never even saw the manuscript."

"Beats hell," said Pharoah. "A lost manuscript by Dashiell Hammett supposedly turns up after all these years." He leaned back and stretched his arms. "Nice title. *The Thin Woman*."

Dora Lester was a thin woman. She was also a very determined woman. She was an ardent collector of rare books and manuscripts. She possessed more than enough wealth to indulge her literary passion. She traveled the world in search of rare treasures. She made tenacity a respected word. She was in Otto Penzler's office the day after Jonathan Lake's murder, though Penzler wished she were somewhere else, like maybe climbing a mountain in the Himalayas. The office was his private library, an immense room in a converted brownstone, covering almost half of the second floor. The walls held shelves on every available space and the shelves held thousands of rare volumes—all mysteries and detective stories, a treasure. Otto was attempting an inventory with the aid of Alex Giddons, the young man who managed his book store. Alex stood on a ladder rattling off titles to Otto, who checked them against a list on his desk. At least that's what they would have been doing if Dora Lester hadn't entered unannounced.

"Otto, I must have the Hammett."

Otto folded his arm and leaned back in the swivel chair. "I don't have it. If it exists, I don't know who does. It's never been offered to me." He wished he had a magic wand with which to tap her on the shoulder and cry "Vanish!"

"I do a lot of business with you," Dora reminded him.

"And you know I'm grateful. I hope we continue to do a lot of business."

"Find the Hammett. *The Thin Woman*."

Otto said to Alex Giddons who was stifling a yawn, "*Cherchez la femme*."

"*La Thin Femme*," said Alex.

Otto turned to Dora Lester. "Dora, I wish I could conjure up some kind of genie to locate that manuscript . . ."

Pharoah Love entered.

"Speak of the devil," said Penzler. Albert West followed Pharoah into the room. He was eating a hot dog. "Albert," said Penzler, "you're always eating."

"I think he's pregnant," said Pharoah.

"Really!" exclaimed Dora Lester.

Otto made the introductions.

Pharoah didn't like thin lips. Dora's lips were painfully thin, covered with lavish dollops of rouge to make them look fat. It didn't help. Pharoah loathed heavy make-up on women almost as much as he loathed it on men. He asked Penzler, "Am I interrupting business?"

"No," said Penzler. "Mrs. Lester is interested in buying the Hammett manuscript."

"Do you know where it is?" Pharoah asked the woman.

"If I did, I'd be there."

"Christmas present?" asked Pharoah.

She favored him with a thin smile. "To myself."

"I'd be careful," said Pharoah. "Seems to me there's a curse on it. Three dead men. You know any of them?"

"I knew them all," said Dora. "I know every rare book dealer in the world."

"You should be in *Guinness*. Or else drink it." He said to Penzler, "Will you be long?"

Dora Lester picked up the cue. "I'm leaving. Don't let me down, Otto. Whatever you do, don't let me down. Nice to meet you," she said to the detectives. "Seasons Greetings. Alex, would you see me out?"

Alex climbed down from the ladder, looked at Otto who winked, and followed Dora Lester out of the room, closing the door behind him at Pharoah's request. Otto said to the detectives, "Sit." They sat.

Pharoah asked Otto, "You ever hear of a book collector named Wylie Emerson?"

"Wylie Emerson. My God. He still alive? If he is, he's ancient."

"He's alive. Living in the West Nineties. Was a close friend of Hammett and Lillian Hellman. I asked him about *The Thin Woman*."

Otto leaned forward eagerly. "And?"

"And he said come up and see me sometime. I thought I'd collect you and have you along for immoral support."

"I wouldn't miss this for the world. Wylie Emerson. I'll be damned. Don't be disappointed by the size of his collection. As I recall being told, it's quite modest."

"I was never a size queen," said Pharoah. "Right Albert?"

"Leave me out if it!" said Albert.

"Ever since he was a reluctant boy scout, Albert has detested camping. Sit up and paw the air, Albert, and I'll buy you *souvlaki*."

Penzler was still dwelling on Wylie Emerson. "It was Hammett who put Emerson on to collecting. I'll bet he has some Hammett first editions."

"Stop slavering," cautioned Pharoah.

"If he does, I hope he needs money. You know, Emerson wrote some pretty good thrillers of his own. Years ago. He burned out early and turned to acting. Shafted by the blacklist and then little was heard of him. Until Hellman died and left him a nice sum, I was told."

"Nice of her."

"She wasn't all that nice. She was a bona fide, certified, bitch."

"Ah, the good old days!" said Pharoah, "I find myself growing very nostalgic for nostalgia. Let's head uptown."

Otto led the way to the room on the second floor that looked out on 56th Street and where there were more shelves filled with books. Alex Giddons sat behind a desk and Otto told him they were on their way to see an ancient book collector he'd thought long dead. Otto led the way down the spiral staircase that led to the first floor of the store and its paperback treasury. The paperback division manager was busy writing up a sale but wasn't too busy not to size up the detectives and guess that's what they were. He had long suspected they would catch up with Otto for something or another. He had a mean streak in him which Penzler seemed to appreciate.

Albert West took the wheel of the unmarked police car which he and Pharoah always occupied. Penzler sat in the back. Of course they discussed the three murders, especially the one freshest on their minds. Penzler had known and respected all three victims, but didn't find it necessary to say he liked them. Albert made excellent time going uptown despite the holiday traffic being diverted to Broadway from Columbus Avenue, which was being torn up from 59th Street to 96th Street to replace old sewer pipes, which were probably the only things in New York older than Wylie Emerson.

Albert found a parking space in front of the building in which Wylie Emerson lived. "This old building," said Albert West, "is a very old building. It probably has a very old elevator."

They entered the foyer and Pharoah found Wylie's apartment number. Pharoah pressed the intercom button and began a patient wait, assuming the old man was making slow progress from wherever he had been to answer the intercom. Finally the box squawked and they heard, "Who is it?" It was an old man's voice but one with plenty of moxie still in it. Pharoah announced himself. In response to a series of clicks, Albert West opened the door that led to a hallway with graffiti-painted walls and a variety of odors, none terribly pleasant.

Albert sniffed the air. "Very nostalgic. Reminds me of the morgue."

"Awfully cute graffiti," said Pharoah with irony, "a censor's paradise." They arrived at the elevator at the end of the long narrow hall and Pharoah pressed the Up button. They soon heard creaks and groans and other unpleasant noises that filled them with apprehension. The elevator's descent was a slow one. From the upper floors they could hear hard rock and sappy soap opera dialogue and a few screams and a woman yelling at someone called "Puta," probably a daughter.

The elevator arrived. Pharoah opened the door. More graffiti on the walls, including some racial slurs. The men entered, Albert pulling the door closed behind him. Pharoah pressed the third floor button. "Third floor," muttered Penzler grimly.

"Keep the faith," urged Pharoah, "God is our co-pilot."

The elevator creaked and groaned its way slowly to the third floor. Finally it came to a halt.

"Third floor," announced Pharoah, "rare books, old manuscripts, fading dreams and lost hope. We want Three-D." Albert found it. He pressed the doorbell.

From behind the door they heard, "I'm coming, I'm coming."

Pharoah asked, "At his age?"

Slowly the door opened a few inches. There was a safety chain. Pharoah spoke up. "Mr. Emerson? I'm Pharoah Love, the detective. Remember? The attorney for the Hammett estate told me to contact you."

"Pharoah Love, fine. Now who are the other two?"

Pharoah identified Albert West and Penzler.

"Penzler the publisher?" His voice had gone up an octave. "Paying Wylie Emerson a visit? Oh my, oh my." He shut the door and then released the chain. Emerson opened the door wide and they saw the remnant of what once must have been a tall, handsome man with the air of a bon vivant. Wylie Emerson, stooped with sloped shoulders, wore an old smoking jacket patched at the elbows. His no longer white shirt was decorated with a woolen scarf wrapped around his neck. He shook hands and indicated they follow their noses down the hall to the living room. He bolted the door and followed them.

Pharoah was startled to see a fireplace with a smoldering fire. The furniture was old and worn. Yellowing manuscripts were piled on a rolltop desk. There were books on shelves and books stacked on the floor; worn velvet drapes covered the windows.

"A real live fireplace," said Pharoah.

Emerson smiled. "I don't use it very often. Only for company. It's very draughty in here. It's an old building, even older than I am. Please sit, gentlemen. I have tea bags. Are you interested in tea?"

Pharoah said, "We're interested in a Dashiell Hammett manuscript."

"No tea?"

"We haven't much time. Albert and I mustn't be late for choir practice at Riker's Island. We're in a program of Christmas carols."

Emerson eased himself into a straight-back chair with wooden arms. "I have none of Dash's manuscripts. Miss Hellman left me quite a lot of money, but none of the artifacts. Most of his stuff was sold off to pay his bills. What manuscript in particular did you have in mind?"

Pharoah spoke. "The one he was said to have completed shortly before his death. *The Thin Woman*."

Emerson chuckled. "You too? A couple of dealers tracked me down the same way you did, but I had to disappoint them just as I have to disappoint you. I saw in the papers they were murdered. I saw in this morning's *Times* another one was murdered yesterday. He was on his way to see me, you know. Jonathan Lake. He wouldn't believe I didn't have the manuscript. So I invited him for tea. So now, I suppose, he's on a slab in the morgue where I doubt if they're serving tea." He folded his arms. "Gentlemen, I could have told you this over the phone, but I hunger for company, even if only for a few minutes. Nobody visits me anymore. There's nobody left. They're all dead or uninterested." He leaned forward. "Let me tell you, if there had been such a manuscript, Lillian would have had it published." He extended his arms lavishly. "Think of what a publishing coup it would have been! A Hammett novel after three decades of silence." He shook his head sadly. "*The Thin Man* finished him. What little he wrote after that was junk. The plot for a B movie that starred Melvin Douglas and Fay Wray, *Woman In The Dark*. A radio series he created but never wrote. A comic strip he helped create and also never wrote, though the syndicate claimed he did." He sighed. "Dashiell Hammett. Another literary tragedy. Tell me, Mr. Penzler, are you possibly in the market for a detective story with Dash as the protagonist? I've been working on it for years. When it's finished, I'll send it to you."

"I'll look forward to it," lied Otto graciously.

"Oh, yes. I almost forgot. There's a crazy lady who tracked me down."

"Dora Lester?" asked Pharoah.

"That's her. She visited me last week, again no thanks to the lawyer for Dash's estate. She had this young man with her."

Pharoah sat up. "Do you remember his name?"

"She didn't introduce him. He just leaned against the wall staring at me like a character out of *The Maltese Falcon*. Anyway, she was very unpleasant. She examined all of my manuscripts, especially the ones on the desk. She kept insisting I was hiding the one you're all after. Fortunately, the social worker who looks in on me every weekday arrived. He's a big black buck. Name's Tyrone. He hustled them out of here." He favored Pharoah. "Can you tell me something?"

"What do you want to know?"

"Why do the young men today wear their blue jeans torn at the knees? It's so slovenly looking."

"So are most of the young men today," said Pharoah.

Otto had wandered over to the desk, examining the manuscripts while Emerson watched him. Emerson said, "Believe me, the manuscript is not here."

"I'm sure it isn't," said Penzler. He was riffling the pages of a manuscript. "This one of yours?"

Emerson sighed. "Yes. Unpublished. Unwanted. An orphan."

"May I read it?"

Emerson got to his feet with effort. "You want to read it? You really want to read it?"

"Maybe I can do something with it. Maybe as a curio."

Emerson laughed. "It certainly is a curio." He was at Penzler's side reading the manuscript's title page. *Arrows In The Dark.* "Oh, yes! Oh, yes! It's about an insane American Indian on the loose in Central Park. I always thought it was good. Please. Please read it. I'd appreciate it. Here's an envelope." He opened a drawer and extracted an envelope. "And here's my card." There were several on top on the desk. Penzler accepted the card, put the manuscript in the envelope, and said to the detectives, "It's late. I should be getting back."

Pharoah and Albert followed him to the front door with Wylie Emerson bringing up the rear, bubbling with unimportant chatter, once again filled with hope. Someone was going to read his manuscript. At the door they said their goodbyes. The elevator door opened and a massive black man emerged. He saw Emerson with the three strangers. "Pop," he boomed, "you okay?"

"Oh, yes, Tyrone. Oh, yes. These are friends." He gurgled on about Penzler and the manuscript as Albert held the elevator while Pharoah said, "Tyrone, I'm glad you're on our side."

Five minutes later, they were seated in the unmarked police

car, listening to Otto offer a theory. "Alex Giddons, my manager, wears nothing but torn jeans at the knees."

"So do a lot of other guys," said Pharoah.

"He moonlights for Dora Lester."

"Stud?" asked Pharoah, always in the market for a juicy piece of gossip.

"Possibly. Also does odd jobs for her."

Pharoah suddenly remembered. "In your office, when she was leaving, she asked Giddons to see her out. Does he usually escort the ladies to the exit?"

"He usually ignores them. He's a very strange man. A damned good manager, but a very strange man. He never receives personal calls. He never makes any. No friends visit him at the store."

"There was no way Giddons could have known we were going to see Emerson unless he was listening at the door after I asked him to close it."

"He wouldn't dare. My assistant, Linda, works in the space separating the two offices. My editorial staff on the third floor frequently comes down to talk to me. There's a lot of traffic on my floor."

Pharoah now held the envelope containing the manuscript. "You going to read this?"

"Yes, and I'm going to buy it, too." Penzler smiled. "Merry Christmas, Pharoah."

"What's the deal on this manuscript?"

"Why, Pharoah. Shame on you. It's *The Thin Woman*, discovered at last!"

Half an hour later, Dora Lester answered her phone. "Yes?" She listened. Her eyes widened. Her lips trembled. "I want it!" she cried. "I don't care what it costs! I want it! I want it!"

When Pharoah and Penzler left the car to enter The Mysterious Bookshop, Albert West hurried across the street to a local delicatessen to buy himself some cookies. Pharoah and Penzler had gone upstairs with Penzler waving the envelope at Giddons. "We've got it! We finally got it!"

Pharoah took the envelope, claiming it as police evidence

while following Penzler into his office. Giddons reached for a phone. In the delicatessen, Albert seemed to be having difficulty choosing his cookies. There was such a tempting array in the showcase. "Hmm," he hmmmed while looking out the window, which afforded him an excellent view of the bookshop.

In the shop, Alex had gone downstairs to the stock room. He put on his heavy sweater and a windbreaker. He reassured himself the handgun was in the windbreaker's right hand pocket. He heard Pharoah descending the staircase shouting a last goodbye to Penzler. The last-minute Christmas shoppers in the store managed to move to one side as Pharoah made his excuses while he pushed his way past them. Alex Giddons wasn't as polite and just missed getting hit over the head with a woman's handbag.

Outside, the street was bustling with pedestrian traffic, everyone ignoring everyone else, their minds on purchases yet to be made or on the Big Macs waiting to be ordered and consumed. Pharoah was at the unmarked car about to open a door when a voice behind him said with menace, "Stand still. Not a move. Don't turn around." Nobody on the street noticed anything was amiss. Pharoah knew better than to be astonished by anything going on in the streets of New York, but he was astonished anyway. Alex had the envelope under his left arm.

From behind him, Alex heard, "Stand still. Not a move. Don't turn around. You might crush my cookies."

Pharoah said, "Albert. If it's toll house cookies again I'll scream."

Alex screamed—the cry of a wounded forest animal. He shoved Pharoah to the sidewalk and turned to shoot Albert. Albert was too quick for him. He pulled his trigger as the bag of cookies fell to the pavement. Several women shrieked, as did several men. Alex crumpled to the pavement atop the bag of cookies. Pharoah moved swiftly and disarmed Alex.

"Oh, my God! What did he do?" asked a handsome woman walking her dog, Emma.

"What did he do? He crushed our cookies, that's what he did!"

Otto and his staff were on the street, Otto taking charge of the envelope. A taxi pulled up and Dora Lester struggled out of the back seat. Alex whimpered from the pain of the bullet in his shoulder as Albert cuffed his hands behind his back. Bystanders wondered why Dora Lester was screaming something about wanting a thin woman. "I suppose nowadays you really can't tell," said one woman to a friend, "but she doesn't strike me as being a lez-bean. What do you think?" Her friend shrugged.

Pharoah held Dora Lester by the arm. "Mrs. Lester, lend me your ear. I'm going to read you your rights." Albert had already read Alex his.

"I want the manuscript! I want the manuscript!" Dora Lester was crazed. Penzler took the manuscript out of the envelope and held up the title page for her to read.

"*Arrows In The Dark*," she whimpered. Then she shouted. "Alex! You said they had the manuscript! This is not the manuscript! Where's the manuscript?"

Pharoah winked at Penzler and helped Dora Lester into the unmarked police car where Alex Giddon sat in pain in the front seat, slumped against the door.

Pharoah lowered his window and shouted, "Merry Christmas, darlings! Have a nice day!"

Uptown, in his apartment, Wylie Emerson had poured another glass of wine for himself and Tyrone. "Just think, Otto Penzler is going to read my novel." He handed the glass of wine to his companion. "You know, Tyrone, because you're my best friend. In fact, you're my only friend." Tyrone said nothing. "I hope Mr. Penzler finds something worthwhile in that manuscript. It's really an embarrassment. It was written by a dear friend who was an alcoholic, but still a dear friend. It had a different title than the one it has now. I gave it a new title to protect it from unscrupulous people who were after it. I wonder if Mr. Penzler will recognize what he got."

The Theft of the Rusty Bookmark

By Edward D. Hoch

Driving through the slushy streets of Greenwich Village on a brisk December afternoon, Nick Velvet saw a clerk standing in front of a flower shop smoking a cigarette. In the old days, when he was growing up in the Village, that man would have been a lookout, ready to sound the alarm if any cops appeared to break up the high-stakes gambling in the back room. But times had changed and now it was just a guy who wasn't allowed to smoke on the job.

Nick had driven down from Westchester, something he hated to do during the Christmas shopping season. An old school chum, Charles O'Neill, had phoned him that morning on an matter, promising to pay double Nick's usual twenty-five thousand fee for a rush job. That was enough to get him into the car, despite Gloria's complaint that he'd promised to go shopping with her. And that was enough to have him squeezing into a parking space on Hudson Street near the White Horse Tavern.

O'Neill was a few years younger than Nick but they'd played baseball together in high school and been casual friends ever since. His classy Greek Revival house was a few blocks back, past the flower shop, and Nick nodded to the smoker as he went by. This was not his first visit to the O'Neill place. Charles owned a sports catering service that had brought him into contact with certain mob elements in the past. He was a good family man with a pretty wife and a couple of cute kids. But his troubles with the mob wouldn't go away. His brother-in-law, Bob Temple, had been killed at home a year earlier and no one really believed the knife had been wielded by a crack addict breaking into houses at random. Charles feared the mob had sent a warning that he should sell the business and go into some other line of work.

"Good to see you again, Nick," Charles O'Neill greeted him at the front door. "Merry Christmas."

"You're five days early but I'll take a drink anyway if you're offering one. What's up? More trouble with the mob?"

O'Neill led him into the big living room with its polished hardwood floor and oversized mirrors reflecting the myriad ferns and flowering plants with which his wife Ida had decorated the place. "I have no mob contacts, Nick. You should know that." He picked up a decanter from the sideboard. "Too early in the day for bourbon?"

"A bit. A cold beer would be fine if you have one."

Charles O'Neill chuckled. "The first time we ever met you were drinking a beer." He opened a small refrigerator below the sideboard and took out a bottle. "I think you were eighteen at the time."

Nick declined a glass and took a sip. Even on a chilly day it tasted good. "How are Ida and the kids?"

"Fine. They're out seeing Santa Claus with my sister."

Nick took another sip of beer. "Now what's your problem?"

"Are you familiar with The Mysterious Bookshop on West 56th Street?"

"I've passed it. Down the street from Carnegie Hall's stage door."

"That's the place. A man named Otto Penzler owns it, and in addition to selling new books he buys and sells used mysteries, especially valuable first editions. Buys them from all over the world."

Nick glanced at the single bookcase with its collection of book club titles. "Are you a collector?"

"I'm barely a reader. Those are Ida's books. My brother-in-law Bob was the mystery fan. Did you know him?"

"Bob Temple? Never met him but I saw your sister once."

"His death was a terrible blow to Marci. And then there were all the rumors of a mob killing. No truth to it, of course. He was probably stabbed by some drug addict looking for money." O'Neill laughed sadly. "The house was full of books, not money."

"Where does The Mysterious Bookshop figure in to all this?"

"My sister Marci has been wanting to clear out Bob's things ever since he was killed. She thinks it's morbid to keep them and I agree. But she just can't bring herself to go through everything. Just after Thanksgiving she and Ida spent a week at a beauty spa on Long Island. While they were gone I packed up all Bob's mysteries and sold them to Otto Penzler. He paid a pretty good price for them and best of all it got them out of the house—about four hundred books in ten boxes."

"Then what's the problem?"

"I sold something I shouldn't have. Now I need to get it back. I need you to steal it for me."

"Valuable books are like cash or jewels. You know I don't touch anything of value."

"This isn't a book. It's a bookmark in one of the mysteries I sold."

"Go in and tell Penzler about it."

"I can't do that. He'd probably want a fortune for it."

"Nowhere near the fortune you're offering me to steal it."

O'Neill looked pained. "It's got a little silhouette of Sherlock Holmes on it. Penzler collects things like that. He might not sell it at any price. Besides, I know you'll keep your mouth shut about it."

"All right," Nick said with a sigh. "What does it look like and what book is it in?"

"It's a thin strip of copper with some rust on it—a combination bookmark and letter opener, really. But I don't know just where it is."

"How many books are there?"

"He bought them all—over four hundred, all hardcover. I took them to the store in my van and helped carry them up to his private study. It's a big room on the second floor with his personal library in it. He said he'd have to store the books there until he could price them after Christmas. This is their busy season at the store. So that gives us a few days, at least."

"I'll need time to flip through four hundred books. That means breaking in at night."

Charles O'Neill shook his head. "The store has a good alarm system, and Penzler lives right upstairs. You wouldn't have time to find it before you were discovered."

"Then I'll go in while the store is open."

"I can tell you Penzler and his assistant are in and out of that study all the time. There are several other employees too, and they make sure no one goes in there."

"I'll find a way."

"It has to be before Christmas, and that's Monday. The store will probably be closed on Sunday too. So you've only got till Saturday."

He was interrupted by the opening of the front door and the voices of women and children. Ida O'Neill, a dark-haired, pale-skinned beauty, entered with her two young daughters and Charles's sister Marci. Nick put down his empty bottle and said hello to them all.

"We saw Santa, Daddy!" the youngest girl hurried to tell her father. The older one, at an age to know better, simply smirked.

Ida O'Neill turned to Nick. "It's good to see you again. You know Charles's sister, don't you?"

"I believe we met once years ago," Nick said. Marci Temple was one of those almost-pretty women who relied on cosmetics to complete the job nature had left undone. She was a bit younger than her brother and Ida, and seeing her now Nick couldn't help but remember how her husband had died. He and Marci had been awakened around three a.m. by an intruder. Bob had gone to investigate and Marci had heard a tussle and a scream from her husband. She found him dying from a throat wound and immediately phoned the police. He was dead when they arrived a few minutes later. The knife-wielding slasher had escaped.

"*I* remember you," Marci Temple said, shaking Nick's hand. "It was when we were both a lot younger."

"What brings you into town today?" Ida asked, shucking the winter coats from her daughters. "Christmas shopping?"

"I suppose you could call it that," Nick said. He glanced at his watch and told Charles O'Neill, "I really must be getting back. Gloria will wonder what's happened to me."

"I'll be hearing from you?"

"Before the end of the week," Nick promised. When Charles walked him to the door he noticed the man was still smoking in front of the flower shop. "That guy must really be hooked on cigarettes."

O'Neill chuckled. "No, they run a craps game in the back of the flower shop and he's the lookout for the cops. It's just like the old days."

"Yeah," Nick said and walked to his car.

🌲🌲🌲

The first thing he did, that same afternoon, was to drive uptown to 56th Street and leave his car in a parking garage while he paid a visit to The Mysterious Bookshop, a narrow brownstone building about halfway down the block between Sixth and Seventh Avenues. Its front window was decorated for the holidays, with tinsel and Christmas ornaments mixed among the books. A sign in one corner announced that mystery writer Lawrence Block would be signing copies of his newest Matt Scudder novel the following afternoon from four to six.

He walked down a few steps to the door. It was locked and he had to press a buzzer to be admitted. The store itself was small and crowded, the shelves stocked with paperbacks and a central table featuring new hardcover books. It took him a moment to realize there was another floor upstairs. He made his way up a spiral staircase to the hardcover department, where bookshelves stretched from floor to ceiling and a ladder was necessary to reach the top. Comfortable chairs seemed to invite reading but here too there were more buyers than browsers as Christmas approached. He glanced at the books, at an extensive Sherlock Holmes section, and even at a pile of back issues of *Ellery Queen's Mystery Magazine,* where somewhat fictionalized accounts of his exploits appeared regularly.

A man he quickly identified as Otto Penzler was speaking on the telephone with someone, apparently a collector, making notes as he talked. When he finished he went quickly through a small connecting room into a large rear study. Nick caught a glimpse of bookshelves, with boxes piled on the floor, before an employee informed him that the area was private. He glanced around some more, noting a large metal fire door that led out to the building's staircase. There were apartments and offices on the upper floors, but he could see no way that these would help him. He had to be in that back room long enough to go through four hundred books, and that was a problem. The alarm system seemed to be a good one, making a night visit difficult and dangerous. Doing it by day meant keeping Penzler and the other employees out of that room for a half-hour or longer.

Nick shifted ideas around in his head, weighing each in turn. He could have Gloria phone the store at a prearranged time, pretending to be a collector with a large library to sell. Nick could slip into the study while Penzler was occupied on the phone. But he realized a flaw in the idea almost at once. Surely there was another phone in the study, and it was only by chance that Penzler had taken today's call out in the store itself. The odds were greater that he'd speak to a collector from his study.

Still, he had the beginning of another idea. The big problem was time, but there might be a way to work around that. The rusty bookmark wasn't made of paper or cloth or plastic, after all. It was made of metal.

🎄🎄🎄

By the following morning he'd worked it out. He would do it that day because the appearance by Lawrence Block would bring more traffic to the bookshop, and more traffic would mean more confusion with the Christmas crowds. A call to the public library brought him the names of a half-dozen well-known book collectors who specialized in mysteries. He looted Gloria's shelves of a handful of old mysteries she'd planned to donate to the Salvation Army, and then went out to purchase a particular piece of equipment that he'd need.

Gloria came upon him as he was fitting everything into a large box. "You just bought that thing this morning and you're taking it away already?"

"I need it for a job," he answered vaguely. He stuffed paper into the box along with his gadget, then arranged the books on top of it. After sealing the box with tape he typed a label to Otto Penzler, using the name of one of the book collectors for the return address. Beneath the collector's address he typed and underlined: Letter follows!

From his closet he chose a brown shirt and a pair of brown slacks, with a brown jacket to wear over it. Gloria was doing some computer work when she saw him and groaned. "It's the UPS man again!"

"It works, doesn't it? Everyone trusts a UPS man."

"What if they ask about your truck?"

"It's parked down the block. Couldn't get any closer."

"I hope he's paying you enough for working Christmas week."

"Double."

She nodded and went back to her computer. "Good luck."

🌲🌲🌲

At exactly ten minutes to five that afternoon Nick Velvet crossed the street in front of The Mysterious Bookshop carrying a large brown box. At the bookshop door he rested it on the steps and rang the bell for admittance. He could see the place was jammed with customers and autograph seekers.

When the door buzzed he poked his head in and said, "Delivery for Otto Penzler."

"I can't take care of you with all these people waiting," the bearded man behind the desk said. "Otto is upstairs. We're having an author signing. Can you get up there with that box?"

"I'll make it," Nick assured him, edging toward the spiral staircase.

Otto Penzler stood near the top of the stairs, refilling a guest's wine glass. "Who's this from?" he asked, bending to read the label. "Carl Fox! I wonder what he's sending me. Haven't spoken to him in years."

"On the label it says Letter follows. Probably got delayed in the Christmas mail."

Penzler led Nick through the crowd toward the study door. "All right. Put it in the back room, will you? On the floor against the wall."

"Sure thing!"

"You're not our usual UPS man."

"Working a double shift for Christmas. It's our busy time."

Penzler glanced at the sea of faces surrounding the table where Lawrence Block was signing books. "You're telling me!"

Nick hurried through the doors into the book-lined study. There seemed to be boxes everywhere, but he quickly spotted the group of ten that O'Neill had described. He'd expected Penzler to open the box he'd delivered, at least for a look, but he'd been too busy for that. Now Nick opened it and reached beneath Gloria's books for the hand-held metal detector he'd hidden there. It was the type sometimes used at airports and high-security events to search for weapons. He adjusted it to its most sensitive setting and ran it quickly over the boxes of books. He figured he had less than a minute before Penzler or someone else came looking for him.

Nothing sounded the warning beep on the first pass over the boxes so he moved a couple of them and tried it again from a different angle. This time he was rewarded with a buzz and a blinking light. He opened the box and quickly flipped through a couple of the books. A slender piece of copper, tapered to a point at one end, slid out of the second book. From its shape and size it looked more like a letter-opener than a bookmark, but he could see the rust along the edges. He slipped it into a plastic bag in his pocket and turned off the metal detector, placing it under his jacket. Then he quickly resealed the box with a piece of tape and left the study, returning to the crowded bookshop.

Otto Penzler was busy trying to line up people waiting for autographed books. He never looked in Nick's direction as Nick slipped down the stairs and out the front door to the street. In another moment he was mingling with the Christmas crowd.

🌲🌲🌲

Charles O'Neill sighed gently as Nick took the plastic bag from his pocket and laid it on the coffee table. "One rusty bookmark, as ordered."

"You're a wizard, Nick. Always have been." He produced an envelope full of currency and slid it across the table.

They were seated in O'Neill's living room later that same evening. Ida was upstairs with the children, getting them ready for bed, and the sounds of laughter drifted down to them. Children were always happy in the days before Christmas.

"There's just one thing—"

"What's that?"

"Those spots of rust along the edges of the bookmark. Copper doesn't rust. Only iron does. Copper is slow to corrode and when it does the corrosion products are green, not rust-colored. This is something else, something like dried blood."

O'Neill was silent for a moment. "Take the money, Nick. You've earned it."

But Nick Velvet wasn't quite through talking. "Bob Temple was killed with that bookmark or letter opener, wasn't he? There was never a burglar. The killer had to dispose of the weapon quickly so it went into one of the hundreds of books in Temple's collection, just before the police arrived. Who killed him? Who slashed his throat with that thin strip of copper with its pointed end? It had to be Marci, of course. Your sister Marci. It couldn't have been anyone else."

"Don't get into this, Nick. We've been friends for too long."

"You wouldn't pay fifty grand for just anyone. If you'd killed him yourself you'd know where the weapon was hidden and you wouldn't have sold the books to Penzler without removing it. Likewise if your wife Ida had done it she would have removed the weapon on one of her visits to Marci's place over the past year. Only Marci could safely leave that bloodstained bookmark where it was. With Bob dead the books were hers, and they were in her house. She never dreamed you'd do her the favor of packing them up and selling them while she was out of town."

Charles O'Neill shook his head, and there may have been tears in his eyes. "When she got back and found the books gone, she was wild with fear. She had to tell me. They'd both been drinking and he hit her. It wasn't the first time. She grabbed up that bookmark—it's actually sold as a combination bookmark and letter opener—and struck out at him. She didn't mean to kill him."

"The police have to be told, Charles," Nick said quietly. "It's for a jury to decide what she meant to do."

The sounds from upstairs had finally ceased, and Ida came down alone. "They're in bed," she said. "Let's get the Christmas tree up."

"I'll speak to Marci after Christmas," O'Neill told Nick quietly. "Then I'll tell her what she has to do."

Nick nodded and slid the envelope back across the coffee table. "Use this to hire a good lawyer."

"Nick—"

He turned to Ida. "Could you use some help in putting up that Christmas tree?"

♣♣♣

It was after Christmas before Otto Penzler had an opportunity to look into the big box that had arrived from Carl Fox. No letter had followed as promised, and he was puzzled by the wads of paper with a dozen or so books on top. Finally he phoned Carl on the west coast, but the collector knew nothing of the package.

"It wasn't from me, Otto. You know I don't work that way."

"I'm baffled by the whole thing. Why should anyone send it to me and put your name on it?"

"Is there anything of value inside?"

Otto was staring down at the box as he spoke. "That's the funny thing about it, Carl. Most of the books are junk, but among them is a mint first edition of Sue Grafton's *"A" Is For Alibi*. It could bring a thousand dollars. Why would anyone just give it away like that?"

Murder for Dummies

By Ron Goulart

In a way, it was The Mysterious Bookshop that inspired him to commit the crimes he did.

Rufe Petticord was a tall, thin man, red-haired and freckled, a year shy of fifty. He usually dropped into the West 56th Street store whenever he was in Manhattan to have lunch with an editor or an argument with his literary agent.

On this particular white afternoon in late December of last year Rufe was standing there leafing through various books in the display of new hardcover mystery novels. His aging overcoat was speckled with melting snowflakes and he was muttering and cursing.

"Oh, sure, for crying out loud, this is just exactly what we need," he observed in his thin nasal voice. "Another halfwit book about yet another lady private eye. Fourth big printing yet."

Slamming the fat book shut, he selected another and scanned the first page.

"Lousy opening, geeze. Flatfooted prose." He brought the book closer to his eyes, squinting. "Crappy typography, too."

Shutting that, he sampled a new one.

"Oy, good golly, I write much better stuff than this. Heck, a baboon with nothing but a third grade education could write something superior to this bilge."

The next book he sampled drew no comment from Rufe. "Tripe," he decided after perusing two paragraphs of yet one more.

Otto Penzler, dapper and grey-bearded, was descending the spiral staircase from the second floor, eying the disgruntled author. "Merry Christmas, Rufe," he said as his foot touched the final step.

"Garbage." Rufe held up a bestseller. "What you've got on display here is garbage."

"We would have preferred a manger with a bunch of little sheep, but it wouldn't fit on the table."

Rufe turned, spread his thin arms wide and indicated the walls of shelves and the thousands of paperback mysteries. "A ton of crapola and not one book by me."

"We don't get much call for juvenile mysteries, Rufe, so I can't really stock too—"

"Young adult," he corrected. "I don't write for juveniles. I'm the favored mystery novelist of the young adult reader."

"We don't get much demand for YA books either."

"Do you know what's been said about my Dibble Triplets, Teen Detectives series?"

"Behind your back, you mean?"

"By critics, Otto, by respected literary figures. They say my stuff is *inspired, unputdownable* and *chillingly original.*"

Nodding, Penzler said, "By the way, Rufe, I don't mind your coming in every so often and messing up the displays, but some of the customers have been objecting to your muttering and cursing."

"Yes, honesty and truth often meet with suppression."

"Well, I'd better—"

"I bet you haven't even read my latest Dibble Triplets mystery for Jugend House Books—*The Mystery of the Scary Old Cemetery*—have you?"

"No, but it's on my bedside stack," Penzler assured him.

"Everybody in this business is a wiseass," complained Rufe. "Well, I'm a damned good writer and eventually you're all going to have to admit it."

"Have you thought about trying an adult mystery?"

"I've written seventeen of the damned things." Rufe tightened his faded muffler. "They remain unsold because I've been unfairly labeled as a kids' writer. And my halfwit agent, Bix Gretter, won't lift a finger to help me out of the young adult ghetto."

Buttoning up his overcoat, the red-haired writer strode to the door. "I'll make it onto the bestseller list one way or the other," he promised. "Then you'll have to display my work."

Rufe yanked open the glass door and dived out into the afternoon snow storm.

"Who was that?" asked the young man at the cash register.

"Nobody," answered Penzler.

As Rufe drove his 9-year old Toyota home from the train station, the twilight snow suddenly changed to hail. Big pellets of the stuff came crashing down on the rusted hood.

"The end," he observed, "of a perfect day."

Windward was a small town that sat on the Connecticut side of the Long Island Sound. Its homes were a mix of heavy Victorian, 1930s modern and an occasional gross misunderstanding of the basic theories of Frank Lloyd Wright.

Rufe turned the car into the white gravel drive that led to the three-story Victorian mansion he was living in at the moment. The house rose up at the rear of an acre of wooded grounds and belonged to a cousin who was spending the winter in a warm spot in the Caribbean.

As he parked the car in the big shadowy garage between his absent cousin's two gleaming Mercedes, he heard the phone ringing inside the house. A dog also started barking.

Carefully, he let himself into the house. "It's only me, Aldo," he called out.

Hurrying across the long hallway, he ducked into the parlor and picked up the telephone. "Yeah—what?"

"You're sure overflowing with the Christmas spirit, buddy." It was his agent.

"Now what, Bix? Didn't you unload sufficient bad news on me at lunch?"

Bix Gretter said, "Hey, don't kill the messenger. I'd spare you this if I could."

Barking and galloping sounded in the hall.

"Hold on a second, Bix. Back, Aldo. It's me, your interim master. Get back, schmuck!"

A huge white dog came hurtling at him, snarling, growling. It hit him in the chest and knocked him over.

Rufe scrambled to get free, whapping the snarling animal over the head with the phone. "Down. Sit. Be a good dog."

Aldo whimpered, rubbed a paw across his head and eyed the redheaded writer. Reluctantly, he backed off a few feet and sat, glowering at him.

"Sorry, Bix. You were saying?"

"What the heck just occurred at your end, buddy?"

"The usual homecoming welcome. My cousin's dog suffers from bouts of amnesia," Rufe explained. "So what's wrong now?"

"I got a call from Aunt Jane at Jugend Books just after I returned from having —"

"There's one reason why I'm not getting anywhere in the literary world. Having to deal with an editor who insists on being called Aunt Jane."

"It's their policy at Jugend, since they deal with kids' books and such," reminded his agent. "As their CEO, Uncle Bob, was telling me only the—"

"What's the bloated old skwack want now?" He made his way, watchful of the grumpy hound, over to a loveseat and sat.

"She's unhappy about the manuscript we just turned in— *The Mystery of the Spooky Old Haunted House.*"

"Specifics?"

"Aunt Jane feels the characterizations on the Triplets aren't right in this one. The kids seem too much alike."

"They're supposed to, Bix. They're *triplets.*"

"Tell that to your editor. She thinks Don and Dean tend to make the same kind of clever remarks—and so does their sister Dora."

He watched the dog who was sitting there glowering up at

him. Rufe sighed and said, "Okay, all right. I'll take a look at the manuscript and see what I can do. How does Aunt Jane feel about the idea of increasing the size of the advance when we sign the contracts for the next three Dibble Triplets books?"

There was only silence from his agent.

"Bix?"

"Don't get ticked off, Rufe, buddy, but—well, there may not be three more."

"Geeze, why not? The sales have been—"

"Been dropping. In fact, they're rotten."

"I'm paying alimony to two wives, Bix. Isn't there anything you can do to—"

"That's what I'm trying to tell you, buddy. I've just about got her persuaded to sign for at least *one* more."

"Good, that $7500 will help."

Another silence from Manhattan.

"Bix?"

"Aunt Jane says they couldn't go beyond $5,000 for any further books.

"$5,000? Hell, I can make more flipping burgers."

"Maybe it is, seriously, time to think about a career change."

Rufe glanced at the grandfather clock in the corner. "Try to get the old dear up to $6,000, huh?" he told his agent. "Now I've got to go."

"You're not tangled up with some new psychotic woman?"

"I'm teaching that new creative writing class at the Windward Adult Ed Centre," he reminded. "Pays $32 per hour."

"Okay, don't despair."

"I'm way beyond despair already," Rufe assured him.

♣♣♣

The class, the fifth in a weekly series of eight, did not go especially well. Attendance had been dwindling and tonight only two pupils showed up in the small, chilly underground classroom.

The skinny teenage boy—Rufe never could remember his name—fell asleep just after the 8:00 p.m. break and old Mr. DeAngelo, a retired pharmacist from Bridgeport, got miffed because the young man kept snoring while he was reading aloud from the first chapter of his mystery novel in progress.

After he abruptly quit and sat, angry, back down, Rufe told him, "I'm wondering if a tough LA private detective is the best sort of protagonist for you to be working with, Mr. DeAngelo."

"Don't you start in, too. My wretched wife keeps nagging me about the same damn—"

"What I mean is—well, your private eye seems to base most of his similes and metaphors on the drug store business."

"Fooey." The erstwhile pharmacist stuffed his pages into his battered briefcase, stood up and headed for the door. "You're a lousy writer, Petticord, and a rotten teacher. You don't know your backside from your elbow."

"You, DeAngelo, can't write for sour beans," countered Rufe from behind his lopsided desk. "In fact, it's a shame they don't put out the same sort of books for halfwit mystery writers as they do for computer nerds. Then I'd advise you to rush out and grab up a copy of *Murder for Dummies*.

"Up yours." DeAngelo's feet slapped on the linoleum tiles of the shadowy hall as he took his leave.

A moment later a plump gray-haired woman in her middle sixties appeared in the doorway. Wearing slacks and a red mackinaw, she clutched a large plastic shopping bag to her bosom. "Am I too late in the semester to sign up, Mr. Petticord?" She crossed the threshold and fished a fat manuscript out of the snow-flecked bag. "I'm Donna Wimbler Harp."

"Did you ask at the office?"

"It's all closed up—probably because of the dreadful weather."

"Well, come in and sit down anyway."

The woman shed her coat and took a seat near the slumbering youth. After giving the boy a maternal smile and shaking her head, she held up her manuscript toward Rufe. "In the meantime, would you possibly be able to critique my suspense novel?"

"Well, I don't usually—"

"I'm an enormous admirer of your Dibble Triplets books, Mr. Petticord. Especially *The Mystery of the Creepy Old Church.* I couldn't put it down."

"Really? Well, thanks." He grinned. "Sure, I suppose I could read the book. Of course, I'd have to charge a token fee."

"Would $100 be enough?" She approached the desk, holding the book in both hands. "I'm a widowed beautician and I still have to watch my—"

"That's an acceptable fee, yeah." He could skim the damned thing in a couple of hours, give her a few pages of bull when he handed it back to her. And he'd clear more than he got for an evening of teaching this dimwit class.

"It's my first effort," she explained as she, gently, placed the thick stack of pages atop the desk. "It's called *Flight to Dark Death.*"

He nodded, glancing at the title page. "By Doug Harpman?"

"I prefer to use a pen name," she explained. "I really would like to know what you feel my chances of selling it are. It would be wonderful to be able to support oneself as a writer."

"Wouldn't it, though," he agreed.

♣♣♣

Standing near the high wide window of the editorial office was a small, thin young woman. She wore a short-skirted and sleeveless black dress, had a silver ring in her left nostril and a swooping vulture tattooed on her right upper arm. Her hair was a deep, dark black and she held a tiny unlit cigar clenched between her teeth. When she turned away from the view of the grey February afternoon outside, both her large earrings clicked and rattled. "So?"

Rufe smiled and took a step into the office. "Is your mother around someplace?"

"My mother, the old lush, drank herself to death during my second year in college and is now six feet under the sod out in Glendale. Her passing saddened a lot of San Pedro sailors but didn't affect me much." She came over to the large metal desk at the room's center and sat.

"Oh, then you're Morgana Bindloss?"

"Who else? Park your butt, Petticord," she invited. "I know that to a doddering old coot like you I look like a teenager."

"Well, you are sort of youthful."

"I'm twenty-four and I've been Editor-in-Chief here at Maxx Books for over two years. I came right in after the Germans bought them out—and I've doubled the damned sales."

"I'm still getting used to the fact that I'm older than most of the editors," Rufe explained. "When I started out, why, it seemed—"

"I'm not interested in sitting through a pathetic account of your shabby life, Petticord," she explained to him. "But I have to tell you that I love this book of yours—*Flight to Dark Death*. That's why I asked your dipstick agent to have you come to Manhattan for this talk."

"Yeah, Bix mentioned you were interested in the novel."

"I love it."

"Bix feels it has a sort of classic English thriller feel," he told the small young editor. "You know, in the tradition of Eric Ambler, Victor Canning, Desmond Bagley—"

"Old coots. I've never read any of that crap."

Neither had Bix, for that matter. But the agent figured the names might help sell the book.

Morgana continued, "You know, Petticord, this book of yours is about ten gazillion times better than the crap you've been turning out for Jugend Books."

"You've read my Dibble Triplets books?"

Morgana held up a forefinger. "One of the dippy things. Had it forced on me in my youth by a sow of an aunt." Her nose wrinkled. "You've sure as hell improved since then. How's $300,000?"

"It's fine—but for what?"

"As an advance, stupid," said the editor. "I want to push this one big—and I've come up with a new category. We'll push it as a historical thriller."

"It takes place in the 1970s."

"That's way back in the dim, dark past."

"Historical thriller. Sounds great."

"Let's make it, now that I think about the potential for this book, let's make it $400,000."

Rufe swallowed. "You're offering me $400,000 for this—for my book?"

"What else?" Certainly not for your body."

He cleared his throat, rubbed at his cheek. "You'll have to talk to Bix—he handles all the financial details."

Morgana rested her elbows on her desk top. "There are a couple of things I want to change."

"Oh, so?"

"First off—the title. *Flight to Dark Death.* Smells."

"Change it to what?"

"Something better. If you don't object?"

"No, call it whatever you like."

"And I want to dump this Doug Harpman penname. We're going to put your name on it."

"My name?"

"As wretched as those Dribble, Dibble, whatever—as god awful as those things are, Petticord, I figure there must be thousands of people out there who read them and know your name."

"The sales figures indicate—"

"The sales figures indicate that you and Jugend Books are about three steps from going down the old toilet," said the editor. "But your name probably has some recognition factor." Using her dead cigar as a pen, she inscribed a line of copy on the air above her desk. "*His Best Book Yet! Rufe Petticord Grows Up—With A Bang!*"

"That sounds good, yeah."

"So you have no objection to putting your own name on this book?"

This was where Rufe could have backed down and admitted the truth. He sat there for a quiet minute, eyes on the young editor's tattooed vulture. "No," he told her, "that'll be just fine."

Early in March, on a rainy evening, Rufe finally went and had a talk with Dora Wimbler Harp. She lived alone in a small cottage that sat by itself at the edge of a seventy-acre nature preserve in the nearby town of Brimstone.

He parked his car behind a stand of maples near the brown shingle house and ran through the downpour to the front door.

Dora, just home from work and still wearing her pale blue beautician's uniform, opened the door wide and smiled out at him. "Well, finally, Mr. Petticord. I was really wondering when I'd be hearing from you again,"

"I'm sorry if I've seemed to be avoiding you, Mrs. Harp, but—"

"I know you've had other things on your mind, what with your class being canceled and all," she said, inviting him in. "But I did, you know, give you my manuscript *and* my $100 way back before Christmas last year."

"I really want to apologize about that, yes." He followed the plump gray-haired woman into a small, cozy, cluttered parlor.

"I left several messages on your answering machine, but I didn't want you to feel I was hounding you." Dora nodded him into a fat Morris chair. "Coffee?"

"Not just yet."

She looked at him, frowning. "Was my book so awful that you didn't want to give me the bad news?"

"No, not at all. In fact, it's quite good."

"Really now? You aren't simply saying that?"

"It's extremely well done."

She seated herself on a loveseat facing him. "And do you think there's a chance of selling it to a publisher?"

Leaving his chair, Rufe wandered to the mantelpiece and tapped his finger on a marble bust of Edgar Allan Poe. "Well, as a matter of fact," he began. "Well, it's. . ."

She leaned forward on her chair. "I can't quite hear you, Mr. Petticord. Speak up."

Rufe returned to his chair and sat. "Okay, here's actually what's happened," he said, slowly, not exactly looking at her. "I started to read your *Flight to Dark Death* that same night that you turned it over to me, Mrs. Harp. Expecting the usual amateur effort, I was—well, bowled over."

She chuckled. "Really? My, that's certainly nice to hear." She reached down and picked a large framed photo off the coffee table. "This is my nephew, Charlie Wimbler."

"Nice looking young man. Now let me explain what—"

"I think I like him better without this curly beard." Dora set the photo down. "Charlie's a freelance Egyptologist and I'm not exactly sure where he is now. But, when he's in the States he stays here with me. I've told him all about my novel and I know he'll love to hear what you're telling me."

"Good, fine." He cleared his throat. "See, about your book. I found myself sitting up all night reading it. It was—"

"Unputdownable?"

"Exactly. So what I decided to do was show it to my agent."

"Oh, that was extremely thoughtful of you. I never dreamed I'd be able to get a big-time literary agent to look at my novel."

"The point is, Mrs. Harp," said Rufe, looking over at Poe. "Well, you'll have to believe that, initially, I wasn't planning any sort of dishonest—"

"I'm afraid I don't quite understand."

"You have to remember that the name signed to the book was Doug Harpman," he told her. "What I did, I dropped the manuscript off at my agent's office. I plumped it down on his desk and said, 'I'd like your opinion of this, Bix.'"

"Bix—that's an unusual name."

"It is, yes. Anyway, Bix was just on his way out to lunch with an important magazine editor—and, well, I didn't exactly get to explain that it was *your* book he was getting."

"New York agents are awfully busy I imagine."

"About a month later Bix finally got around to looking at the manuscript. He thought it was absolutely terrific, sat up all night, felt it was—"

"Unputdownable?"

"Right. In fact, without even telling me, he sent it over to the top editor at Maxx Books."

"Oh, that's a very prestigious publishing house. Yes, they publish all those wonderful best selling mysteries by William F. Nolan."

"They do," agreed Rufe. "The editor at Maxx loved the book—and she made a substantial offer."

Dora clapped her hands together and chuckled again. "How substantial?"

He-studied his shoes. "A half a million dollars."

She gasped, pressing her palms against her chest. "Good gracious, that's an enormous amount of money."

He nodded his agreement. "We're coming to the part of the story that I'm not especially proud of, Mrs. Harp," he said in a faraway voice. "But this became a sort of comedy of errors and—well, the bottom line is that my agent and everybody at Maxx think I wrote that book."

She rose up slowly, frowning. "You've put them straight, haven't you?"

Rufe stood up, too, facing her. "I've been a freelance writer for twenty five years—a quarter of a century—half my damned life. I've never earned more than $46,000 a year. Then I had an offer of $500,000."

Her voice became a whisper. "You didn't tell them?"

"I didn't, no. And three days ago I signed the contracts," he said.

"That's completely dishonest."

"It is, which is why I'm confessing to you now," Rufe said. "Now, here's what I'd like to suggest as a way out of this dilemma." He returned to the mantel, turned to look at the plump woman. "You wouldn't have had a chance of getting to a publisher if I hadn't helped out. I feel, therefore, that a 50-50 split is fair. That's $250,000 for me, Mrs. Harp, and $250,000 for you."

"And whose name gets on the book?"

He coughed into his left hand. "All the publicity is already in the works—listing me as the author," he said. "But, listen, I'll dedicate the book to you. 'To Dora Wimbler Harp, without whom I could never have written this novel.'"

She put hands on her hips. "Bullshit," she observed.

"Okay, how about 'To my dear friend, Dora—'"

"I mean, bozo, that I want every flapping penny of that half a million bucks." She poked her bosom with a fat thumb. "*And*, you simpleminded jerk, the only name that's going to be on it is my penname."

"That's not right. I helped you get this deal."

"You also, schmuck, stole my book and passed it off as yours."

"Technically, Mrs. Harp, I acted as your agent and negotiated a deal for you," he pointed out. "Things, admittedly, did get out of—"

"Hooey." She scowled at him once before moving toward the doorway. "I think I'd better phone my attorney right now."

"No, don't do that." He grabbed the Poe bust off the mantel and went sprinting after her.

Catching up, he whapped her over the skull with it.

Dora groaned, took three wobbly steps, dropped to her knees on a throw rug.

He lunged, struck her head, hard, twice more.

She died and hit the rug flat out.

♣♣♣

During Christmas week this year there was an autographing party held at The Mysterious Bookshop. Rufe's novel was now titled *Death Flight* and great piles of fresh-off-the-presses copies were stacked up at the desk on the second floor of the store.

Rufe, wearing one of his favorite expensive Italian suits and tinted glasses, was sipping champagne and smiling to himself as he watched the people crowded into the small room.

Penzler, in a tuxedo, stopped beside him. "Well, you did get your signing, Rufe."

"It was inevitable." He took a sip of his champagne. "By the way, what did you think of the book?"

"Haven't had a chance to read it yet," he admitted. But it's—"

"On your bedside table. I know."

Morgana Bindloss' head appeared in the stairwell as she, clad in a crimson dress, came climbing up the spiral staircase from below. She threw him a kiss, then yelled, "Fifth printing, dear heart."

Penzler drifted away to shake hands with a short, mustached old writer that Rufe didn't know. Not anybody important.

Someone tapped Rufe on the elbow.

He turned and saw a vaguely familiar bearded man smiling at him. "Congratulations, Mr. Petticord, he said as he took hold of Rufe's arm and led him over to the corner by the Sherlock Holmes books and items. "For you." He handed him a buff-colored envelope.

"Sorry, I can only sign books."

"No, there's something inside this one you'll want to see."

Setting his glass aside, Rufe reached into the unsealed envelope. There was a Polaroid photo inside and he fished it out to look at. "Holy Christ." He made a gagging noise, shoved the picture into his coat pocket.

The photo showed a dead Dora Wimbler Harp sitting in a big white wicker chair in front of a brick wall. Her eyes were open and staring; she had a leathery, yellow look.

"I'm Charlie Wimbler," said the bearded man.

"The freelance Egyptologist," he said, remembering. "But I don't see how you could get a photograph of—"

"Of a body you buried deep in the nature preserve back in March?"

"Yeah, exactly."

"You worked it all fairly cleverly," said the nephew in a low voice that only the two of them could hear. "Burying my aunt, cleaning up the mess, then writing a suicide note on her computer. You print the damned note out, leave it with a folded uniform and her undies on the edge of the Long Island Sound. Fooled just about everybody, since Aunt Dora was known far and wide, especially to the ladies who frequented the beauty shop, as being goofy as a bedbug."

"But you were supposed to be away someplace."

He chuckled. "Nope, I'd been shacked up with a terrible woman over in New Haven," Charlie said. "As fate would have it, I got back to the cottage just as you and Aunt Dora were having your final discussion of her book."

"Why didn't you break in and—"

"I always like to listen awhile before I bust in on a party," explained Charlie. "I figured I could get a bigger share of the proceeds from you than I could from my daffy aunt."

"So you just watched and waited?"

"Sure, until the book was out and you had all sorts of dough pouring in—and you couldn't call anything off."

Rufe touched at his pocket. "This picture?"

"Oh, I dug Aunt Dora up soon after you laid her to rest, mummified the old dear and stored her in a safe place."

"And now what?"

"I want 60% of everything you make off the book."

"50%"

"60%"

"Okay, all right." Nobody had suspected him of anything all these months since he'd killed Dora Wimbler Harp. 40% of several million wasn't bad. It sure beat the hell out of grinding out more rotten Dibble Triplets books. He could coast on that kind of money for years and eventually write a really good book on his own. Once he paid off Charlie Wimbler, there'd be no way to connect him with anything criminal. "You've got a deal, Charlie."

After shaking hands, Charlie said, "Oh, and there's one more thing."

He retrieved his hand. "What now?"

"You have to turn out more thrillers like this one. And share the profits with me."

"How the hell can I do that? This was her first book and she's dead and gone."

Charlie chucked again. "Easy," he said, "we just copy them from old Desmond Bagley books the way she did."

As Dark As Christmas Gets

By Lawrence Block

It was 9:54 in the morning when I got to the little bookshop on West 56th Street. Before I went to work for Leo Haig I probably wouldn't have bothered to look at my watch, if I was even wearing one in the first place, and the best I'd have been able to say was it was around ten o'clock. But Haig wanted me to be his legs and eyes, and sometimes his ear, nose and throat, and if he was going to play in Nero Wolfe's league, that meant I had to turn into Archie Goodwin, for Pete's sake, noticing everything and getting the details right and reporting conversations verbatim.

Well, forget that last part. My memory's getting better— Haig's right about that part—but what follows won't be word for word, because all I am is a human being. If you want a tape recorder, buy one.

There was a lot of fake snow in the window, and a Santa Claus doll in handcuffs, and some toy guns and knives, and a lot of mysteries with a Christmas theme, including the one by Fredric Brown where the murderer dresses up as a department store Santa. Someone pulled that a year ago, put on a red suit and a white beard and shot a man at the corner of Broadway and 37th, and I told Haig how ingenious I thought it was. He gave me a look, left the room, and came back with a book. I read it—that's what I do when Haig hands me a book—and found out Brown had had the idea fifty years earlier. Which doesn't mean that's where the killer got the idea. The book's long out of print—the one I read was a paperback, and falling apart, not like the handsome hardcover copy in the window. And how many killers get their ideas out of old books?

Now if you're a detective yourself you'll have figured out two things by now—the bookshop specialized in mysteries, and it was the Christmas season. And if you'd noticed the sign in the window you'd have made one more deduction: i.e., that they were closed.

I went down the half flight of steps and poked the buzzer. When nothing happened I poked it again, and eventually the door was opened by a little man with white hair and a white beard—all he needed was padding and a red suit, and someone to teach him to be jolly. "I'm terribly sorry," he said, "but I'm afraid we're closed. It's Christmas morning, and it's not even ten o'clock."

"You called us," I said, "and it wasn't even nine o'clock."

He took a good look at me, and light dawned. "You're Harrison," he said. "And I know your first name, but I can't—"

"Chip," I supplied.

"Of course. But where's Haig? I know he thinks he's Nero Wolfe, but he's not gone housebound, has he? He's been here often enough in the past."

"Haig gets out and about," I agreed, "but Wolfe went all the way to Montana once, as far as that goes. What Wolfe refused to do was leave the house on business, and Haig's with him on that one. Besides, he just spawned some unspawnable cichlids from Lake Chad, and you'd think the aquarium was a television set and they were showing *Midnight Blue*."

"Fish." He sounded more reflective than contemptuous. "Well, at least you're here. That's something." He locked the door and led me up a spiral staircase to a room full of books, and full as well with the residue of a party. There were empty glasses here and there, hors d'oeuvres trays that held nothing but crumbs, and a cut glass dish with a sole remaining cashew.

"Christmas," he said, and shuddered. "I had a houseful of people here last night. All of them eating, all of them drinking, and many of them actually singing." He made a face. "I didn't sing," he said, "but I certainly ate and drank. And eventually they all went home and I went upstairs to bed. I must have, because that's where I was when I woke up two hours ago."

"But you don't remember."

"Well, no," he said, "but then what would there be to remember? The guests leave and you're alone with vague feelings of sadness." His gaze turned inward. "If she'd stayed," he said, "I'd have remembered."

"She?"

"Never mind. I awoke this morning, alone in my own bed. I swallowed some aspirin and came downstairs. I went into the library."

"You mean this room?"

"This is the salesroom. These books are for sale."

"Well, I figured. I mean, this is a bookshop."

"You've never seen the library?" He didn't wait for an answer but turned to open a door and lead me down a hallway to another room twice the size of the first. It was lined with floor-to-ceiling hardwood shelves, and the shelves were filled with double rows of hardcover books. It was hard to identify the books, though, because all but one section was wrapped in plastic sheeting.

"'This is my collection," he announced. "These books are not for sale. I'll only part with one if I've replaced it with a finer copy. Your employer doesn't collect, does he?"

"Haig? He's got thousands of books."

"Yes, and he's bought some of them from me. But he doesn't give a damn about first editions. He doesn't care what kind of shape a book is in, or even if it's got a dust jacket. He'd as soon have a Grosset reprint or a book-club edition or even a paperback."

"He just wants to read them."

"It takes all kinds, doesn't it?" He shook his head in wonder. "Last night's party filled this room as well as the salesroom. I put up plastic to keep the books from getting handled and possibly damaged. Or—how shall I put this?"

Anyway you want, I thought. You're the client.

"Some of these books are extremely valuable," he said. "And my guests were all extremely reputable people, but many of them are good customers, and that means they're collectors. Ardent, even rabid collectors."

"And you didn't want them stealing the books."

"You're very direct," he said. "I suppose that's a useful quality in your line of work. But no, I didn't want to tempt anyone, especially when alcoholic indulgence might make temptation particularly difficult to resist."

"So you hung up plastic sheets."

"And came downstairs this morning to remove the plastic, and pick up some dirty glasses and clear some of the debris. I puttered around. I took down the plastic from this one section, as you can see. I did a bit of tidying. And then I saw it."

"Saw what?"

He pointed to a set of glassed-in shelves, on top of which stood a three-foot row of leather-bound volumes. "There," he said. "What do you see?"

"Leather-bound books, but—"

"Boxes," he corrected. "Wrapped in leather and stamped in gold, and each one holding a manuscript. They're fashioned to look like finely-bound books, but they're original manuscripts."

"Very nice," I said. "I suppose they must be very rare."

"They're unique."

"That too."

He made a face. "One of a kind. The author's original manuscript, with corrections in his own hand. Most are typed, but the Elmore Leonard is handwritten. The Westlake, of course, is typed on that famous Smith-Corona manual portable of his. The Paul Kavanagh is the author's first novel. He only wrote three, you know."

I didn't, but Haig would.

"They're very nice," I said politely. "And I don't suppose they're for sale."

"Of course not. They're in the library. They're part of the collection."

"Right," I said, and paused for him to continue. When he didn't I said, "Uh, I was thinking. Maybe you could tell me. . ."

"Why I summoned you here." He sighed. "Look at the boxed manuscript between the Westlake and the Kavanagh."

"Between them?"

"Yes."

"The Kavanagh is *Such Men Are Dangerous*," I said, "and the Westlake is *Drowned Hopes*. But there's nothing at all between them but a three-inch gap."

"Exactly," he said.

🌲🌲🌲

"*As Dark As It Gets*," I said. "By Cornell Woolrich."

Haig frowned. "I don't know the book," he said. "Not under that title, not with Woolrich's name on it, nor William Irish or George Hopley. Those were his pen names."

"I know," I said. "You don't know the book because it was never published. The manuscript was found among Woolrich's effects after his death."

"There was a posthumous book, Chip."

"*Into the Night*," I said. "Another writer completed it, writing replacement scenes for some that had gone missing in the original. It wound up being publishable."

"It wound up being published," Haig said. "That's not necessarily the same thing. But this manuscript, *As Dark—*"

"*As It Gets*. It wasn't publishable, according to our client. Woolrich evidently worked on it over the years, and what survived him incorporated unresolved portions of several drafts. There are characters who die early on and then reappear with no explanation. There's supposed to be some great writing and plenty of Woolrich's trademark paranoid suspense, but it doesn't add up to a book, or even something that could be edited into a book. But to a collector—"

"Collectors," Haig said heavily.

"Yes, sir. I asked what the manuscript was worth. He said, 'Well, I paid five thousand dollars for it.' That's verbatim, but don't ask me if the thing's worth more or less than that, because I don't know if he was bragging that he was a big spender or a slick trader."

"It doesn't matter," Haig said. "The money's the least of it. He added it to his collection and he wants it back."

"And the person who stole it," I said, "is either a friend or a customer or both."

"And so he called us and not the police. The manuscript was there when the party started?"

"Yes."

"And gone this morning?"

"Yes."

"And there were how many in attendance?"

"Forty or fifty," I said, "including the caterer and her staff."

"If the party was catered," he mused, "why was the room a mess when you saw it? Wouldn't the catering staff have cleaned up at the party's end?"

"I asked him that question myself. The party lasted longer than the caterer had signed on for. She hung around herself for a while after her employees packed it in, but she stopped working and became a guest. Our client was hoping she would stay."

"But you just said she did."

"After everybody else went home. He lives upstairs from the bookshop, and he was hoping for a chance to show her his living quarters."

Haig shrugged. He's not quite the misogynist his idol is, but he hasn't been at it as long. Give him time. He said, "Chip, it's hopeless. Fifty suspects?"

"Six."

"How so?"

"By two o'clock," I said, "just about everybody had called it a night. The ones remaining got a reward."

"And what was that?"

"Some 50-year-old Armagnac, served in Waterford pony

glasses. We counted the glasses, and there were seven of them. Six guests and the host."

"And the manuscript?"

"Was still there at the time, and still sheathed in plastic. See, he'd covered all the boxed manuscripts, same as the books on the shelves. But the cut-glass ship's decanter was serving as a sort of bookend to the manuscript section, and he took off the plastic to get at it. And while he was at it he took out one of the manuscripts and showed it off to his guests."

"Not the Woolrich, I don't suppose."

"No, it was a Peter Straub novel, elegantly handwritten in a leatherbound journal. Straub collects Chandler, and our client had traded a couple of Chandler firsts for the manuscript, and he was proud of himself."

"I shouldn't wonder."

"But the Woolrich was present and accounted for when he took off the plastic wrap, and it may have been there when he put the Straub back. He didn't notice."

"And this morning it was gone."

"Yes."

"Six suspects," he said. "Name them."

I took out my notebook. "Jon and Jayne Corn-Wallace," I said. "He's a retired stockbroker, she's an actress in a daytime drama. That's a soap opera."

"Piffle."

"Yes, sir. They've been friends of our client for years, and customers for about as long. They were mystery fans, and he got them started on first editions."

"Including Woolrich?"

"He's a favorite of Jayne's. I gather Jon can take him or leave him."

"I wonder which he did last night. Do the Corn-Wallace's collect manuscripts?"

"Just books. First editions, though they're starting to get interested in fancy bindings and limited editions. The one with a special interest in manuscripts is Zoltan Mihalyi."

"The violinist?"

Trust Haig to know that. I'd never heard of him myself. "A big mystery fan," I said. "I guess reading passes the time on those long concert tours."

"I don't suppose a man can spend all his free hours with other men's wives," Haig said. "And who's to say that all the stories are true? He collects manuscripts, does he?"

"He was begging for a chance to buy the Straub, but our friend wouldn't sell."

"Which would make him a likely suspect. Who else?"

"Philip Perigord."

"The writer?"

"Right, and I didn't even know he was still alive. He hasn't written anything in years."

"Almost twenty years. *More Than Murder* was published in 1980."

Trust him to know that, too. "Anyway," I said, "he didn't die. He didn't even stop writing. He just quit writing books. He went to Hollywood and became a screenwriter."

"That's the same as stopping writing," Haig reflected. "It's very nearly the same as being dead. Does he collect books?"

"No."

"Manuscripts?"

"No."

"Perhaps he wanted the manuscripts for scrap paper," Haig said. "He could turn the pages over and write on their backs. Who else was present?"

"Edward Everett Stokes."

"The small-press publisher. Bought out his partner, Geoffrey Poges, to became sole owner of Stokes-Poges Press."

"They do limited editions, according to our client. Leather bindings, small runs, special tip-in sheets."

"All well and good," he said, "but what's useful about Stokes-Poges is that they issue a reasonably priced trade edition of each title as well, and publish works otherwise unavailable, including collections of short fiction from otherwise uncollected writers."

"Do they publish Woolrich?"

"All his work has been published by mainstream publishers,

and all his stories collected. Is Stokes a collector himself?"

"Our client didn't say."

"No matter. How many is that? The Corn-Wallaces, Zoltan Mihalyi, Philip Perigord, E. E. Stokes. And the sixth is—"

"Harriet Quinlan."

He looked puzzled, then nodded in recognition. "The literary agent."

"She represents Perigord," I said, "or at least she would, if he ever went back to novel-writing. She's placed books with Stokes-Poges. And she may have left the party with Zoltan Mihalyi."

"I don't suppose her client list includes the Woolrich estate. Or that she's a rabid collector of books and manuscripts."

"He didn't say."

"No matter. You said six suspects. Chip. I count seven."

I ticked them off. "Jon Corn-Wallace. Jayne Corn-Wallace. Zoltan Mihalyi. Philip Perigord. Edward Everett Stokes. Harriet Quinlan. Isn't that six? Or do you want to include our client, the little man with the palindromic first name? That seems farfetched to me, but—"

"The caterer. Chip."

"Oh. Well, he says she was just there to do a job. No interest in books, no interest in manuscripts, no real interest in the world of mysteries. Certainly no interest in Cornell Woolrich."

"And she stayed when her staff went home."

"To have a drink and be sociable. He had hopes she'd spend the night, but it didn't happen. I suppose technically she's a suspect, but—"

"At the very least she's a witness," he said. "Bring her."

"Bring her?"

He nodded. "Bring them all."

♣ ♣ ♣

It's a shame this is a short story. If it were a novel, now would be the time for me to give you a full description of the off-street carriage house on West Twentieth Street, which Leo

Haig owns and where he occupies the top two floors, having rented out the lower two stories to Madam Juana and her All-Girl Enterprise. You'd hear how Haig had lived for years in two rooms in the Bronx, breeding tropical fish and reading detective stories, until a modest inheritance allowed him to set up shop as a poor man's Nero Wolfe.

He's quirky, God knows, and I could fill a few pleasant pages recounting his quirks, including his having hired me as much for my writing ability as for my potential value as a detective. I'm expected to write up his cases the same way Archie Goodwin writes up Wolfe's, and this case was a slam-dunk, really, and he says it wouldn't stretch into a novel, but that it should work nicely as a short story.

So all I'll say is this. Haig's best quirk is his unshakable belief that Nero Wolfe exists. Under another name, of course, to protect his inviolable privacy. And the legendary brownstone, with all its different fictitious street numbers, isn't on West 35th Street at all but in another part of town entirely.

And someday, if Leo Haig performs with sufficient brilliance as a private investigator, he hopes to get the ultimate reward—an invitation to dinner at Nero Wolfe's table.

Well, that gives you an idea. If you want more in the way of background, I can only refer you to my previous writings on the subject. There have been two novels so far, *Make Out With Murder* and *The Topless Tulip Caper*, and they're full of inside stuff about Leo Haig. (There were two earlier books from before I met Haig, *No Score* and *Chip Harrison Scores Again*, but they're not mysteries and Haig's not in them. All they do, really, is tell you more than you'd probably care to know about me.)

Well, end of commercial. Haig said I should put it in, and I generally do what he tells me. After all, the man pays my salary.

And, in his own quiet way, he's a genius. As you'll see.

♣♣♣

"They'll never come here," I told him. "Not today. I know it will always live in your memory as The Day the Cichlids

Spawned, but to everybody else it's Christmas, and they'll want to spend it in the bosoms of their families, and—"

"Not everyone has a family," he pointed out, "and not every family has a bosom."

"The Corn-Wallaces have a family. Zoltan Mihalyi doesn't, but he's probably got somebody with a bosom lined up to spend the day with. I don't know about the others, but—"

"Bring them," he said, "but not here. I want them all assembled at five o'clock this afternoon at the scene of the crime."

"The bookshop? You're willing to leave the house?"

"It's not entirely business," he said. "Our client is more than a client. He's a friend, and an important source of books. The reading copies he so disdains have enriched our own library immeasurably. And you know how important that is."

If there's anything you need to know, you can find it in the pages of a detective novel. That's Haig's personal conviction, and I'm beginning to believe he's right.

"I'll pay him a visit," he went on. "I'll arrive at 4:30 or so, and perhaps I'll come across a book or two that I'll want for our library. You'll arrange that they all arrive around five, and we'll clear up this little business." He frowned in thought. "I'll tell Wong we'll want Christmas dinner at eight tonight. That should give us more than enough time."

♣♣♣

Again, if this were a novel, I'd spend a full chapter telling you what I went through getting them all present and accounted for. It was hard enough finding them, and then I had to sell them on coming. I pitched the event as a second stage of last night's party—their host had arranged, for their entertainment and edification, that they should be present while a real-life private detective solved an actual crime before their very eyes.

According to Haig, all we'd need to spin this yarn into a full-length book would be a dead body, although two would be better. If, say, our client had wandered into his library that morning to find a corpse seated in his favorite chair, *and* the

Woolrich manuscript gone, then I could easily stretch all this to sixty thousand words. If the dead man had been wearing a deerstalker cap and holding a violin, we'd be especially well off; when the book came out, all the Sherlockian completists would be compelled to buy it.

Sorry. No murders, no Baker Street Irregulars, no dogs barking or not barking. I had to get them all there, and I did, but don't ask me how. I can't take the time to tell you.

🌲🌲🌲

"Now," Zoltan Mihalyi said. "We are all here. So can someone please tell me *why* we are all here?" There was a twinkle in his dark eyes as he spoke, and the trace of a knowing smile on his lips. He wanted an answer, but he was going to remain charming while he got it. I could believe he swept a lot of women off their feet.

"First of all," Jeanne Botleigh said, "I think we should each have a glass of eggnog. It's festive, and it will help put us all in the spirit of the day."

She was the caterer, and she was some cupcake, all right. Close-cut brown hair framed her small oval face and set off a pair of China-blue eyes. She had an English accent, roughed up some by ten years in New York, and she was short and slender and curvy, and I could see why our client had hoped she would stick around.

And now she'd whipped up a batch of eggnog, and ladled out cups for each of us. I waited until someone else tasted it—after all the mystery novels Haig's forced on me, I've developed an imagination—but once the Corn-Wallaces had tossed off theirs with no apparent effect, I took a sip. It was smooth and delicious, and it had a kick like a mule. I looked over at Haig, who's not much of a drinker, and he was smacking his lips over it.

"Why are we here?" he said, echoing the violinist's question. "Well, sir, I shall tell you. We are here as friends and customers of our host, whom we may be able to assist in the solution of a puzzle. Last night all of us, with the exception of course of myself and my young assistant, were present in this room. Also present was the original manuscript of an unpublished novel by Cornell Woolrich. This morning we were all gone, and so was the manuscript. Now we have returned. The manuscript, alas, has not."

"Wait a minute," Jon Corn-Wallace said. "You're saying one of us took it?"

"I say only that it has gone, sir. It is possible that someone within this room was involved in its disappearance, but there are diverse other possibilities as well. What impels me, what has prompted me to summon you here, is the likelihood that one or more of you knows something that will shed light on the incident."

"But the only person who would know anything would be the person who took it," Harriet Quinlan said. She was what they call a woman of a certain age, which generally means a woman of an uncertain age. Her figure was a few pounds beyond girlish, and I had a hunch she dyed her hair and might have had her face lifted somewhere along the way, but whatever she'd done had paid off. She was probably old enough to be my mother's older sister, but that didn't keep me from having the sort of ideas a nephew's not supposed to have.

Haig told her anyone could have observed something, and not just the guilty party, and Philip Perigord started to ask a question, and Haig held up a hand and cut him off in mid-sentence. Most people probably would have finished what they were saying, but I guess Perigord was used to studio executives shutting him up at pitch meetings. He bit off his word in the middle of a syllable and stayed mute.

"It is a holiday," Haig said, "and we all have other things to do, so we'd best avoid distraction. Hence I will ask the questions and you will answer them. Mr. Corn-Wallace. You are a book collector. Have you given a thought to collecting manuscripts?"

"I've thought about it," Jon Corn-Wallace said. He was the best-dressed man in the room, looking remarkably comfortable in a dark blue suit and a striped tie. He wore bull and bear cufflinks and one of those watches that's worth $5000 if it's real or $25 if you bought it from a Nigerian street vendor. "He tried to get me interested," he said, with a nod toward our client. "But I was always the kind of trader who stuck to listed stocks."

"Meaning?"

"Meaning it's impossible to pinpoint the market value of a one-of-a-kind item like a manuscript. There's too much guess-work involved. I'm not buying books with an eye to selling them, that's something my heirs will have to worry about, but I do like to know what my collection is worth and whether or not it's been a good investment. It's part of the pleasure of collecting, as far as I'm concerned. So I've stayed away from manuscripts. They're too iffy."

"And had you had a look at *As Dark As It Gets*?"

"No. I'm not interested in manuscripts, and I don't care at all for Woolrich."

"Jon likes hardboiled fiction," his wife put in, "but Woolrich is a little weird for his taste. I think he was a genius myself. Quirky and tormented, maybe, but what genius isn't?"

Haig, I thought. You couldn't call him tormented, but maybe he made up for it by exceeding the usual quota of quirkiness.

"Anyway," Jayne Corn-Wallace said, "I'm the Woolrich fan in the family. Though I agree with Jon as far as manuscripts are concerned. The value is pure speculation. And who wants to buy something and then have to get a box made for it? It's like buying an unframed canvas and having to get it framed."

"The Woolrich manuscript was already boxed," Haig pointed out.

"I mean generally, as an area for collecting. As a collector, I wasn't interested in *As Dark As It Gets*. If someone fixed it up and completed it, and if someone published it, I'd have been glad to buy it. I'd have bought two copies."

"Two copies, madam?"

She nodded. "One to read and one to own."

Haig's face darkened, and I thought he might offer his opinion of people who were afraid to damage their books by reading them. But he kept it to himself, and I was just as glad.

Jayne Corn-Wallace was a tall, handsome woman, radiating self-confidence, and I sensed she'd give as good as she got in an exchange with Haig.

"You might have wanted to read the manuscript," Haig suggested.

She shook her head. "I like Woolrich," she said, "but as a stylist he was choppy enough *after* editing and polishing. I wouldn't want to try him in manuscript, let alone an unfinished manuscript like that one."

"Mr. Mihalyi," Haig said. "You collect manuscripts, don't you?"

"I do."

"And do you care for Woolrich?"

The violinist smiled. "If I had the chance to buy the original manuscript of *The Bride Wore Black*," he said, "I would leap at it. If it were close at hand, and if strong drink had undermined my moral fiber, I might even slip it under my coat and walk off with it." A wink showed us he was kidding. "Or at least I'd have been tempted. The work in question, however, tempted me not a whit."

"And why is that, sir?"

Mihalyi frowned. "There are people," he said, "who attend open rehearsals and make surreptitious recordings of the music. They treasure them and even bootleg them to other like-minded fans. I despise such people."

"Why?"

"They violate the artist's privacy," he said. "A rehearsal is a time when one refines one's approach to a piece of music. One takes chances, one uses the occasion as the equivalent of an artist's sketch pad. The person who records it is in essence spraying a rough sketch with fixative and hanging it on the wall of his personal museum. I find it unsettling enough that listeners record concert performances, making permanent what was supposed to be a transitory experience. But to record a rehearsal is an atrocity."

"And a manuscript?"

"A manuscript is the writer's completed work. It provides a record of how he arranged and revised his ideas, and how they were in turn adjusted for better or worse by an editor. But it is finished work. An unfinished manuscript. . ."

"Is a rehearsal?"

"That or something worse. I ask myself, what would Woolrich have wanted?"

"Another drink," Edward Everett Stokes said, and leaned forward to help himself to more eggnog. "I take your point, Mihalyi. And Woolrich might well have preferred to have his unfinished work destroyed upon his death, but he left no instructions to that effect, so how can we presume to guess his wishes? Perhaps, for all we know, there is a single scene in the book that meant as much to him as anything he'd written. Or less than a scene—a bit of dialogue, a paragraph of description, perhaps no more than a single sentence. Who are we to say it should not survive?"

"Perigord," Mihalyi said. "You are a writer. Would you care to have your unfinished work published after your death? Would you not recoil at that, or at having it completed by others?"

Philip Perigord cocked an eyebrow. "I'm the wrong person to ask," he said. "I've spent twenty years in Hollywood. Forget unfinished work. My *finished* work doesn't get published, or 'produced,' as they so revealingly term it. I get paid, and the work winds up on a shelf. And, when it comes to having one's work completed by others, in Hollywood you don't have to wait until you're dead. It happens during your lifetime, and you learn to live with it."

"We don't know the author's wishes," Harriet Quinlan put in, "and I wonder how relevant they are."

"But it's his work," Mihalyi pointed out.

"Is it, Zoltan? Or does it belong to the ages? Finished or not, the author has left it to us. Schubert did not finish one of his greatest symphonies. Would you have laid its two completed movements in the casket with him?"

"It has been argued that the work was complete, that he intended it to be but two movements long."

"That begs the question, Zoltan."

"It does, dear lady," he said with a wink. "I'd rather beg the question than be undone by it. Of course I'd keep the Unfinished Symphony in the repertoire. On the other hand, I'd hate to see some fool attempt to finish it."

"No one has, have they?"

"Not to my knowledge. But several writers have had the effrontery to finish *The Mystery of Edwin Drood*, and I do think Dickens would have been better served if the manuscript had gone in the box with his bones. And as for sequels, like those for *Pride and Prejudice* and *The Big Sleep*, or that young fellow who had the colossal gall to tread in Rex Stout's immortal footsteps."

Now we were getting onto sensitive ground. As far as Leo Haig was concerned, Archie Goodwin had always written up Wolfe's cases, using the transparent pseudonym of Rex Stout. (Rex Stout = fat king, an allusion to Wolfe's own regal corpulence.) Robert Goldsborough, credited with the books written since the "death" of Stout, was, as Haig saw it, a ghostwriter employed by Goodwin, who was no longer up to the chore of hammering out the books. He'd relate them to Goldsborough, who transcribed them and polished them up. While they might not have all the narrative verve of Goodwin's own work, still they provided an important and accurate account of Wolfe's more recent cases.

See, Haig feels the great man's still alive and still raising orchids and nailing killers. Maybe somewhere on the Upper East Side. Maybe in Murray Hill, or just off Gramercy Park. . .

The discussion about Goldsborough, and about sequels in general, roused Haig from a torpor that Wolfe himself might have envied. "Enough," he said with authority. "There's no time for meandering literary conversations, nor would Chip have room for them in a short-story-length report. So let us get to it. One of you took the manuscript, box and all, from its place on the shelf. Mr. Mihalyi, you have the air of one who protests too much. You profess no interest in the manuscripts of unpublished novels, and I can accept that you did not yearn to possess *As Dark As It Gets*, but you wanted a look at it, didn't you?"

"I don't own a Woolrich manuscript," he said, "and of course

I was interested in seeing what one looked like. How he typed, how he entered corrections. . ."

"So you took the manuscript from the shelf."

"Yes," the violinist agreed. "I went into the other room with it, opened the box and flipped through the pages. You can taste the flavor of the man's work in the visual appearance of his manuscript pages. The words and phrases x'd out, the pencil notations, the crossovers, even the typographical errors. The computer age puts paid to all that, doesn't it? Imagine Chandler running Spell Check, or Hammett with justified margins." He sighed. "A few minutes with the script made me long to own one of Woolrich's. But not this one, for reasons I've already explained."

"You spent how long with the book?"

"Fifteen minutes at the most. Probably more like ten."

"And returned to this room?"

"Yes."

"And brought the manuscript with you?"

"Yes. I intended to return it to the shelf, but someone was standing in the way. It may have been you, Jon. It was someone tall, and you're the tallest person here." He turned to our client. "It wasn't you. But I think you may have been talking with Jon. Someone was, at any rate, and I'd have had to step between the two of you to put the box back, and that might have led to questions as to why I'd picked it up in the first place. So I put it down."

"Where?"

"On a table. That one, I think."

"It's not there now," Jon Corn-Wallace said.

"It's not," Haig agreed. "One of you took it from that table. I could, through an exhausting process of cross-questioning, establish who that person is. But it would save us all time if the person would simply recount what happened next."

There was a silence while they all looked at each other. "Well, I guess this is where I come in," Jayne Corn-Wallace said. "I was sitting in the red chair, where Phil Perigord is sitting now. And whoever I'd been talking to went to get another drink, and I looked around, and there it was on the table."

"The manuscript, madam?"

"Yes, but I didn't know that was what it was, not at first. I thought it was a finely bound limited edition. Because the manuscripts are all kept on that shelf, you know, and this one wasn't. And it hadn't been on the table a few minutes earlier, either. I knew that much. So I assumed it was a book someone had been leafing through, and I saw it was by Cornell Woolrich, and I didn't recognize the title, so I thought I'd try leafing through it myself."

"And you found it was a manuscript."

"Well, that didn't take too keen an eye, did it? I suppose I glanced at the first twenty pages, just riffled through them while the party went on around me. I stopped after a chapter or so. That was plenty."

"You didn't like what you read?"

"There were corrections," she said disdainfully. "Words and whole sentences crossed out, new words penciled in. I realize writers have to work that way, but when I read a book I like to believe it emerged from the writer's mind fully formed."

"Like Athena from the brow of What's-his-name," her husband said.

"Zeus. I don't want to know there was a writer at work, making decisions, putting words down and then changing them. I want to forget about the writer entirely and lose myself in the story."

"Everybody wants to forget about the writer," Philip Perigord said, helping himself to more eggnog. "At the Oscars each year some ninny intones, 'In the beginning was the Word,' before he hands out the screenwriting awards. And you hear the usual crap about how they owe it all to chaps like me who put words in their mouths. They say it, but nobody believes it. Jack Warner called us schmucks with Underwoods. Well, we've come a long way. Now we're schmucks with Power Macs."

"Indeed," Haig said. "You looked at the manuscript, didn't you, Mr. Perigord?"

"I never read unpublished work. Can't risk leaving myself open to a plagiarism charge."

"Oh? But didn't you have a special interest in Woolrich? Didn't you once adapt a story of his?"

"How did you know about that? I was one of several who made a living off that particular piece of crap. It was never produced."

"And you looked at this manuscript in the hope that you might adapt it?"

The writer shook his head. "I'm through wasting myself out there."

"They're through with you," Harriet Quinlan said. "Nothing personal, Phil, but it's a town that uses up writers and throws them away. You couldn't get arrested out there. So you've come back east to write books."

"And you'll be representing him, madam?"

"I may, if he brings me something I can sell. I saw him paging through a manuscript and figured he was looking for something he could steal. Oh, don't look so outraged, Phil. Why not steal from Woolrich, for God's sake? He's not going to sue. He left everything to Columbia University, and you could knock off anything of his, published or unpublished, and they'd never know the difference. Ever since I saw you reading, I've been wondering. Did you come across anything worth stealing?"

"I don't steal," Perigord said. "Still, perfectly legitimate inspiration *can* result from a glance at another man's work—"

"I'll say it can. And did it?"

He shook his head. "If there was a strong idea anywhere in that manuscript, I couldn't find it in the few minutes I spent looking. What about you, Harriet? I know you had a look at it, because I saw you."

"I just wanted to see what it was you'd been so caught up in. And I wondered if the manuscript might be salvageable. One of my writers might be able to pull it off, and do a better job than the hack who finished *Into the Night*."

"Ah," Haig said. "And what did you determine, madam?"

"I didn't read enough to form a judgment. Anyway, *Into the Night* was no great commercial success, so why tag along in its wake?"

"So you put the manuscript. . ."

"Back in its box, and left it on the table where I'd found it."

Our client shook his head in wonder. "*Murder on the Orient Express*," he said. "Or in the Calais coach, depending on whether you're English or American. It's beginning to look as though *everyone* read that manuscript. And I never noticed a thing!"

"Well, you were hitting the sauce pretty good," Jon Corn-Wallace reminded him. "And you were, uh, concentrating all your social energy in one direction."

"How's that?"

Corn-Wallace nodded toward Jeanne Botleigh, who was re-filling someone's cup. "As far as you were concerned, our lovely caterer was the only person in the room."

There was an awkward silence, with our host coloring and his caterer lowering her eyes demurely. Haig broke it. "To continue," he said abruptly. "Miss Quinlan returned the manuscript to its box and to its place upon the table. Then—"

"But she didn't," Perigord said. "Harriet, I wanted another look at Woolrich. Maybe I'd missed something. But first I saw you reading it, and when I looked a second time it was gone. You weren't reading it and it wasn't on the table, either."

"I put it back," the agent said.

"But not where you found it," said Edward Everett Stokes. "You set it down not on the table but on that revolving bookcase."

"Did I? I suppose it's possible. But how did you know that?"

"Because I saw you," said the small-press publisher. "And because I wanted a look at the manuscript myself. I knew about it, including the fact that it was not restorable in the fashion of *Into the Night*. That made it valueless to a commercial publisher, but the idea of a Woolrich novel going unpublished ate away at me. I mean, we're talking about Cornell Woolrich."

"And you thought—"

"I thought why not publish it as is, warts and all? I could do it, in an edition of two or three hundred copies, for collectors who'd happily accept inconsistencies and omissions for the sake of having something otherwise unobtainable. I wanted a few minutes peace and quiet with the book, so I took it into the lavatory."

"And?"

"And I read it, or at least paged through it. I must have spent half an hour in there, or close to it."

"I remember you were gone a while," Jon Corn-Wallace said. "I thought you'd headed on home."

"I thought he was in the other room," Jayne said, "cavorting on the pile of coats with Harriet here. But I guess that must have been someone else."

"It was Zoltan," the agent said, "and we were hardly cavorting."

"Canoodling, then, but—"

"He was teaching me a yogic breathing technique, not that it's any of your business. Stokes, you took the manuscript into the John. I trust you brought it back?"

"Well, no."

"You took it home? You're the person responsible for its disappearance?"

"Certainly not. I didn't take it home, and I hope I'm not responsible for its disappearance. I left it in the lavatory."

"You just left it there?"

"In its box, on the shelf over the vanity. I set it down there while I washed my hands, and I'm afraid I forgot it. And no, it's not there now. I went and looked as soon as I realized what all this was about, and I'm afraid some other hands than mine must have moved it. I'll tell you this—when it does turn up, I definitely want to publish it."

"*If* it turns up," our client said darkly. "Once E. E. left it in the bathroom, anyone could have slipped it under his coat without being seen. And I'll probably never see it again."

"But that means one of us is a thief," somebody said.

"I know, and that's out of the question. You're all my friends. But we were all drinking last night, and drink can confuse a person. Suppose one of you did take it from the bathroom and carried it home as a joke, the kind of joke that can seem funny after a few drinks. If you could contrive to return it, perhaps in such a way that no one could know your identity. . .Haig, you ought to be able to work that out."

"I could," Haig agreed. "If that were how it happened. But it didn't."

"It didn't?"

"You forget the least obvious suspect."

"Me? Dammit, Haig, are you saying I stole my own manuscript?"

"I'm saying the butler did it," Haig said, "or the closest thing we have to a butler. Miss Botleigh, your upper lip has been trembling almost since we all sat down. You've been on the point of an admission throughout and haven't said a word. Have you in fact read the manuscript of *As Dark As It Gets*?"

"Yes."

The client gasped. "You have? When?"

"Last night."

"But—"

"I had to use the lavatory," she said, "and the book was there, although I could see it wasn't an ordinary bound book but pages in a box. I didn't think I would hurt it by looking at it. So I sat there and read the first two chapters."

"What did you think?" Haig asked her.

"It was very powerful. Parts of it were hard to follow, but the scenes were strong, and I got caught up in them."

"That's Woolrich," Jayne Corn-Wallace said. "He can grab you, all right."

"And then you took it with you when you went home," our client said. "You were so involved you couldn't bear to leave it unfinished, so you, uh, borrowed it." He reached to pat her hand. "Perfectly understandable," he said, "and perfectly innocent. You were going to bring it back once you'd finished it. So all this fuss has been over nothing."

"That's not what happened."

"It's not?"

"I read two chapters," she said, "and I thought I'd ask to borrow it some other time, or maybe not. But I put the pages back in the box and left them there."

"In the bathroom?"

"Yes."

"So you never did finish the book," our client said. "Well, if it ever turns up I'll be more than happy to lend it to you, but until then—"

"But perhaps Miss Botleigh has already finished the book," Haig suggested.

"How could she? She just told you she left it in the bathroom."

Haig said, "Miss Botleigh?"

"I finished the book," she said. "When everybody else went home, I stayed."

"My word," Zoltan Mihalyi said. "Woolrich never had a more devoted fan, or one half so beautiful."

"Not to finish the manuscript," she said, and turned to our host. "You asked me to stay," she said.

"I *wanted* you to stay," he agreed. "I wanted to *ask* you to stay. But I don't remember. . ."

"I guess you'd had quite a bit to drink," she said, "although you didn't show it. But you asked me to stay, and I'd been hoping you would ask me, because I wanted to stay."

"You must have had rather a lot to drink yourself," Harriet Quinlan murmured.

"Not that much," said the caterer. "I wanted to stay because he's a very attractive man."

Our client positively glowed, then turned red with embarrassment. "I knew I had a hole in my memory," he said, "but I didn't think anything significant could have fallen through it. So you actually stayed? God. What, uh, happened?"

"We went upstairs," Jeanne Botleigh said. "And we went to the bedroom, and we went to bed."

"Indeed," said Haig.

"And it was . . ."

"Quite wonderful," she said.

"And I don't remember. I think I'm going to kill myself."

"Not on Christmas Day," E. E. Stokes said. "And not with a mystery still unsolved. Haig, what became of the bloody manuscript?"

"Miss Botleigh?"

She looked at our host, then lowered her eyes. "You went to sleep afterward," she said, "and I felt entirely energized, and knew I couldn't sleep, and I thought I'd read for a while. And I remembered the manuscript, so I came down here and fetched it."

"And read it?"

"In bed. I thought you might wake up, in fact I was hoping you would. But you didn't."

"Damn it," our client said, with feeling.

"So I finished the manuscript and still didn't feel sleepy. And I got dressed and let myself out and went home."

There was a silence, broken at length by Zoltan Mihalyi, offering our client congratulations on his triumph and sympathy for the memory loss. "When you write your memoirs," he said, "you'll have to leave that chapter blank."

"Or have someone ghost it for you," Philip Perigord offered.

"The manuscript," Stokes said. "What became of it?"

"I don't know," the caterer said. "I finished it—"

"Which is more than Woolrich could say," Jayne Corn Wallace said.

"—and I left it there."

"There?"

"In its box. On the bedside table, where you'd be sure to find it first thing in the morning. But I guess you didn't."

♣♣♣

"The manuscript? Haig, you're telling me you want the *manuscript*?"

"You find my fee excessive?"

"But it wasn't even lost. No one took it. It was next to my bed. I'd have found it sooner or later."

"But you didn't," Haig said. "Not until you'd cost me and my young associate the better part of our holiday. You've been reading mysteries all your life. Now you got to see one solved in front of you, and in your own magnificent library."

He brightened. "It is a nice room, isn't it?"

"It's first-rate."

"Thanks. But Haig, listen to reason. You did solve the puzzle and recover the manuscript, but now you're demanding what you recovered as compensation. That's like rescuing a kidnap victim and insisting on adopting the child yourself."

"Nonsense. It's nothing like that."

"All right, then it's like recovering stolen jewels and demanding the jewels themselves as reward. It's just plain disproportionate. I hired you because I wanted the manuscript in my collection, and now you expect to wind up with it in *your* collection."

It did sound a little weird to me, but I kept my mouth shut. Haig had the ball, and I wanted to see where he'd go with it.

He put his fingertips together. "In *Black Orchids*," he said, "Wolfe's client was his friend Lewis Hewitt. As recompense for his work, Wolfe insisted on all of the black orchid plants Hewitt had bred. Not one. All of them."

"That always seemed greedy to me."

"If we were speaking of fish," Haig went on, "I might be similarly inclined. But books are of use to me only as reading material. I want to *read* that book, sir, and I want to have it close to hand if I need to refer to it." He shrugged. "But I don't need the original that you prize so highly. Make me a copy."

"A copy?"

"Indeed. Have the manuscript photocopied."

"You'd be content with a . . . a copy?"

"And a credit," I said quickly, before Haig could give away the store. We'd put in a full day, and he ought to get more than a few hours' reading out of it. "A two thousand dollar store credit," I added, "which Mr. Haig can use up as he sees fit."

"Buying paperbacks and book-club editions," our client said. "It should last you for years." He heaved a sigh. "A photocopy and a store credit. Well, if that makes you happy. . ."

And that pretty much wrapped it up. I ran straight home

and sat down at the typewriter, and if the story seems a little hurried it's because I was in a rush when I wrote it. See, our client tried for a second date with Jeanne Botleigh, to refresh his memory, I suppose, but a woman tends to feel less than flattered when you forget having gone to bed with her, and she wasn't having any.

So I called her the minute I got home, and we talked about this and that, and we've got a date in an hour and a half. I'll tell you this much, if I get lucky, I'll remember. So wish me luck, huh?

And, by the way . . .

Merry Christmas!

The Holiday Fairy

By Jeremiah Healy

"You must be the private investigator from Boston," said the tall, slim woman who'd buzzed me into the book store at 129 West 56th Street.

Shaking off the cold of a late December day, I set the corrugated box I was carrying on her desk, which seemed to function as a combination retail counter and security station. "Just another Christmas courier."

She looked at the box. "Let me call Otto."

As the woman picked up a phone, I glanced around the first floor of the old brownstone, inhaling that relaxing patina of age that wafts off shelves and moldings into the air itself. From the titles displayed cover-out—mostly paperbacks and all crime novels—you could guess the name of the place was The Mysterious Bookshop. Once in a while, I do a courier run to New York City, usually with jewelry or negotiable bonds for clients who want the incremental assurance that a private license and a permit to carry provide. That day, though, it'd been a rare book dealer who'd asked me to carry a first-edition somebody-or-other to a man named Otto Penzler.

As the woman hung up, I could hear footsteps above me, the last few onto the metal rungs of a black, spiral staircase at the rear of the store. A voice like one you'd hear on an evening news program said, "Mr. Cuddy, you can leave the package downstairs, but come up. Please."

I climbed the narrow steps, which resolved—revolved, actually—into a view of a man somewhere over fifty, with carefully groomed hair and beard just on the gray side of white. He looked sharp in a dress shirt and slacks, body fit but blue eyes filled with troubles.

"Mr. Penzler," I said, reaching the top rung and his outstretched hand at the same time.

"I'd prefer Otto if you'd prefer John."

I stopped. "You usually get on a first-name basis with first-time couriers?"

A wise smile. "Let's say I'd like your expert opinion on a different matter. Follow me, please."

The staircase ended in a front room with very high ceilings and a lot of hardcover books that looked old even as I moved by them behind Penzler. He led me through a short corridor containing a refrigerator and sink to the rear room on the floor, a magnificent library with the more rarefied atmosphere of a gentleman's club. Something about the arrangement of the books on those shelves gave me the impression that we'd upscaled from Cadillacs to Mercedes.

Penzler closed the door behind us. "Have a seat, John."

I took one of the leather chairs, Penzler perching his butt on the arm of its mate.

He said, "When Kate told me who she was using to send the Wilkie Collins, I made it a point to be here."

"The 'Wilkie Collins' part is more than she told me."

Another smile. "Actually, that rare book is the excuse rather than the reason why you're here."

"Which would be?"

Penzler moved off the arm, stepping around the room as though timing his movements to synchronize with his words. "I've experienced three odd. . .occurrences over the last few weeks, and I'd like someone to look into them for me. Discreetly."

"Otto, if there aren't a thousand private investigators licensed in this town—"

"I know. And I doubt you're one of them."

"I am not."

"All right then, here's my dilemma. I need three friends . . . 'interviewed' by a professional, without them realizing that person is working for me. But all three have had contact with a lot of private investigators here, certainly any I'd trust with my own business."

"Who are your friends?"

"I'll name them in a minute, but for now, assume they're prominent mystery authors in Manhattan."

"Otto, even three local crime writers can't know all the trustworthy investigators in the city. And besides, my Massachusetts license wouldn't provide the kind of confidentiality protection on our conversations that would make me 'trustworthy' for you."

A third smile. "Kate said I'd like you. A 'motherlode of honesty,' in her words." Penzler paused by an empty table with a top just big enough to hold a flower vase. "How about this, then. You hear me out, and if you don't feel comfortable, no problem. If you're intrigued, though, as I think you might be, I'll pay half again your usual rate."

I decided listening would take less time than debating. "Go ahead."

Penzler tapped the tabletop. "There used to be a skull here, one that once belonged to Agatha Christie. Two days ago, it disappeared, replaced by a plain white envelope." Penzler opened the only drawer in the table, drawing out three number 10's. "In the envelope was the exact amount of cash that a collector's handbook suggested as the current value for such an artifact."

"You figure the Tooth Fairy might be branching out?"

Penzler didn't smile this time. "I've thought of it as the 'Holiday Fairy.'"

I tilted my head toward the other two envelopes. "What else was taken?"

Penzler glided over to his desk. "Two weeks ago, a letter opener in the shape of a miniature cavalry saber that Erle Stanley Gardner used on his mail."

"He wrote 'Perry Mason,' right?"

"Among other series." Penzler moved toward a wall where an eight-by-ten space of brighter paint was framed by duller. "Then, a week later, the third item. A facsimile of the first page from the will of Edgar Allan Poe."

"And money was left for each?"

Penzler fanned the three envelopes in his hand as though they were mutant playing cards. "Exactly the right amount, collectorwise."

"Otto, I've heard of people commissioning gangs to steal works of art—"

"—but never somebody doing a forced exchange—"

"—especially where the 'purchaser' won't get more money from somebody else for the item involved."

Penzler finally sank into the cushions on the opposite chair. "Now you see why I need a professional."

"Maybe not, if you've somehow narrowed down the suspect list to three."

"That was the easy part, actually. I could eliminate most of the customers, because they never come back into my private library. And given that we're talking about only two weeks, I can remember the three people who visited during the time each item went missing."

"Saber, then will, then skull."

"Right." Penzler signed. "Frankly, when I'd used the letter opener the day before and then couldn't find it the day after, I thought I'd just misplaced the thing. But following that, one of my staff was taking down all the framed items to give the glass a Christmas cleaning. When they went back up, the Poe wasn't among them."

"I know this is a painful suggestion, but. . .maybe one of your employees?"

"No. No, my staff is pretty small, and given their flex hours, nobody was here on all three days at the necessary times'."

"Though three of your friends were."

"Yes, separately." Penzler's brow knit. "It isn't the value of the items that bothers me. Hell, our 'Holiday Fairy' has already given me that. What gnaws at my gut, John, is that a friend could do this for no apparent reason."

"Maybe you'd best give me the names of these people."

"Then you'll help me?"

"If we can come up with a credible cover story for my seeing them."

A twinkle in the eye, like Santa Claus might still have after Richard Simmons got through with him. "I have an idea for that."

♣♣♣

Standing outside a thirty-story high-rise overlooking Central Park, I looked down at the notes I'd taken on three-by-five index cards at the bookshop. The first writer was Maury Bronstein, though Penzler told me most readers would know him by his pen name of "Ace Stark," collaborator on mysteries by famous tennis stars. The man apparently favored punning titles, as in one where Chris Evert Lloyd ventured to a dude ranch (*Mount Evert*) and another where Michael Stich saved a fashion designer (*A Stich In Time*). Bronstein/Stark was also the only one who over the years expressed any interest to Penzler regarding all three items. Inside the double-entrance was a doorman, who led me to a bank of elevators. Getting off on the twenty-seventh floor, I knocked on the door standing partially ajar.

"Just push your way in, please," a hoarse but pleasant male voice.

The door was on a strong spring, so I had to put my shoulder to it. Inside, the weak light of the December sun flowed into the room through seven windows across its front wall, giving this first-time visitor the disorienting sensation that Central Park was the city and the buildings a receding necklace around it.

"Rather like suddenly discovering the world really is round, eh?"

I cleared a corner of the entry hall and saw a man sitting at a computer hutch integrated into a wall unit longer than a stretch limo. His shoulders were stooped, a sweater he wore seeming a size too large. Even his hair, almost jet-black, looked a little big for his scalp. The hollows under eyes and cheeks reminded me of people I'd seen when I visited my wife, Beth, at the hospital.

In the cancer ward.

"Otto called me about you," said the man without getting up. "But from the look on your face, he didn't mention my illness. Ace Stark, lymphoma."

If Bronstein wanted to use his pen name, I wasn't about to correct him. "John Cuddy, Mr. Stark."

"Ace, please. I rather like the sound of it." Stark paused. "Otto did tell you about my tennis mysteries?"

"Yes." I took a chair against a second wall as he swiveled in his. "But not about the view."

Stark half-turned to take it in "Yes, when I was lucky enough to be able to buy this place, I thought it felt as though I were watching the city from the sky." Another pause. "Which, unfortunately, I might be soon. But that's not why you're here. Otto said you were doing a necessary background check on him?"

"That's right," I said, bringing out a blank note card. "He's been proposed for a national literary post, and given the events of the last year in Washington, any kind of nominee has to be vetted."

"Understandable. I'd recommend Otto highly. I suppose, however, that you have more specific questions?"

"A few. How did you come to know Mr. Penzler?"

We reviewed Stark's early career. Writing part-time while a journeyman player on the pro tennis tour. Penzler seeing some of his short stories in magazines and eventually getting him published in book form.

"So," I said, "you know Mr. Penzler well."

"Quite well. And rather biased, as I mentioned earlier, in his favor."

"Anyone who doesn't quite lean that way?"

A frown."Meaning, a potentially negative person you should speak with?"

"That's what I mean."

"Well, I'm sure there must be a couple. One can't live over a half century on this earth and express passionate professional opinions without ticking off somebody."

I made as if to glance down at the other two names Penzler had given me."How about Tanya Washington and Kyle McKray?"

"Tanya and Kyle? Well, they're rather different sorts. Tanya writes a police procedural series about a female African-American homicide lieutenant, and Kyle about a male Irish-American private investigator."

There was a faint smile toying with the corners of Stark's mouth during that last comment, but I didn't bite. "I meant more how they'd feel about Mr. Penzler."

"Oh, very positive I would say. Otto has praised both Tanya's gritty realism and Kyle's wisecracking dialogue. Will you be talking with them as well?"

"Possibly."

"Well, if you do, please be sure to give both my best."

"You know each personally, then?"

"We served together as judges on an Edgar Award committee several years ago."

"Edgar?"

"The Oscar of the mystery-writing industry, in the form of a bust of Edgar Allan Poe. He was—"

"Yes," I said,"I know."

🌲🌲🌲

After asking some more detail questions to grease the skids for my cover story, I left Bronstein/Stark and headed for the Upper West Side. Even my cabbie had a little trouble finding the address, which turned out to be a mansion overlooking a leafy strip separating it from the Hudson River. Based on the homes of the first two people on Penzler's list, I was beginning to think I'd chosen the wrong profession.

However, when I climbed the stoop, I could see there were a dozen names block-printed on the elaborate buzzer system at the doorjamb, though Washington (in 5A) did seem to have at least the front of the top floor. A minute after pressing her button, the door opened to reveal a slim woman in yellow and black spandex standing and puffing behind it. Her modest Afro was held back by a terry cloth sweatband, but the eyes were what caught you: the golden fire of a leopard's.

"Ms. Washington?"

"Otto's a good guy with descriptions. John Cuddy, right?"

"Right."

"Tanya Washington. Come on up."

We climbed four flights of a pre-War—Spanish-American—staircase before arriving at an apartment with a spectacular view across the river of some high-rises in New Jersey.

On the whole, I preferred the earlier vista of Central Park.

"Make yourself comfortable."

As Washington brought over two already-poured glasses of what looked like lemonade, I took the couch with a dashiki-patterned slipcover.

Handing me a glass, she said, "Fresh-squeezed."

I tried it. "Like grandma used to keep on her back porch."

Washington flopped into an easy chair with a different dashiki design. "And where was grandma's house?"

"South Boston."

"Where that bussing controversy went down?"

"Twenty years ago. Things are better now."

Washington's eyes told me she wasn't quite buying it. "Otto said you're checking him out for some literary gig?"

"Yes, What can you tell me?"

A shrug, "He's always been good to me."

Not exactly a ringing endorsement. "But he hasn't been to others?"

"Otto's not crazy about the cozy-style mysteries. You know, like Agatha Christie?"

Christie's skull was the last item taken. "What does he enjoy?"

"Mysteries, you mean? Oh, legal procedurals, like Erle Stanley Gardner used to write."

Gardner's saber replica. "How about Edgar Allan Poe?"

"Him, too," said Washington, same fire in the eyes but otherwise a perfectly neutral expression on her face.

We went through the laundry list of cover-story questions I'd used once already.

Then Washington came forward a little in her chair. "Who else you talking to?"

"Maury Bronstein and Kyle McKray."

She clucked her tongue off the roof of her mouth. "Damn shame about Maury. But you'll like Kyle. He's a real throwback."

I went downstairs alone. Turning right and walking up toward Broadway for another taxi, though, I had to ask myself how Washington could know I'd get her allusion to Bronstein/Stark's illness without also knowing I'd already spoken with him.

♣♣♣

Kyle McKray lived in the West Village, a long baseball throw from Washington Square Park and New York University. When I rang the bell of a small, white-brick townhouse that appeared to belong all to him, a woman's voice–disembodied and squawky—came through the speaker.

"Yeah?"

"John Cuddy to see Kyle McKray."

"Try the Sheep's Head."

"I'm sorry?"

"It's a bar, a block east and three south."

I looked at my watch. Two-twenty p.m. "You think he'll be there?"

"Beats me. But he isn't here, and the Sheep's Head is where lover-boy picked me up last night."

♣♣♣

The entrance under the painted and chipped sheep's head on a wooden plaque gave a view of a bar sunk half-a-level below the sidewalk, with that peanuts and stale beer smell of a hard-drinking joint. Counting the bartender, there were maybe six people in the dark cavern. When I walked up to the brass rail and asked for "lover-boy" by his proper name, a swab-towel flicked toward the guy on the corner stool.

Sitting, McKray seemed broader than he was tall, with a divot-scar through one eyebrow and a nose that hadn't pointed straight ahead since Watergate. Despite the December weather outside, he wore just an orange-and-blue Mets baseball jersey over cut-off shorts. There was a short tumbler in front of him containing three fingers of amber liquid with no ice. By the time I crossed the ten feet toward him, his glass was empty.

"Innkeeper, innkeeper. Another Jim Beam, if you would."

The kind of bad, thick brogue you hear in a grade-C movie with no dialogue coach in the budget. "Kyle McKray?"

"And who would you be, lad?"

I probably had ten years on him, but I said, "John Cuddy."

"I knew it. Another Irishman. I can sense these things"

The bartender brought McKray's bourbon. I ordered a Harp.

"Ah, lager," said the man on the corner stool. "Reminds me of the idea for a novel I never got around to writing."

"About beer?"

"About a lad like yourself who liked Harp so much, he wanted a case of it distributed around his wake at the funeral home. A memento mori, the Romans called it."

I wasn't sure McKray was right in his linguistics, but that didn't appear to be the point. When my beer arrived, I clinked the pint against his tumbler. "To literature."

"Ah, no finer occasion for a drink."

McKray drained half of the bourbon, and I realized I'd have to cut to the car chase if I wanted anything useful from him. "I understand you're a mystery author yourself."

"'Writer,' lad. Writer. 'Author' sounds pretentious."

"Some of my favorites are Agatha Christie—"

"—Brit pap—"

"Erie Stanley Gardner—"

"—legal hack—"

"And Edgar Allan Poe."

"—over-rated, and dead like the rest of them."

"The rest?"

"Christie and Gardner. Who've we been talking about just now?"

Either McKray was a hell of an actor, or the names meant no more to him than headings in an encyclopedia. "Did Otto Penzler by any chance speak to you today?"

"Otto? A fine lad himself. But no, I'm afraid I was otherwise engaged this morning, and beyond the fine damsel I met here last night and this equally fine lad behind the bar who's about to grace me with another Jim Beam, I've not talked to a soul but you the livelong day."

And at that, Kyle McKray winked at me conspiratorially and downed the rest of his bourbon of the moment.

🌲🌲🌲

The afternoon sun stayed out, so I decided to walk back to Midtown, shuffling my thoughts as though they were index cards, trying to see if they'd fit into some kind of pattern. Waiting for the light at Seventh Avenue and Fifty-Fourth, a random combination of information made sense, and I refined it during the last two and a half blocks to The Mysterious Bookshop.

🌲🌲🌲

A redheaded woman with the springy walk of a good dancer was walking away from Penzler and toward me as I crested the spiral staircase.

She said, "He's all yours."

I followed him back into the library, where he closed the door again, something that now felt as though it happened only rarely.

When we were settled in our chairs, I said, "Maury Bron-stein—or 'Ace Stark'—told me you'd called him ahead of time with my cover story."

"And Tanya Washington, too. I couldn't reach Kyle McKray."

"How do you mean?"

Penzler looked at me a little strangely. "I called his house, but just got his tape machine."

"And left a message."

"Yes."

"Would he have been able to hear your voice from his bed?"

Stranger look. "I suppose so. I've been to his place, and the door to the writing study is just off his bedroom."

I nodded.

Penzler waited—impatiently but politely—before saying, "Well, did you find out anything?"

"Yes."

"And?"

"I think I've got it, but I'd like to spin it out for you before sharing my conclusion."

"Oh, God. That bad?"

"You be the judge."

Penzler tried to relax. "Okay, go ahead."

I took out the index cards I'd written on earlier. "Three items are missing, each from a different, and famous, but dead mystery writer. Three current authors stand suspected, one of them even expressing interest in the items over the years. Now, none of your friends could have known whether there'd be other potential suspects—other people who were back here in your library each of the three days in question. However, at a minimum we have these three."

"Yes, but go back to your prior point. Maury, Tanya, and Kyle were all here separately, so even they wouldn't know about each other."

"I'm coming to that. All three are acquainted—the first told me they served on an award committee together. The second seemed to know I'd already seen the first and just 'happened' to mention the three famous authors whose artifacts were taken. The third claimed not even to have talked with you, but did share out of the blue a projected novel he probably hasn't touched for years about items somebody contemplating their own death might cherish. He used the term memento—"

"Wait a minute, John. Your third writer's obviously Kyle, but was Tanya or Maury the first?"

"In a way it doesn't matter, because they couldn't have known who would be."

"I'm sorry?"

"Which of them you—or, as it happened, I as your delegate—would start with."

Penzler shook his head. "You're saying they're all involved?"

"Yes."

"In a conspiracy to steal—or have me involuntarily 'sell' these items?"

"No. The artifacts are just the excuse, not the reason. Kind of like my bringing that rare book down from Boston for you."

"The. . .excuse? Then what the hell are they doing?"

"Giving you a present."

"A what?" said Penzler.

"A present. For the holidays."

"John, are you all right?"

"You've been good to all three of these writers, Otto. They knew each other from that committee, and one of them isn't sure he'll see another December. What better present to give you than a live mystery?"

"A live mystery."

"In which you participate as apparent victim."

Penzler sat blinking. He opened his mouth twice to speak, but closed it each time to think a little longer.

Then he showed me the wise smile. "Maury. I'll bet it was his idea."

"I think so, too, since the others probably wouldn't have known about his interest in the three items involved."

"Plus, it's like him to balance out the cast. Two men and a woman's artifacts, two men and a woman as suspects."

"And, all being mystery writers, they're adept at planting the appropriate clues, regardless of who got called on first."

Penzler shook his head again, but this time in a marveling way. "I'd even bet Maury's the one holding the saber, the will, and the skull."

"He admired them," I said softly, "and he's thinking about no longer being a live writer himself."

"Yes, though even more because doing so echoes his titles."

My turn to be stumped. "His titles?"

"I told you about the Ace Stark series when we first spoke this morning. '*Mount Evert*,' '*A Stich in Time*.'"

"Puns."

"Yes."

"And Kyle McKray mentioned that old dog of a book he was thinking of writing."

I still didn't get it. "So?"

Penzler sat back in his chair, lacing fingers behind his head obviously quite pleased with himself. And with the present from his 'Holiday Fairy' friends.

"Okay, John. Put the Ace Stark Titles together with the subject of Kyle's novel and you get..."

Finally. "Memento Maury."

Otto Penzler lifted his face to the library's high ceiling and roared out a laugh. "God, but I love this business!"

I Saw Mommy Killing Santa Claus

By Ed McBain

Christmas Eve at The Mysterious Bookshop is not normally a crowded time. We'll get the usual rush of last-minute shoppers eager to find something a distant mystery-reading uncle or aunt my enjoy, but if there are a dozen shoppers still on the premises when we close at five o'clock, that's a lot.

I had been working there for a bit more than two years now, and I must say I liked the job a lot. I have always loved books—in fact, my previous job had been at a book store—but there is something especially intense about the feeling mystery lovers share. Working at The Mysterious, I often felt as if I were performing a public service. Matching readers with the perfect books for them became something of an obsession. This was especially true at Christmas time, when I knew the book would be a gift and when I could imagine the delight of unwrapping it on Christmas morning. At Christmas time, I truly felt like one of Santa's helpers, listening to a shopper telling me his cousin liked "puzzles, you know, but not violence," listening to yet another shopper telling me her brother-in-law liked to read "something by the name of Leonard Elmore? Does that sound familiar?"

There were perhaps nine or ten people in the shop at four-fifteen that Christmas Eve, some of them browsing upstairs, a handful scattered around downstairs, none of them looking particularly harried or rushed despite the fact that we would be closing in forty-five minutes. I always hate to tell people we'll be closing because it sounds as if we're shoving them out into the cold, when instead we should be offering them a noggin of grog. I hadn't seen the little boy when he came into the shop, and so I was surprised to see him coming down the spiral staircase from above. We get a lot of kids in the store, accompanying their mothers or fathers, and most of them are well behaved, perhaps because they sense the sort of reverence for mysteries I mentioned a moment ago. This one seemed to be about eight, a skinny little kid wearing a blue stocking cap over blond hair, a blue ski parka over darker blue corduroys and L.L. Bean boots. He sidled down the staircase with one hand on the banister, watching his own hand as it glided downstairs, and then he smiled somewhat shyly, and drifted toward the bookshelves where he began browsing titles. He finally pulled an illustrated book from one of the shelves, leafed through the pages, and then put it back neatly in its slot.

"Hi," I said. "Can I help you?"

"No, thank you," he said.

"Where's your mommy?" I asked.

"Still upstairs," he said, and glanced toward the front door as if he might suddenly bolt.

"That's okay," I said. "Feel free to browse."

"Thanks," he said, and went hesitantly to the bookshelves again.

"Do you like to read mysteries?" I asked.

"Sometimes."

"Which ones are your favorites?"

"The ones where a kid solves them."

A woman standing at one of the shelves smiled when she heard this, and then asked if I thought Lawrence Block might be good for a woman who'd just passed a kidney stone.

"Or would Donald Westlake be better?" she asked.

"You can't miss with either one," I said.

"Maybe I ought to take one of each," she said. "What do you think?"

"Did she pass *two* kidney stones?" I asked, and smiled.

"I'm not sure how many she passed, she's my husband's supervisor."

"In that case, I wouldn't take any chances," I said.

"If *you'd* just passed a kidney stone, which of these would *you* take?"

"They're both very good," I said. "You can't go wrong."

"Do you think Bergdorf's is still open?" she asked, and put both books back on the counter and walked out.

"Why didn't she buy one?" the kid asked.

"I don't know. Maybe she didn't trust me."

"She said she wanted two, and then she didn't even take one."

"Well, she was trying to decide, I guess."

"What's a supervisor?"

"A boss."

"Are you a boss?"

"No, I just work here."

"What's you name?"

"Alan," I said. "What's yours?"

"Max. What's a kidney stone?"

"A stone the kidney manufactures."

"Why?"

"I have no idea."

"Do you believe in Santa Claus?" he asked.

There was suddenly an intensely serious look on his face. I had learned a long time ago that you can't ever make the mistake of believing kids aren't at least as serious as grownups. I didn't for a moment believe Max's question ranked up there with peace in the Middle East or pollution of the environment, but the look on his face told me at once that he was having very grave reservations about the existence of the bearded man in the red suit.

"Do *you* believe in him?" I asked.

"I used to."

"When did you stop?"

"When he died," Max said.

A sandy-haired man wearing a Burberry trench coat walked over to me, a copy of the latest Janet Evanovich mystery in his hand.

"Is this a pseudonym?" he asked.

"I don't think so."

"Evanovich?"

"I don't think so, sir."

"It's not one of Evan Hunter's pseudonyms, is it?"

"No, that's her name. Janet Evanovich."

"Cause I don't want to buy the book and then find out it's just another one of his goddamn pseudonyms."

"There's her picture and everything," I said.

The man looked at the picture on the back jacket.

"Is it a good book?"

"It's very good."

"It's for my daughter who has no sense of humor."

"It'll make her laugh."

"*Nothing* makes her laugh."

"Try it," I said. "It's very funny. She's very funny."

"Where do I pay for it?" he said, though he was standing not three feet from the cash register. Max stepped out of his way as he turned. The serious look was still on his face.

"What makes *you* laugh?" I asked him.

"Dirty jokes," he said.

"What's your favorite dirty joke?"

"Mommy wouldn't want me to tell it."

"That's okay, she's upstairs."

"She'd find out," he said, and looked up into my face, his blue eyes wide. "If you knew Santa was dead," he asked, "would you still believe in him?"

"Santa can't be dead," I said.

"But he is."

"No, he isn't. Santa can't die."

"Why can't he?"

"Because he's magic. That's why you see him on every street corner at the same time."

"If I saw him die, then he can't be on *any* street corner at *all*."

"Yes, but you couldn't have seen him die."

"But I did," the kid said.

"Excuse me," a man at my elbow said.

He was wearing a brown coat with velvet lapels. He was wearing a homburg. He was carrying a furled black umbrella. He had a neat little mustache under a somewhat bulbous nose.

"I'm looking for something called *The Poison Cookbook*," he said. "Does that title ring a bell?"

"I'm not familiar with that title, no, sir."

"You're not?"

"Is it fiction or non-fiction?"

"It's a collection of recipes for poisoned dishes," he said.

"I don't believe we have such a book, sir."

"Isn't this a mystery bookshop?"

"It is *The* Mysterious Bookshop, yes, sir."

"Then why don't you carry this book?"

"I don't think such a book exists, sir."

"Then how would I know the title?"

"I don't even think such a book would be legal, sir."

"Well, I certainly don't plan to *kill* anyone with it," he said.

"Santa Claus is dead, you know," Max told him solemnly.

"I'm afraid I don't care," the man said. "Are you positive you don't have this book? A friend of mine is *aching* to have it."

"I feel certain, sir."

The man looked down at Max and said, "You don't *still* believe in Santa Claus, do you? A big boy like you?"

"Not anymore," Max said.

"Good for you," the man said, and marched out of the shop. It was almost four-thirty.

"Listen," I said, "you have to stop telling people Santa Claus is dead."

"But he is."

"That's what you keep saying. But it might destroy their faith in this joyous holiday season, if you know what I mean."

"I'm sorry, but it's true."

"What'd you do, witness some accident on the street?"

"No."

"Did some street Santa get hit by a car or something?"

"No."

"Then what is it? What makes you think Santa Claus is dead?"

"I saw him die."

"Uh-huh."

"I did."

A blond woman coming down the spiral staircase said, "When I was a little girl, I saw Santa die, too." She was wearing a sable coat that dusted her ankles; a matching sable hat tilted rakishly over one eye.

"You did?" Max asked.

"Yes, little boy," she said. "Where do I pay for these?"

"At the register," Max said, and nodded toward it. "Where was this?" he asked.

"At Macy's," she said.

"How old were you," he asked.

"Never ask a woman her age," she said. "I was six."

"What happened?"

"I was sitting on Santa's lap when he had a fatal heart attack."

"That must have been *horrible* for you," I said.

"Yes," she said dryly. "I always felt I'd caused it somehow."

"But you didn't, of course."

"Well, I'm not actually sure. I was a pretty sexy little thing, you know." She winked at me, turned to Max, and said, "The point is, little boy, we *all* have Santas die on us sooner or later, so I wouldn't take it too much to heart, really. Do you gift wrap?" she asked the cashier.

I knelt beside Max and said, "You see? That nice lady thinks *she* saw him die, too, but of course that can't be. He's still everywhere you look."

"Not anymore," Max said. "He's been dead for half an hour."

Which was when Rosie Prochak came into the shop.

"*Who's* been dead for half an hour?" she asked.

"Santa Claus," Max said.

"Oh," Rosie said, and dismissed the notion with a wave of her hand. "Hello, Alan," she said. "Merry Christmas."

"Merry Christmas, Rosie."

Rosie is a Detective/Second Grade working out of the Fifth Precinct downtown. She is five-feet-seven inches tall, with very long legs and a wonderful chest and red hair and green eyes that make her look more Irish than Polish—which I think she is, but have never asked. You can set your clock by Rosie's arrival times because she usually takes the subway uptown after her shift ends, and spends an hour or so browsing the shop before going home to her three cats. Rosie hates police procedurals. She has told me in confidence that not anybody writing about cops ever gets it right. She hates cat mysteries, too. She says she has never in her lifetime known a cat who solved a homicide. Never. Not even her own three sterling specimens. There is always an air of excitement about Rosie. Maybe it's because she's the only cop I know who wears expensive perfume. Maybe it's because she carries an automatic pistol in her tote bag.

"You know we close at five tonight," I said.

"I need a rare edition costing fifty thousand dollars," she said.

"We'll stay open."

"Actually, I need something for my grandmother. She's in the hospital."

"Did she just pass a stone?" I asked.

"No, she fell getting out of the bathtub. Have you got something that costs a buck ninety-five?"

"Santa got stabbed," Max said.

"What kind of mysteries does she like?" I asked.

"Nothing with cops or cats."

"I remember."

"What's this with Santa?" she asked Max.

"He got stabbed."

"Gee, is that right?" Rosie asked. "How do you know that?"

"I saw him."

"Yeah?" she said, and looked at him curiously. "Where'd you see this?"

"Upstairs," he said.

"So when are you due back?" I asked her.

"The job, you mean?"

"Yeah."

"Monday morning. Why?"

"Just wondering."

"Uh-huh," Rosie said, and her eyes met mine and I could suddenly smell her expensive perfume and I wondered what kind of lingerie tall redheaded detective ladies wore under their skirts. Max was looking up at both of us.

"Maybe you ought to go tell your Mommy we'll be closing in half an hour, huh?" I said.

He seemed puzzled.

"Your mother?" I said. "Upstairs?" I said, and winked at him and nodded toward the spiral staircase. He nodded back and began climbing upward. As he went, he glanced over his shoulder toward the front door, and again there was that apprehensive, almost frightened look in his blue eyes.

"So what's this all at once?" Rosie asked.

Not for nothing was she a detective.

"What do you mean?" I said.

"You want to take me out or something?"

"Yes, I do."

"So ask me."

"I'm asking."

"When?"

"How about tonight?"

"Tonight's Christmas Eve."

"What's wrong with that?"

"I ought to go see Grandma."

"See me instead."

"What time?"

"Eight?"

"What'll we do?"

"You like to dance?"

"I love to dance."

"Good," I said.

Rosie grinned.

"Yeah, good," she said. "What's with the little kid? Have you got a stabbed Santa Claus upstairs?"

"Nope."

"Then what's he talking about?"

"Who knows?"

"I hate spooky kids," Rosie said. "So what can I get Grandma?"

"A bottle of scotch."

"I think she'd prefer that to a book, you want the truth. How's the new Grafton?"

"Excellent. Let me get it for you."

"I'll browse," she said.

I started up the spiral staircase, looked back down at her, and smiled. She smiled back. I was thinking Santa Claus *can't* be dead. Not if he dropped Rosie Prochak into my lap on Christmas Eve.

Max was looking at a book he'd taken down from one of the Sherlock Holmes shelves on the second floor. A man wearing a red parka open over a red and black plaid shirt was standing beside him, leafing through another book. There were three women up here, in addition to Daisy, who worked for us. I wondered which of them was Max's mother. The man who looked as if he'd just come back from a hunting trip spotted me as I came onto the floor, and said, "Excuse me, do you work here?"

"Yes, sir, I do."

"What would a first edition of *Hound of the Baskervilles* cost?" he asked.

"That's not a first edition you've got there, sir."

"I realize that. But what *would* a first edition cost? Ballpark."

"Anywhere from three thousand to eight thousand dollars," I said. "Depending on its condition. Were you interested in seeing something like that, sir?"

"I might be."

"Otto's in his office; he'd be the one to talk to about that."

"Eight thousand dollars, huh?"

"Shall I tell him you'd like to see him?"

"Maybe next Christmas," the man said, and went down the staircase, sighing heavily.

Daisy signaled me over. She was a woman in her forties, I guessed, wearing what looked like a French butcher's apron, blue, over a tidy skirt and blouse. She peered at Max over her little Benjamin Franklin spectacles, and asked, "Who's the kid?"

"Max," I said.

"Is his mother downstairs?"

"I though his mother was up here."

"No, he wandered up here alone."

"When?"

"Fifteen, twenty minutes ago? Told me Santa was dead."

"Yeah," I said.

"You think he's okay?"

"I don't know," I said.

I plucked the new Grafton from the shelf and went over to where Max was standing, seemingly absorbed in Sherlockiana.

"Max," I said, "didn't you tell me your mother was upstairs?"

"Yes?" he said, cautiously.

"Which one of these ladies is your mother, Max?"

Max looked them over.

"Why do you want to know who my mother is?" he asked.

"Because you're a little kid, Max, and if you're out at night all alone. . ."

"She's not here, okay?"

"She's not here in the shop?"

"No."

"You told me she was upstairs."

"Upstairs *home*."

Daisy was watching us intently. I was wondering if I should go downstairs and tell Rosie there was a lost little kid in the shop.

"Where's home?" I asked.

"Fifty-fifth Street."

"You live on Fifty-fifth Street?"

He nodded.

"Do you know which building you live in, Max?"

He nodded again.

"How'd you get here?" I asked him.

"I walked."

"Well, we're going to walk right back, Max. Come on, I'm taking you home."

"I don't *want* to go home," he said.

"Max, listen to me. . ."

"No!" he said.

A girl wearing a short, fake leopard coat, black slacks tucked into knee high boots, a long green scarf that trailed almost to her knees, and sunglasses, indoors, on Christmas Eve, came over to where I was kneeling before Max.

"Excuse me," she said. "Are you this boy's father."

She was nineteen or so, I guessed, with frizzed hair that echoed the tawny color of the fake fur. In her right hand, she was holding a copy of a used Jonathan Kellerman paperback, which presumably gave her the authority to question me about adult-child relationships.

"It's okay," I said, "I work here."

"No, it's *not* okay," she said. "You're terrifying him."

"Miss," I said, "this really is not your affair. I know this boy, it's all right."

"Do you know this man?" she asked Max.

"No," he said.

"Then let him go," she said.

"Miss. . ."

"Let him go this *instant* or I'll call the police!"

In the next instant, there was no longer an instant. In the next instant, Max was on the spiral staircase. "Police!" the girl yelled, and I yelled "Rosie, *stop* him!" But Max was already down the stairs and across the shop and had just reached the front door when it burst open to let in a blast of wintry air and a tall blond woman in a blue cloth coat.

"So *there* you are!" she said.

Max stopped dead in the center of the shop.

He seemed about to run back toward the staircase, away from the woman who now closed the door behind her and smiled at him, her blue eyes echoing his, the facial resemblance unmistakable.

"You had me scared to death," she said, and opened her arms to him, but he did not go to her. Instead, and surprisingly, he went to Rosie and buried himself in her skirt. The girl with the sunglasses and the frizzed hair was just coming down the steps, still yelling "Police!" when Rosie told her, "It's okay, Miss," and showed her a gold and blue-enameled shield which the blond standing just inside the door now took in with a cool, measured look. The girl with the frizzed hair looked at the shield and said, "Are you sure you've got this under control here, Officer?"

"It's *Detective*." Rosie said and gave her a look that sent her scurrying out of the shop.

"Let's go home now, Max," the blond said.

"Are you the boy's mother?" Rosie asked.

"Yes. Let's go, Max."

"I don't want to," Max said.

"Santa will be coming soon," she said. "It's Christmas Eve, Max."

The boy shook his head.

"Maa-aax," she said warningly, virtually singing the name.

"Santa's already been there," he said.

"Max, please don't try my. . ."

"Santa's dead," he said.

"All right, that's enough," she said, and reached for his arm, and was pulling him away from Rosie when he said, "You killed him, Mommy."

♣♣♣

And now he told the story he'd been trying to tell in bits and pieces from the moment he'd entered the shop at a quarter to four this afternoon.

School had let out early for Christmas Eve. The bus had dropped him off on the corner of 55th and Seventh, and he'd walked down the block to the brownstone he lived in, letting himself in with his own latch key, and then tiptoeing upstairs because sometimes his mother took naps in the afternoon. On the second floor of the building, the Christmas tree was ablaze with light in the living room. Max grinned as he walked past it, knowing that Santa would be here later tonight; he had spied on him last year, putting presents under the tree and then drinking the milk and eating the chocolate chip cookies Max had set out for him. He was climbing the steps to the third floor when he heard his mother shrieking at someone. He stopped dead on the staircase, and looked up the steps to the landing above, and realized that the someone she was screaming at was Santa Claus, rushing down the hallway in his red suit and black boots and white beard and whiskers, big belly thrusting, red hat with white fur trim and a white fur pom-pom bouncing as he ran—what was he doing here so early?

And then Max saw his mother coming down the hall behind Santa. There was a pair of scissors in her hand. She kept slashing at the air with the scissors, screaming, until at last she caught up with him, just at the top of the stairs, just five or six feet above Max where he stood watching, terrified. The twin blades of the scissors caught Santa between the shoulder blades. He groped at the air with his open hands, and then fell to the floor, his eyes bulging. Max's mother straddled him where he lay on the floor, plunging the scissors into his back again and again, shrieking "You son of a bitch!" with each deadly thrust. Blood spattered the hallway walls. Blood spattered his mother's face and hands.

Max turned and ran.

He ran down the stairs and out of the house, leaving the door open behind him, rushing out into the night, running blindly, running anywhere, finally seeing the bright lights of the shop and coming in where he thought he would be safe.

Now, in the six o'clock stillness of the shop, police cars angled into the curb outside, dome lights flashing, Max's mother seemed oddly calm. Sitting in a chair near the cash register, her hands folded in the lap of the blue cloth coat, her blue eyes vacant, she told Rosie that she'd been married to Frank Prescott for twelve years, that he'd always been a wonderful father to little Max, a kind and generous man who merely *happened* to have a penchant for other women.

"I've known this for some time now," she said.

Her face was as still and as wan as a funeral mask. The pale hands in her lap were unmoving.

"I simply couldn't take it anymore," she said.

Rosie stood beside the chair, head bent, red hair partially falling over her face, listening, her focus intense. I realized all at once that this was the same concentration mystery readers brought to their passion. Rosie was that very rare individual, a cop who actually loved a good mystery. Totally absorbed, she listened. . .

There was afternoon sunlight slanting through the third floor windows of the brownstone. Frank, slightly drunk after his office Christmas party, insisted on modeling the Santa Claus costume before Max got home from school. Raucously singing "Deck the halls with boughs of holly," he stood before the bathroom mirror, trying on the beard and the boots and the big belly. In the bedroom, Max's mother was going through his briefcase, a faithful loving wife reduced to the role of sneak thief. She recognized the woman in the framed photograph at once, though she had never before seen her so exposed. The inscription was intimate, as utterly candid as the pose: "Come to me, Frank, I'm yours." It was signed "Sybil."

"Frank is a lawyer," she said now. "They work together in the same office. I knew she was the one all along."

It occurred to me that she was still talking about him in the present tense. It occurred to me that perhaps she didn't yet realize she'd stabbed her husband however many times in the back.

"There was a scissors in my sewing basket," she said. "He came out of the bathroom wanting to know how he looked. I told him '*This* is how you look, you son of a bitch!'" and suddenly demonstrated the motion, bringing her hand high above her head, her fist clutched around an imaginary pair of scissors, bringing the hand down again in a sharp plunging thrust. And then, just as suddenly, she folded her hands in her lap again, and sat still and silent for what seemed the longest time.

"He got what he deserved," she said at last. "Mr. *Santa* Claus."

I suddenly remembered what the lady in the sable coat had told Max not an hour earlier.

The point is, little boy, we all *have Santas die on us sooner or later, so I wouldn't take it too much to heart, really. Do you gift wrap?*

But who was going to tell little Max that it wasn't merely Santa who'd died tonight?

Who was going to look into his eight-year-old eyes and tell him *that?*

The Grift of the Magi

By S. J. Rozan

Everybody in the book-collecting world knew what Otto Penzler wanted for Christmas.

Not that everybody cared. Some people didn't say "Mysterious Bookshop" when you asked what their favorite New York book store was; but they were generally bottom-feeders, underdogs, low-lifes, and Otto took the high road, peering down from his pinnacle through his monocle, ignoring them. But he never ignored his good customers. He kept track of our collections, invited us over for drinks (or, in the case of total teetotalers, tea), sent us little stories at Christmas; he never ignored his friends, and he never ignored me.

"Impossible," he said gallantly, waiting at the top as I climbed the thirteen steps on December 24th to the second floor of his first shop on 56th Street. "In fact, Kitty, when you're around I ignore everyone else."

"Uh-huh," I said, giving him a Christmas kiss. "I bet you say that to all the cat burglars. Where'd you get the monocle?"

"Only when they're blond and beautiful. It was a present from Pascal."

"Your mother's French brother?"

"That's right, Mononcle. Did you have trouble getting here?"

"No, except I had to climb over all that snow in front of the bar next door."

Otto nodded. "The drift of the Mayfly. Anyway," he said as I followed him through the shop, "what you do for a living is no business of mine." We entered the book-lined study in the back. Pastry and tea were arrayed on a tray. Outside the windows, snowflakes the color of Otto's hair drifted gently down.

"Snow in the city is so noir," I said. "And I happen to know my profession's your favorite thing about me."

"No, that's—"

"Never mind." Quick on the uptake, I took a teacup and a cupcake from the tea set and settled on the settee. "I adore you, Otto, but let's just stay friends. I don't need romance in my life right now."

"You're wrong, Kitty Manx, you minx. It's what everyone needs."

My look was stern. He bowed.

"Maybe not with me," he went on. "But I have a friend—"

"Never mind your friends, too," I said. "And the mice in their pockets. What do you want for Christmas, Otto?"

"I want my friends to be happy. Did you like that sports mystery, by the way?"

"*Take Me Out at the Ball Game?* No, I got annoyed at how dumb the villain was."

Otto nodded. "Miffed at the bad guy?"

"Right. So, what do you want for Christmas?"

He selected a CD from the stack and slipped it in the stereo. As he started to sit, and the soprano to sing, the song skipped. "It's off-kilter since I cleaned the filter. Could you wedge this on the ledge?"

I got up and helped Otto with the lift of the hi-fi.

"Seriously," he softly sighed as we serenely sat. "There's one thing I want for Christmas. As a collector you'll appreciate it. But I don't think I'll ever find it."

"What's that?"

"A copy of *The Trip to the Outhouse*, by Willy Makit."

"Willy Makit? Isn't that one of Evan Hunter's pen names?"

"Yes. In his 82nd 87th Precinct book—"

"The piano one?"

"No, not *88*, that was '85. The one from '84—"

"Oh, *Pieces of Eight*. I used to own it, but I '86ed it."

"Well, Makit is the name of the guy who claimed he got framed."

"Oh, the one who tried without shame to blame the lame dame?"

"The same. Anyway, *Outhouse* is Hunter's first book, from when he was six. He wasn't nearly as fast then as he is now; they say it took two weeks. There's a beautiful edition, illustrated by Betty Wont."

"That's the one published by Andy Didnt?"

"You know it?"

"Yes, I've seen it. But it's very rare."

"You bet your booty. That's why I don't think I'll ever have one. I do have a customer who has a perfect dust jacket, but he doesn't have the book."

"Forget about my booty."

"That was your booties, my beauty. For your sweet feet."

"That's a neat retreat. But a perfect jacket? Otto, that was a St. Martin's Press book. There can't be a perfect jacket."

"I've seen it. A customer named Felix Gato. South American, new in town. You'd like him—"

"Don't even start."

"But you have something in common."

"I don't like people who're common."

"C'mon."

"No," I said. "Otto, don't play Cupid, it's stupid." I got up to leave, kissed him again. "Merry Christmas, darling, and thanks for the tea."

"Don't thank me."

"Why would that be?"

"Come sit on my knee."

"Go climb a tree."

"Without you I'm all at sea."

"When we get down to one syllable," I said, "it's really time to go."

So I went.

♣♣♣

On my way home, I passed the Chinese take-out place, caught a whiff of the stir-fry. Upstairs, I unlocked the glass-door bookcase. From the center shelf, on cue, I drew what I knew by its hue: a perfect first of Willy Makit's *Trip to the Outhouse*.

I hadn't bought it from Otto, so he wouldn't know I had it. I loved it, but if Otto wanted it for Christmas, then Otto would have it. I smiled. This was the first time I'd be able to surprise Otto: he's usually a step ahead of everyone. But this gift wasn't complete. I went to the window, looked out over the city. Christmas Eve, traffic flowing, red and green lights glowing in the snow, which was blowing. The street was hopping, people not stopping, doing last-minute Christmas shopping.

Well, me too.

I changed into my work clothes—black boots, black sweater, black hood, black slacks—took my black sack, cracked the door and slipped out the back.

Gato's place wasn't hard to find. There was only one F. Gato according to Verizon, whose veracity I couldn't verify but of whom I had heard they were ruthless about truth.

He lived in a townhouse on a side street, so I picked a doorway in a high-rise on the sidewalk near a brownstone by the snow bank at the streetlight. I waited until Gato's lights went out; a minute later, so did he. Well, that was okay: asleep or away was the same to me. Tall, dark and handsome in a black leather vest, Gato came down his steps and headed west. He was so good-looking it was nerve-wracking, enough to make me rethink my leave-taking when Otto started matchmaking.

I won't bore you with the details of how I broke in to Gato's house. I'm what they used to call a second-story man, except I'm a woman. And this is my first story. But break in I did. I expected his place, like mine, to be in tip-top shape, but no, it was a slip-shod hodge-podge, with what-nots, lobster pots, army cots, bibelots, cache pots, old clothes, china, japonica, Lepidoptera, andirons, flat irons, and leg irons in the environs. This was unexpected: but being a bookworm, I found his bookroom easy to find, and in it, in a glass case with a brass base, I found the cover to the Makit book.

It was in perfect shape, as Otto had said. That made it clearly a St. Martin's erratum edition, and very valuable. From my sack I took my supplies: I Brodarted the cover, Bogarted a cigarette, and hotfooted it from this hotbed of surprise.

But the surprises weren't over. When I got home, I found someone had broken into *my* place, and my Makit was gone.

I looked the place over; nothing else had been touched.

I sat.

I thought.

The phone rang.

"We must talk," said the voice on the other end.

"Yes," I said, "we must."

I thrust a blunderbuss under my duster, brushed my hair so it wouldn't be mussed, and took off over the snow's crust.

As I entered the bar called the Cheshire Cat I saw him in a dark booth. When he smiled light flashed off his gold tooth.

"Senorita Manx."

"Mr. Gato."

"You came. Thanks."

"I had to."

His eyes smoldered. I wondered why they didn't set fire to his face.

I sat. Gato was drinking rum and Gatorade, but the table held tea, too. I said, "How did you know, Gato?"

"Otto. He also said you were pretty. It's a pity; I should listen to him, Kitty."

"I was just thinking I ought to, too, Gato."

"About Otto?"

I said in a *voce* more *sotto*, "You're from South America?"

"I am. You'd like it there. We have a wonderful game they play nowhere else—"

"Never mind," I said, giving short shrift to the jai-lai. "Have you ever eaten here? You should try it, especially around Passover."

"No, that food's too heavy for me."

"Oh, the heft of the matzoh brei. So, Otto told you I had the Makit?"

"Si. He told you I had the jacket?"

"I see. And he said we had something in common. But he didn't say what."

"Didn't give him a chance, did you?"

"No-o-o-o-o."

"Me too."

"You do what I do."

"I do. Who knew?"

I sipped my tea. "Your place is. . .crowded," I said.

He shrugged. "I keep almost everything I steal."

"The thrift of the magpie."

He nodded. "But I didn't steal your book to keep it."

"You stole it to give to Otto. Same as I stole your jacket."

"True."

"So let's do."

He gave a holler to the waitress at the till while I took out some dollar bills.

"No, it's on me."

"That's too macho." I ate a nacho. "Don't try to be a gonzo honcho, Pancho. If we're going to be friends—"

"Is that how this ends?"

"This is too deep, I'm getting the bends. Let's go see Otto, Gato, before you're blotto."

We left before he could get quaffed on the Mai-Tai. We split the check, and split for the shop.

The shop, of course, was closed; even Otto gives his staff a few hours off on Christmas Eve. But we rang the bell, and we could tell he heard the knell.

"Ah," he said, smiling. "Kitty Manx and Felix Gato. Please come in."

"We've brought you Christmas cheer, dear," I said. We went

through the shop to the staircase, ascended—don't even think about it—and followed Otto to the study.

"Would it be," Otto asked, smiling more broadly, "one of these?"

From a shelf he himself plucked a book. I took a look.

"*The Trip to the Outhouse*. With a perfect jacket," I gasped. "Otto, you had it all along."

"Of course." Otto beamed.

I looked at Gato. "Not happy, Felix?"

"The beatitude in his attitude—"

"Where's your gratitude, dude? Give him some latitude."

"That's a platitude."

"You're a platypus."

"You're an octopus."

I gave him a kiss on the puss.

Otto's eyes twinkled. "I tried to tell you, both of you. I knew you'd be crazy about each other once you met. But you wouldn't listen."

"So you set us up?" said Felix.

"How did you know I had the book?" I asked.

"You said in the second paragraph that I keep track of my good customers' collections," Otto said. "I know what you buy, from me or some other guy. You also said somewhere around paragraph fifty-five I'm always a step ahead."

I said, "I think I said 'usually,'" but I think no one heard what I said.

Felix and I, stepping on each other's lines, said, "And you knew—"

"—just what we'd do."

"Yes. I knew that in getting each of you to try to give me the gift you thought I wanted, I could give to you both the gift I wanted to give you. Each other."

"Which is why—"

"Yes," said Otto, and we all sang as church bells rang and well-laid plans agley did gang: "It's why the true title of this story is *The Grift of the Magi*."

My Object All Sublime

By Anne Perry

Half past four in the afternoon on Christmas Eve. The odd flurry of snow drifted out of a darkening sky, but there was always someone who had not got a gift for aunt so-and-so, or uncle someone, so the shops were still lit and no one dared close up and go home. That was particularly true of The Mysterious Bookshop at 129 W. 56th St., New York. Whoever it is you may have forgotten, there's bound to be a book that will suit them, and at "Mysterious" they will be able to put their hands on it for you. Problem solved.

The man who buzzed the door to be let in on this particular occasion was of average height, perhaps a trifle thin, although it was hard to judge under his enveloping raincoat. But he was bareheaded and there was no mistaking the sharp eagerness of his face, the nervous chewing of his lips as the latch was undone and he went down the steps inside.

"I'm looking for a gift. I want something special!" he said almost before his foot was on the bottom step.

The woman behind the desk with the cash register smiled helpfully at him. "Do you have anything in mind?" she asked.

He had thought about this very carefully, in fact he had thought of little else for quite a long time. Every word was planned, but now that the reality was here it was not quite the same. "Yes! Yes, yes," he nodded. "It's for my uncle. He's been extraordinarily good to me. I've. . . I've racked my mind for ages what to get him. That's why I'm so late. But now I have the idea. . ." He gulped with tension and excitement.

She was trying to be helpful, but he must get beyond her. She was no use at all. He must speak to Otto Penzler, the expert, the owner, the man who was the power behind it all. This woman was nothing, not part of it. But he must not be rude. Quite apart from the fact that it would get him nowhere, there was the immorality of it. It was unforgivable to be rude to waiters, servers, the people you pass by and think of no account. That was one of life's great sins!

He made himself smile at her. "I want a book he will treasure, for itself, not just for what's written in it. Something he can hold, touch, turn the pages and think of its history. I want it to have meaning. It must be a mark of my feelings for him, my respect, my regard."

She looked really interested. Here was a book lover, not just someone who merely liked the entertainment of a story. "You would like something rare, perhaps?" she suggested. "An early edition, maybe a first?"

"Yes! Yes, yes," he agreed, nodding his head up and down with enthusiasm. Thank heaven she was intelligent enough he did not have to labor the point and lead her step by step. "How clever of you. That is exactly the right thing. Uncle Horace will be thrilled. It would be in good taste, interesting, valuable but discreet. I do not wish to be ostentatious, show up my other relations, you understand?"

"Very sensitive of you," she approved.

"Thank you. Yes, thank you. I like to think I am aware of other people's feelings," he accepted. He leaned forward a trifle, staring at her. "It matters, you know!"

"Of course it does," she agreed. "What type of book is your uncle most likely to enjoy? Hard-boiled, cozy, thriller, police procedural, private eye?" She enumerated the possibilities. "American or foreign? British perhaps? Present day, sixties or seventies, Golden Age?"

"My goodness, you do have a choice," he marvelled. "I'm afraid that's where I need a little advice. Who is the expert on these things? I don't mean to be offensive, but if I am spending three or four thousand dollars," he watched her face carefully, "or even more, then I do need to be sure I am doing it wisely. And you see I have very little idea myself."

Her eyes widened. He was pleased to see it. He was talking a lot of money; it was right that he should be respected. That was as much as some of those writers had been paid for the entire work originally. And to think that now a single copy of the book was worth that much!

But he pushed the thought away. This was not the time for it.

"I think perhaps I should call Mr. Penzler," she answered him. "He can tell you anything you need to know."

He feigned ignorance. "He's the expert?"

She could not help smiling. "Oh, absolutely! Anything he doesn't know is not worth bothering with. He'll give you the best advice possible, and find you the perfect gift for your uncle. If you'll just excuse me, I'll go upstairs and see if he is free to help you right now."

"Up that spiral staircase?" he asked, opening his eyes very wide and staring at the black wrought iron steps that wound up in a tight corkscrew to the floor above.

"Yes," she took the handrail and began to climb with considerable care.

He watched her all the way, all but holding his breath. It was working! It really was working. He gave a tiny hiccup of excitement. He had waited so long for this, thought over so many plans before he came up with the right one.

She was gone several minutes, but he did not even once glance away at all the shelves and shelves of books along both sides of the room before the staircase and beyond it, thousands of titles, every type and kind of mystery, thriller and espionage story every written. There really was something here for every possible taste, past, present and future.

A couple of customers came from the far end, one empty-handed, the other with a pile of books eight or nine high. Another assistant materialized from behind a stack, took the books and rang them up, accepted the money and wished the customer a happy Christmas. The door opened and closed as a gust of icy air blew in.

It was just about a quarter to five. Exactly right.

He still stood staring at the black spiral steps.

There was a noise above him, the murmur of voices, a man and a woman. She must be telling Otto that there was a customer willing to spend several thousand dollars. That would bring him! Nobody ignores the possibility of a sale like that! What are most books? Five or six dollars for a paperback? Twenty to thirty at most for a hardback, more if you go into coffee table books with photographs, or some kind of an encyclopedia?

Another customer came in, bought a book hastily, a forgotten gift, and went out. It was darker outside and there was a real smell of ice on the wind.

Was she going to come back with a list of books, forcing him to have to argue with her to get to see Otto personally? He began to fidget. His hands were cold. Why was it taking so long?

Then at last she appeared, climbing down slowly, clinging onto the handrail. But she was smiling, and there were no books in her other hand.

His heart leapt. He gulped air and hiccupped again.

"If you would like to come upstairs, Mr. . . . ?"

"Wilson," he replied. It was as good a name as any other, ordinary but not suspicious like "Smith" or "Jones."

"Mr. Wilson," she repeated politely. "Otto will see you, and he has quite a few suggestions, depending on your uncle's taste, and what he might already have. But he'll certainly be able to find something for you."

"Good!" he said with startling feeling. He heard his own voice with the ring of intensity in it. Listening to him, anyone would believe he really wanted this gift for his uncle. And the emotion was genuine. It gave him a fierce satisfaction that Otto Penzler really wanted to sell him an expensive book!

That could be rolled around the mouth and savored, like a good liqueur. "Thank you," he added, smiling at her.

"If you would like to go up?" she invited, stepping away from the stairs and indicating them.

"Oh, yes!" he accepted. "Thank you very much." He put out his hand and gripped the rail, then put his foot on the first iron rung. It was very steep. He had to be careful going up. A misstep and he could slip and fall. Oh, indeed, it would not be too difficult at all! A step short and he could slither all the way back, bounce off the rail at the outside, or the central post in the middle, a step too long and his foot could shoot right through into the space beyond and he could break his leg! Again he would fall backwards. The thought made his stomach knot up, and he felt a little sick. But he had never liked heights.

His head emerged over the floor level of the room above and he stared around. It was an elegant gentleman's study, comfortable leather sofas and chairs, a polished desk, but above all the walls were lined floor to ceiling with books, and not just any books! These were beautiful old books, precious books, rare first editions, works long out of print. The whole history of the genre was here from Edgar Allan Poe to the present day writers whose early work was now collectable. How many millions of readers the world over had been thrilled, mystified, taken into other realms and other lives turning the pages of the books that sat quietly in this wonderful room? The ideas spanned the earth, time, ideologies and passions.

But he must pay attention to what he was here for, or he would not succeed. And he must succeed!

He stared at the man standing in front of the bookshelves. Otto Penzler. It must be. Extraordinary. It was the first time he had actually seen him. They were probably of a height, but that was where the resemblance ended. Otto was not thin, he was quite well built. He had a full head of silver hair and a perfectly trimmed beard. In fact he was perfectly turned out altogether, a dark finely tailored suit, better than just good, a silk handkerchief just tipping his breast pocket, an immaculate white shirt and a silk cravat. The man was almost a dandy! One would expect him to have his shoes handmade! He probably ate Beluga caviar and drank Napoleon brandy.

"Good afternoon," Otto said cautiously, offering a hand as Wilson teetered on the last step before regaining his balance, unassisted. "I believe you are looking for a special gift for an uncle you're particularly fond of?"

"Yes,"Wilson agreed, gulping. It was not so easy now that he was actually here. He had played this out in his mind a dozen times, more, twenty, thirty times. But somehow it was different in reality. In his dreams Penzler had not been so confident, so very smooth. He had not smiled like this! "Yes I am. I'm. . . I'm sorry I left it so late. I realize. . ."

"It's not a problem," Otto said cheerfully. "Come in and sit down, Mr. Wilson." He gestured to the leather sofa. He must have heard the woman address him by name. "Tell me something about your uncle."

Wilson sat down. Or rather more accurately, he buckled at the knees and found himself slumped on the sofa. He must make sense! This was important! A mistake now could cost him everything! He had thought of all this before! It was an essential part of it, or it would not make sense, and it was imperative that Penzler understood, or it all just failed. It would be without purpose, without satisfaction. Justice must make sense or it was not justice at all. Why did they portray it as blind? That was stupid! It must have sight and understanding above everything. That was the very essence of it!

"Your uncle?" Otto prompted.

"Oh, yes! Uncle Horace." He must collect his thoughts. Say what he had prepared. "I am afraid he is a far greater connoisseur of mysteries than I am."

"Then we shall find him something very special," Otto promised.

"Oh. . .that is why I have come here! I could have got just anything at Barnes & Noble." He saw the slightly pained look on Penzler's face. Good. "He has a keen sense of justice," he went on. "Not the law, which is often quite separate. I mean the kind of retribution that catches up with a man, or a woman, of course, for the acts that the law cannot always reach. Not vengeance, you understand? There is a difference. It must be right, and preferably it should bear a relation to the sin, in some way."

"'To make the punishment fit the crime,'" Otto quoted.

"Yes, yes, precisely!" This was most satisfactory. He even found himself smiling. It was going very well, better even than he had dared hope. His earlier fear slipped away. Penzler was not so frightening after all. Let him be confident. So much the better! "You have it perfectly!"

"Mr. Gilbert, actually," Otto murmured.

"I beg your pardon?"

"I was quoting from W. S. Gilbert, from the words to the Mikado. 'My object all sublime, I shall achieve in time, to make the punishment fit the crime.'"

"Oh, I see. You are inspired, sir. That is precisely it. I would like a book which will perfectly answer the greatest injustice done to my uncle. I think it will satisfy him as nothing else could."

A look of puzzlement crossed Otto's face, but his smile faded only very slightly. He would never be discourteous to a customer, unless his behavior was insufferable. There had been one or two—but they had richly deserved their ostracism. "This is injustice?" he enquired. "Should it be addressed openly, or might that be offensive to him?"

"Oh, no!" Wilson said quickly. "I think it should be quite open. That way he will know that I understand. What do you think is a man's most precious possession, Mr. Penzler?"

Otto looked a little lost. It was an impossible question. There were degrees of answers.

"I heard of you when I was in Omaha," Wilson went on helpfully.

"Did you?"

"Yes! And in San Francisco. And in Houston, and Denver, and Chicago—and Albany."

Otto's eyebrows rose. "Albany?"

"Yes, even there."

"As a book dealer?"

"A dealer in rare books, a connoisseur, an expert in hard-boiled American detective fiction in particular, but everything in general, and of course as an editor, and a publisher too."

Otto looked pleased, he just about avoided looking down-right smug. "Really. . ." he murmured.

"Yes," Wilson said decisively. "Your good name is nation-wide!"

"Thank you!"

"You might be said to be at the top of your profession, in your particular niche."

"Thank you!"

"That pleases you?" Wilson asked.

"Well, yes. . .of course." He did look smug. Definitely.

"You value that?"

Otto understood. "You mean a man's good name is his most precious possession!"

"Quite! Oh, exactly so!" Wilson nodded several times. "You have it precisely. And once it is gone, it is extraordinarily difficult to get it back. It is part of your identity, don't you agree?"

Otto was a little reluctant, not in principle, but because he was uncertain where the conversation was leading. There seemed to be more emotion in it that was readily explainable. "Your uncle in some way lost his good name?" he asked. He stood up and moved a step or two further away from Wilson, towards his own chair, and away from the top of the spiral staircase.

"Not in some way," Wilson corrected, rising also. "He was robbed of it. . ." He waited for Otto to ask how, and when he did not, he went on anyway. "By a man so arrogant, so consumed with his own importance, he was hardly even aware he was doing it!" Wilson heard his own voice high and sharp with tension, and deliberately tried to lower it. It was too soon to allow such heat. Anyway, he was still behind Penzler, farther from the gaping hole in the floor with the black iron spiraling downwards.

He gulped, steadying himself. He made his tone level, quite calm. "Of course one is always biased towards one's own family, and Uncle Horace has always been very good to me, and indeed to my mother as well. So I would like to give him something that would not only be a gift of monetary value, but one of personal understanding as well. I'm sure you can see why it is important, and that of course is why I tell you these things." That was a lie, but a necessary one. Penzler would realize the need for it in time. He had to, or there would be no point in all this, no symmetry, and no justice!

"A first edition of a classic story of retribution for some libel or slander," Otto grasped the point that was agreed between them.

"Exactly! Exactly!" Wilson said eagerly, restraining himself with difficulty from moving even closer. "A story that begins with a powerful man, arrogant." He used the word again fiercely, rolling it over his tongue. "A man in a position of trust who can make decisions that raise other men to the skies, or crush them to pieces—a man others listen to—a man whose very word can establish—or ruin!"

"I'm not sure that anyone has quite that power," Otto demurred. There was something a little wild in this man's eyes that he did not care for. Still, more than a few book collectors were eccentric, to say the least. One could not pick and choose all one's customers.

"A modest man would say that!" Wilson seemed almost accusatory. Then he looked away, down at the lowest shelf of books, and his voice was quiet again. "The revenge should be slow. . .take the whole book. That is necessary, isn't it? Otherwise it would be a mere short story."

"Some short stories are very powerful," Otto pointed out. He saw the anger flush up Wilson's cheeks. "But I realize you are looking for a complete book as a gift. There's probably quite a choice and we'll find exactly the right one." He started to move towards the shelves where his American hard-boiled first editions were. It must be nearly dark outside now and he could hear nothing from the shop downstairs, although the lights were still on. Surely they would not have gone home without speaking to him, wishing him goodnight and Merry Christmas. They would not mind interrupting, on such an occasion. After all it was Christmas Eve! He would much rather have heard voices down there, or at least movement.

Wilson's words came clear and resonant behind him, charged with emotion. "It should go turn after turn, like a twisting path downwards."

Otto had been about to bend down and pick out a book, but instead he straightened up. "I beg your pardon?"

"Revenge," Wilson replied, raising his eyebrows. "It must be delicate, don't you agree?"

"Not necessarily." Otto did not agree at all. "It could be sudden. It could be violent or subtle, or of a dozen different natures."

"An artist must have it balanced, appropriate." Wilson made a sudden gesture with his hand, a downward spiral. "Like a vortex! Sucking one down, helplessly, only realizing what it is about when it is too late to escape. . ." He took a deep breath, his eyes very wide open. "Don't you agree, that would be a very dramatic story? Very satisfying?"

Otto was now distinctly uncomfortable. The word "delicate" in connection with revenge, and the term "vortex" used in the same breath awoke a memory in him. It was faint and he could not place it, but it was not pleasant. And yet as far as he could recall, even with an effort, he could not recognize Wilson's face, or his voice, or for that matter his name.

"Yes," he said rather more sharply than he had intended. "It would be very dramatic." He felt uncomfortable turning his back to the man, but it was necessary in order to search the shelves. His eye slid over authors—Mickey Spillane, Dashiell Hammett, Raymond Chandler, Erle Stanley Gardner. What could he sell this man to get him out of here?

"There's an art in it," Wilson said from behind him. He sounded very close, less than a yard, as if he had moved silently.

"Of course," Otto agreed, stepping away from him, and closer to the top of the staircase.

"Literature, and revenge," Wilson started nodding again. "But of course you know that, Mr. Penzler. You are an artist yourself." That sounded like an accusation. "Or at least a judge of artists!"

Otto turned to look at the man, and saw a flare of pure hatred in his eyes that was so intense, so wild it awoke a flicker of fear inside him. It dawned on him that Wilson might not be entirely sane. He was about to call out to someone downstairs, but he suppressed the instinct. It was ridiculous. It was probably a trick of the light. Wilson was a complete stranger, eccentric, but hardly dangerous. Apart from that, there was no sound whatever downstairs; there might be no one there. Better, far better, to keep control.

Otto cleared his throat. "An editor," he corrected. "As a publisher, I naturally read all the books I publish, and edit them as necessary."

"And judge them!" Wilson snapped, moving a step closer.

Otto took a step back, almost level with the rail around the top of the staircase. "Of course." There was no choice but to agree. "That's an editor's job. But I think 'choose' would be a better word. I choose which ones to publish and which ones don't suit my list."

"Judge," Wilson repeated. "Judge which is fit to be given life, and which isn't. A bit like an abortionist really! Are you pro-life, Mr. Penzler? Or do you think some people aren't fit to live—Mr. Penzler?"

Wilson really was mad! Why was there such an awful silence downstairs? Had they really locked up and gone home without bothering to come up and speak to him? Wish him Merry Christmas?

Wilson took another step, obliging Otto to stand nose to nose with him, or move to the head of the staircase at the top of its steep steps down.

"Thank God that is not my decision to make," Otto said a trifle hoarsely. "I edit books, I never make judgments on people."

"You accept—and reject—isn't that a judgment, Mr. Penzler?" Wilson demanded. His breath was rasping in his throat now. "A man's writing is his self, his passions and beliefs spread out on paper, shared with the word—in a way, his immortality! To reject that, stifle it before it is born, that is the beginning of the downward vortex!"

Now Otto remembered it with hideous clarity! A melodramatic, overblown manuscript, well researched but far too wordy, artificial, unbelievable characters, stilted dialogue—*The Downward Vortex*. He had not only rejected it, he had advised a top agent who had asked him, not to bother with it. "Unpublishable," he had said. And so it was. No amount of editing could have made it a success. And what he published made his own reputation as well. But it would be very much wiser not to say that now!

Wilson must have seen the recognition in his face. His breathing quickened, beads of sweat glistening on his upper lip and his brow.

"It's a curling, twisting path that leads you down to ruin," he said softly. "A kind of death, don't you agree?"

He must try and placate the man until he could get away. But going down the stairs was not so easy with Wilson standing above him. One violent push, hard enough, and the fall would be dangerous. If you pitched down those steps headlong, you could even break your neck.

"Don't you agree?" Wilson repeated more loudly.

"Yes." With a considerable effort, Otto kept his voice level. Wilson had him almost pinned at the top of the steps, and there was a crazy glitter in his eyes. Would he really try to commit murder over a rejected manuscript? If people started doing that there wouldn't be a publisher left alive in New York! Or anywhere else. There must be still an element of reason left in the man's mind. He had planned this with some care.

"But ruin and death are not the same thing," he said, forcing himself to meet Wilson's eyes. "For revenge to be perfect there has to be some equation, some artistry and balance." His spine was pressing against the rail around the stair. He was not subject to vertigo, but he was most unpleasantly aware of the drop behind him.

Wilson was so close he could smell the aftershave, and feel the heat of him. To push him away now he would have to use considerable force, in fact actually punch him. It would have to be very hard if he were to give himself an opportunity to twist away and get down the stairs before Wilson came after him. And sudden. He must give no warning or Wilson would strike first.

"Artistry!" Wilson said with relish. "Oh, yes! You underestimate me, Mr. Penzler. You really do." Excitement glittered in his eyes and his breathing was rapid. He moved a few inches closer. They were almost touching. There was no longer any denying the threat. *The Downward Vortex!* he rasped between clenched teeth, his lips drawn back. "Justice!" He made the word sibilant. "That's what it is—justice." He hunched his shoulders.

Otto gathered his strength. He had no advantage of height, but perhaps a little of weight—but Wilson was crazy, and that gave a strength that was impossible to judge. On the other hand, Otto was fighting for survival, from injury or worse, and that too gave a unique edge.

There was no sound from downstairs. The lights were on, but that was all. Anyone could have come or gone, and he had no way of telling.

"You believe in justice. . .don't you, Mr. Penzler?" Wilson asked, almost caressingly.

Was this the moment? When he was expecting words, excuses, pleas even. . .Otto tensed his body, ready to lash out as hard as he could—send this lunatic staggering back against the farther bookshelves. Then as the weight of his own fall knocked the wind out of his lungs, he would buckle and sprawl onto the floor—giving Otto time to scramble down the stairs to the ground floor, and if necessary the street. Wilson was mad, there was no way to deal with him in a reasonable manner.

Wilson was trembling with suppressed excitement, the

sweat beading on his face, his eyes wild, brilliant. His breath hissed between his lips.

Suddenly Otto saw it all—not his own body crushed at the bottom of the stairs—but Wilson, bruised and bleeding, lying on the floor of Otto's study, his special book room filled with priceless first editions, practically the history of detective literature. There would be law suits, medical bills, punitive damages, but towering over it all the headlines racing though the mystery world—"Otto Penzler attacks customer in The Mysterious Bookshop"—and underneath the story of how he had gone mad and beaten the daylights out of some nameless middle-aged man who had simply come to buy a Christmas gift for his uncle. The physical evidence would be all on Wilson's side. He would be bleeding, bruised, terrified—and there would not be a mark on Otto—nor any sane excuse in the world.

Otto took a long, deep breath and forced himself to relax and to smile, although it felt more like a baring of teeth such as a dog might make as a warning, just before it leapt for your throat.

"You know, Mr. Wilson, you have something of a gift for drama. You create tension rather well, and menace, merely with words." He took a breath and kept his voice perfectly steady, just lifting it a fraction at the end. "Every year I have a short story printed up in a booklet, as a gift for special customers, friends and associates. If you care to write up this little incident, just as it occurred, I would consider it for next year. I think my usual financial arrangement would be acceptable to you—it's not high, but it's fair."

Wilson's jaw fell slack. He was caught so completely by surprise that he had no idea how to react.

Otto waited a moment or two, breathing in and out slowly, his back still pressed against the rail.

"Would you?" Wilson asked, his voice cracking. "How do I know that?"

"Write it just as it happened, and I give you my word," Otto replied. He meant it. He had opinions, likes and dislikes, a sharp tongue at times, but he never lied, and everyone knew that. Apart from personal integrity, it was bad business, and even if Wilson did not believe in his honor, no one had ever thought Otto a fool.

Hope was easing the lines out of Wilson's face, taking the hectic look from his eyes and replacing it with something saner, sweeter. He took a step back, allowing Otto to straighten up and relax properly. Wilson held out his hand. "I'll do that! I'll bring it to you by the New Year. Happy Christmas, Mr. Penzler."

Otto took the proffered hand and shook it. "It's a deal. Happy Christmas, Mr. Wilson."

Christmas Spirit

By Michael Malone

If you live alone, there's nothing lonesomer than Christmas.
Well, one thing maybe: wandering around alone right before
Christmas on a visit to New York City. The air is sharp and the
sky is crisp and cloudless and all these cheerful folks are hurrying past you on crowded sidewalks swinging big bright bags
full of presents they've just bought for each other and they're
all strangers to you, and it's Christmas, and back home you're
living alone.

So there I was, December 23rd, by my lonesome in midtown
Manhattan, and nobody in particular waiting for me in Hill-
ston, North Carolina, where I've been Chief-of-Police so long
I ought to take down that yellow *Newsweek* clipping on my
refrigerator calling me "SMART YOUNG CRIMEFIGHTER IN
THE NEW SOUTH."

I had walked from my hotel over to the little book store on
56th Street that Justin Savile, head of my homicide division,
had told me about. Justin collects old British mysteries (he
likes anything old and Anglophilic), so I figured I'd buy him
one for Christmas, one of the type where everybody wears a
tuxedo to dinner, and the murderer gets left alone in the country house study with a loaded gun on the desk, in case he
wants to avoid the tackiness of a trial.

In the store's display window, a small trim well-dressed man was crawling around fiddling with a row of foot-high angels. He had hair as white as the angels' fiberglass wings but bore no other resemblance to Santa Claus; indeed the way he kept impatiently shoving aside a fat yellow cat that was rubbing against his trousers gave you the feeling that flying around the world with eight tiny reindeer was the last thing this man would have wanted to do on his holidays. He was having a little trouble balancing a hardcover book in the outstretched wire hands of each of the angels. The angels all had wide happy smiles, but the titles of the colorful book jackets ran to corpses and blood and dangerous women—as if the man in the window were trying to tell his customers that the world was not the jolly paradise these Christmas angels innocently supposed.

I tapped on the window. When the man turned, brushing the persistently affectionate cat away, I pointed at the angel on the end, whose book—*The Hearse You Came In On*—was upside down. The man grinned, waved thanks, and flipped the novel right aside up. Then he blew an extravagant kiss in my direction, which was pretty surprising until I heard a woman's voice behind me on the sidewalk. Obviously she, not I, was the object of the man's affectionate gesture.

"My God, Cuddy Mangum! What are you doing at Otto's?"

It's a big city but a small world. The woman behind me was Lauri Wald, an NYPD detective I'd met last spring when we'd both testified to Congress about how to get the homicide rates down. "Get rid of the guns," we'd told the committee, but hey, who listens. Americans shot over eight thousand of each other to death this year, so Lauri and I packed up our charts and graphs and headed out to a Moroccan restaurant. Later on that night, we came close to going to bed together but didn't quite get there.

"Hey, you sweet lady." I gave Lauri a kiss, smelling menthol cigarettes and the Halston I remembered from those Senate chambers. "Merry Christmas. It's been too long."

I'm tall, tall enough to have played ACC basketball in North

Carolina, and Lauri wasn't all that far below me. She had red hair, big strong features and a generous shape she wasn't trying to hide. A tight red sweater under her loose coat was tucked into a wide belt cinched around black Roxy trousers. Lauri was like a woman from the forties. You could imagine her striding along at dawn with her hair in a bandana, and her lunch in a metal box, heading through the factory gates to weld some B-52s together.

"So who's Otto?"

She pointed at the dapper man now crawling out of the window back into the shop. "Otto owns The Mysterious Bookshop. I buy from him." Like Justin, Lauri was one of those busman-holiday detectives who collects mystery fiction. You ask me, the human race's nasty enough on its own without writers making up any more mayhem.

Lauri patted my tie. "I thought maybe you were a friend of his, coming to his Christmas party."

"Darlin', I didn't have a friend in this whole big city till just this minute when I saw you. I flew up to see Reba singing in a Broadway show."

"Sure." She rolled large blue eyes skeptically. I don't know why nobody believes that I really love country singers. She studied me. "What is it really, an extradition?" Another thing nobody seems to believe is I've got a life outside running a police department.

"Just Reba McIntire." I gave her my best smile. "And maybe I had a feeling I'd run into you."

"Sure."

So Lauri invited me to be her date to this fellow Otto's Christmas party that was about to start right there in his store. And that's how it happened that I solved my first murder case, pro bono, in the borough of Manhattan. Well, in fact it was the yellow cat that solved the case. I just helped him.

We were the first guests at this party. Lauri'd come there early so she could leave early because she was pulling graveyard duty for a NYPD pal who was trying to get his marriage back together by taking his wife on a Disney cruise. As it turned out, she had to get another pal to fill in for her filling in for him, because we were busy with a crime scene all that night and the next day too.

Inside the store, we climbed some pretty lethal-looking iron spiral stairs to the second floor. The overweight cat followed us up and into a large paneled room at the end of a corridor. It was handsome, with a high ceiling and clubby furniture and it was decorated for the holidays with a Christmas tree and with swags of pine garlands that hung from the walls of bookshelves. There were books everywhere in that room, thousands and thousands of them. Now it's been said that the only place in Hillston that's got more books than my River Rise condo is Haver University, but this man had me beat. And I admired that about him.

"Otto Penzler, this is Police Chief Cuddy Mangum, from North Carolina."

"Where's that?" the man asked brusquely, shoving aside a stack of little wrapped presents to set down the four champagne bottles he'd carried into the room. "What is it, a state?"

"State of mind," I told him. "Just get on the New Jersey Turnpike and keep going south."

"Why would I?"

He took this tone, like he was hard as Pharaoh's heart, but the fact is, I think he was a marshmallow. It was like with him and the fat yellow cat, which he pretended to despise, claiming he had no use for animals or children or anything else that didn't appreciate a first edition or a *premiere cru*. But the whole time Penzler was telling us how the cat had just sneaked into his life a year ago Christmas, climbed up the fire escape and came in through the bathroom window, he kept dropping bits of pate on the floor for that tubby thing to gobble. The cat spit out the olive he'd been licking the salt off, and tore into this foie gras. His name was Spirit. I thought it was for alcohol but turns out it was Dickens.

"Christmas Past, Christmas Present," Lauri said, "And, Otto, Spirit here's looking to me like Christmas Future."

Penzler shoved the cat away from him with his glossy shoe. "Not if I can get him to eat arsenic."

"I get the feeling he'll eat anything," I said. "That cat looks just like Nero Wolfe in his yellow pajamas."

Penzler liked that. He liked it that I wanted to buy my friend Justin a British mystery from the Twenties or Thirties too, but when he told me the price of an Agatha Christie first edition, I said I'd rather have a new car. Finally we settled on somebody I never heard of, but he said Justin would, so I gave him a check. Studying it dubiously, he said, "Are you sure this place, North Carolina, exists?"

We had some champagne and he told me I ought to marry Lauri, adding that he'd do it himself except she knew him too well to say yes.

"Ha!" she said, and there could have been a whole story behind that syllable.

By this time a stream of guests was flopping up those spiral stairs like salmon. According to Lauri, most of them were writers or cops or blonde women—the three types of people Penzler liked, she said. He was a mighty generous host—the champagne was French, the caviar was Russian, and there was more of both than in *War and Peace*. Lauri and I took our glasses over to a corner, where we had a friendly chat about the world of crime.

Pretty soon the room filled with noisy revelers; they seemed mostly to know each other and to be of extreme types: either they drank non-stop or they'd given up drink entirely, except to talk about how they'd given it up. Or they'd just given up smoking or they planned to soon or they thought quitting was for wimps. There was much joking about Penzler's antipathy to cigarettes. To smoke, guests had to go to the bathroom off the corridor and lean out the window onto the fire escape. There was a line waiting to get in. I mean I'm from North Carolina where it's downright patriotic to smoke, but this group left us in the dust. Also in the bathroom, the champagne sat on ice in the bathtub and the only toilet was in there, so it was a pretty popular place, and all sorts of things turned out to be going on in it, more than anybody knew.

In our corner by the Christmas tree (which was decorated

with little toy guns and knives and skulls and such), Lauri pointed out famous writers to me. There were a lot of them there. Near us, one, thin with a beard, suddenly grabbed hard at the arm of another one, stocky with a moustache, both of them all in black. Beard pointed at someone. "Goddamn it to shit, she's here. Can you believe she'd do that to him? These are his people, these aren't her people."

"Poor old Bart," said the other one. "He told me last night he didn't think he was ever going to get over Claudia. She doesn't make it easy."

The two men were staring at a long-legged woman who was cruising into the party, staggering just a bit like she'd had a few drinks before she'd arrived. Except for these little red bell earrings she was wearing that blinked on and off, she was all in black — black hair, short black dress, sheer black hose and black stiletto heels. She came slipping through that crowd of blondes in a slithery kind of way that gave the general impression of a panther on the Discovery Channel, but a drunk one.

"Who's that?" I asked Lauri. "And who's 'poor old Bart'?"

Well, it was like saying "Who's Dean Smith?" to a Carolina basketball fan. Lauri rolled her eyes at Spirit the cat who was hanging around our feet hoping for some Sacher torte. "Bart Wells! You know. *Fatal Greed, Mortal Envy, Lethal Lust*, Bart Wells, big best-seller." Well, I had heard of him and even recognized him from his jacket photo when she pointed him out talking to Penzler over by the Christmas tree. He was a good-looking man in a pale green cashmere turtleneck, except his face had just turned the color of his sweater, apparently at the sight of his ex-wife Claudia, the black-haired panther lady, who'd divorced him three years earlier. According to Lauri, clearly in the literary know, he'd never gotten over her. It was true; he sure looked like he hadn't.

So that's what the two famous writers next to us, Beard and Moustache, had meant when they were going on about how could Claudia ruin poor old Bart's Christmas by (presumably) crashing a party of his nearest and dearest. Except one of the other guests (a friendly grizzly bear of a fellow, also all in black) took a near and dear approach to the ex-Mrs. Wells herself, wrapping her in a bear hug and hanging on tight while he kissed her, till, watching them, poor old Bart squeezed his champagne flute so tightly he broke it and cut his hand. It looked entirely minor but was bleeding enough to make folks nervous.

Everybody commiserated with him except the panther lady, who just laughed. "Oh Bart, give it a rest." He grimaced at her like she'd slapped him.

Just then Lauri's pager beeped on her belt; handing me her glass, she shoved her way through the crowd to make her call in the bathroom, where she could hear (plus, I bet anything, smoke a few menthols).

Across the room, Penzler stopped pouring champagne into the glasses of anybody that got close to him; he hurried over with a bar towel to wrap up his friend's hand before it bled on his Persian carpet. Ignoring them, the ex-Mrs. Wells swooped up the yellow cat Spirit, smacked him in the mouth when he tried to swat her, took off one of her blinking red earrings and hooked it through the little leather collar around the animal's neck. Spirit hated the ornament but couldn't shake it loose. As he ran off, blinking like a little railroad crossing, she laughed some more. Then she headed my way, close enough for me to smell the gin on her breath, and brushed past Beard and Moustache, floating her hand across their faces like they were water and she was in a canoe. "I'm off, boys. Flying down to Rio tonight, just like in the movie."

I wanted to say, "How's that, Ms. Wells, standing on the wing of the plane?" I know my Fred and Ginger RKO movies, including *Flying Down to Rio*. But I didn't know these people well enough to kid them, so I let it slide.

"Don't indulge Bart," the woman purred at the two writers. "He eats his grief like chocolate-covered cherries." She patted the pocket of Moustache's black cashmere jacket like she knew what she was going to find there, and took out cigarettes and a lighter. Lighting up, she blew smoke in his face with a throaty laugh.

"Go to hell, Claudia," Moustache suggested. "At least go to the bathroom."

Everything struck her funny; she laughed again, slipped through the crowd, puffing smoke rings at the ceiling, and the party swallowed her up.

Right after she left, her rejected spouse, Bart, joined Beard and Moustache. Despite being warned, they were pretty sympathetic. "What a bitch," they told him.

"Don't call her that," Bart said, sucking on his hand like some autoerotic vampire. "I love her."

"Why?" asked Penzler, coming over with another towel; he was either a sweetheart or worried about his rug.

"There's no way I'm going to get over her. If she were dead, maybe I could get over her, but there's no way." The uxorious author then wandered off. After Penzler left us too, to stop one of the young blonde women from drinking cranberry juice while checking out his Dashiell Hammett collection, Beard grabbed at Moustache's arm again. "You think Bart really could get over Claudia if she was dead?"

Moustache thought it over. "So what are you saying, we should kill her for him?"

Beard shrugged. "We do it for a living, shouldn't we be good at it?"

I couldn't help but lean forward. "Well, hey, what are friends for?" They looked at me funny but maybe it was because I had a glass of champagne in each hand, like one wasn't enough, and earlier I'd overheard them comparing AA meetings. "On the other hand," I grinned at them. "I feel like I oughta tell you, I'm a police chief, and she. . ." I gestured with a glass at Lauri as she was squeezing back through the merrymakers. By now they'd gotten so loud and raucous, I was practically shouting. "That's Detective Wald. NYPD Homicide. So the fact is, fellows, if you kill somebody you know, you're probably going to get caught."

Well, it seemed like a joke at the time. And we all laughed and introduced ourselves. Lauri hadn't ever gotten into the bathroom; every time she tried, somebody was in there with the door locked, so she'd gone outside to make her call (and smoke).

She and I were talking about walking over to a nice Italian restaurant she knew nearby, and both of us were thinking that maybe we'd get as far as a hotel room this time, when all of a sudden Spirit shot past us like his tail was on fire; he spun around in a circle and did a couple of high backward flips at my feet. Fat as he was, he got about a foot off the ground.

Moustache thought maybe the cat had epilepsy (you never know with strays, he said), but I figured it was that damn Christmas bell earring with the blinking light in it that Claudia had hooked on the poor animal's collar. So I took it off and he bit me and ran away.

After a while, Bart came back, still looking a little green in the cheeks, but he perked up when our host told him that he thought Claudia was gone; he'd seen her with her coat on.

"Gone to Rio," mumbled Beard. "But not with Joe." He nodded his head at the big bearish man who was hugging somebody else now.

"To Rio?" Bart sighed.

"But not with Joe."

So that was the end of the Wells drama. Or we thought it was. But a few minutes later, I felt Spirit butting at the back of my calf. It was weird; it wasn't like he was trying to get me to pet him or feed him. It was more like he was trying to push me somewhere specific. Now I've got an old poodle, Martha Mitchell, who's been bossing me around for years, so I'm used to it. I jostled along and the cat kept shoving at me and we ended up at the bathroom door, which was fine by me anyhow after all that champagne. No one answered when I knocked, the door opened when I twisted the knob, and nobody was in there when I turned on the light. I let Spirit butt me inside.

Compared to the big party room, which the crowd had quickly warmed up to where Lauri was already complaining about wanting to strip out of that red sweater of hers, the bathroom felt downright nippy. At first I figured it was from all the ice in the tub for the champagne, but then Spirit jumped up on the ledge at the far end of the room and showed me that the big casement window was unlatched and half open.

"Yeah," I nodded. "Your sucker of a landlord told me this is where you came from, Fatso. Off the streets and into the treats, huh?" He ignored my humor, unless his tail twitch was some kind of rejoinder, as he pounced right out the window and landed on the fire escape. I'd gotten so used to thinking of this cat as Nero Wolfe in yellow pjs, that I was surprised he'd ever leave the house. When I leaned out to see what he was up to, he was hanging off the iron ladder like somebody in Cirque du Soleil, and meowing in a panic, like his claws were about to give out on him.

"Damn it!" I had to crawl out the window to reach him.

And that's when I saw Claudia Wells, two stories below us, lying on the asphalt passageway between the two buildings.

I knew it was her and I knew she was dead. Nobody could get those long legs into that contorted position if they'd been alive. Closing the bathroom door behind me, I walked back to the party, took Lauri aside and told her that Mrs. Wells had fallen off the fire escape.

Because that's what I thought at first. And that's what Lauri and I both thought after we slipped downstairs and out into the alley and saw how the woman's neck was broken. I could see the back of her head was bashed in too, but it looked like it could have happened from her banging against the iron landings on the way down.

Lauri got on her cell phone to the precinct dispatcher, so officers and an ambulance were on their way within minutes. We figured the dead woman had been drunk, she was a smoker, maybe she'd gone out on the fire escape to finish a cigarette before getting in a car where she couldn't light up. Or maybe she'd crawled out there with Joe the Bear for a quickie before flying down to Rio. Out there in the dark, tipsy, she'd lost her balance. But something wasn't right. I could feel it. And so apparently could Spirit.

When we gave Penzler the bad news, he handled it pretty

well, got his guests quieted down and told them there'd been an accident, somebody was dead and nobody was going to be able to leave the bookshop until the police could get things sorted out.

"Who's dead?" called out Joe the Bear.

I kept my eyes on Beard and Moustache while Lauri made the announcement that it was Claudia Wells who'd fallen off the bathroom fire escape. After all, just half an hour earlier, I'd heard Beard and Moustache saying how maybe they ought to murder the woman to make the pain of losing her easier on their pal Bart. But I'd been right there with them in the room from the time she'd left it, alive, till I went out to the bathroom and saw her down in the alley. Besides, if those two men weren't truly shocked by her demise, they ought to be playing the leads in their own TV series.

Speaking of poor old Bart, I realized I didn't see him in the crowd. I was looking around fast when a woman suddenly screamed. Across the room, Claudia's ex fell straight forward, as the woman ducked away. He went down like a plumb line, taking the Christmas tree with him.

"Oh, my God," muttered Penzler. Again, from his tone it was hard to tell if it was his collapsing friend or the smashed tree that was upsetting him.

We could already hear the sirens as Bart's friends carried him over to a little leather Victorian couch. He kept moaning, "Claudia, Claudia, Claudia," like the saddest song you ever heard.

I can be as romantic as the next guy and I might have bought into what Claudia had called that chocolate-covered cherry grief of her former husband. But Spirit wasn't falling for it. I swear that cat had a personal crusade going, either to clear things up so Penzler could get back to feeding him, or to help me out because I'd taken that damn light-bulb earring off his neck, or maybe, who knows, he'd been hanging around all those books about smart detectives for so long in that book store, he thought he *was* Nero Wolfe and he was showing off for us. Anyhow he jumped up on the couch in that tubby heavy-footed way of his, walked right along the middle of Bart Wells' body down to his ankles, where he started patting with his paws at the pants.

That's when I noticed that there was a weird pink luminescence glowing on and off through one of Bart's cuffs. I ran my finger inside the cloth and pulled out one of the little Christmas bell earrings with the red blinking light. It was the one Claudia had still been wearing after she gave the other one to Spirit—the one that was still in my pocket. As I stared from the earring to the man on the couch, Spirit looked up at me with a look that said, "Okay, you finally get it?"

I got it. So did Lauri.

After they examined the scene, and ran their tests the next day, CSI and the M.E. got it too. Before Claudia had been tossed off the balcony, she'd been hit on the back of the head with a champagne bottle. The bottle had then been stuck back in the ice-filled tub. Her blood and her hair were on it, no doubt about it. More to the point, poor old Bart's blood was on the bottleneck, where he'd grabbed it with the hand he'd cut earlier. He'd followed her into the bathroom, locked the door, knocked her out and shoved her out the window. Six hours after he was arrested, he changed his story and said she driven him to it in a fit of jealousy.

So it was a whole night later, Christmas Eve, when Lauri and I had our dinner in that Italian restaurant she knew about. She was telling me how she'd found out that on January 2, Bart had been due to make a balloon payment of two million dollars in alimony to Claudia and how *Deadly Pride* hadn't been doing as well as *Greed* and *Lust* and he didn't have the cash.

I raised my little glass of Grappa to her. "Nice job, Detective Wald. But you know what it proves? I got a favorite quote of Will Shakespeare's, I'm always teaching homicide recruits. 'Men have died and worms have eaten them but not for love.'"

Lauri rubbed her hand over mine. She had a good hand, strong and smooth. "Cuddy Mangum, you can believe that tomorrow. But don't believe it tonight. Isn't that what you

Southerners say?" She smiled at me. "'After all, tomorrow is another day'?"

I smiled back. "That's what we say, darlin'. And it's true as rain."

So you know what? All you have to do is know one good person, especially a redhead wearing Halston, and there's nothing nicer in the world than waking up on Christmas day in New York City.

The Lesson of the Season

By Thomas H. Cook

It was the final minutes of the final day before Christmas, and Veronica Cross wanted only to pass these last moments sitting silently behind the register, her attention fixed on the book that rested in her lap. She had worked at The Mysterious Bookshop for almost ten years, but only on Saturdays, when the owner was at his house in Connecticut, and the store's full-time employees were scattered about various apartments throughout the city. Her job was simply to buzz customers into the store, answer whatever questions they asked, take their money, bag their purchases, then buzz them back out onto 56th Street. Almost no intellectual energy was required on Veronica's part, and the small financial supplement her salary added to her "real job" as a freelance copy editor made it possible for her to buy books from other stores, along with an occasional dinner out, or perhaps a discount ticket to a Broadway show.

The dinner and show might be enjoyed alone or with one of her friends, someone like herself, who read good books and could articulately discuss them. As for romance, she'd more or less given up on that. Most men were little boys, needy and selfish, and none had ever struck her as worth the effort it took to dress up and preen and put on a happy face when she well knew that after the first few minutes she'd want only to hail a cab, return home, crawl into bed and open a book

As for dress, she opted for modest elegance, long solid-colored skirts and dark-hued blouses for the most part, though black jeans with an accompanying black turtleneck sweater were not beyond her. Physically, she was tall, lithesome, and incontestably attractive, but for all that she preferred to blend into whatever woodwork surrounded her. That other people chased distant stars, felt imperial urges, sought fame, or at least notoriety, all of that was a mystery to Veronica because she wished only to be left alone with her books.

She glanced at the clock at the rear of the room, then at her watch to verify the clock's correctness. Both sentenced her to fifteen more minutes of minding the store, and given the heavy snow that had begun to fall outside, she thought it quite likely that she might be able to pass those final moments lost in her book, the store silent all around her, with nothing but the soft tick, tick of the clock to remind her that she was part of an all too human world.

Then, it happened.

Someone buzzed.

Veronica glanced toward the door, recognized the mild, faintly hang-dog face she saw behind the glass, then pressed the buzzer and let him in.

His name was Harry Bentham, and he came to the store every Saturday, though usually not during the final minutes of the day, and never during the final minutes of the final day before Christmas when a heavy snow was falling outside.

"Hi," Harry said quietly as he stepped into the shop.

"Hi," Veronica replied in a voice that was not without welcome, but which did nothing to encourage a more extended greeting.

Harry slapped the melting flakes of snow that had accumulated on the shoulders of his worn gray overcoat and stepped nearer to one of the shelves.

Veronica returned to her book, knowing exactly what she would see should she glance up again, Harry facing a shelf of paperback novels, his wiry gray hair blinking dully in the overhanging light, his rounded shoulders slumped, his posture no less slumped, so that he seemed perpetually to be collapsing, or if not that, then held up by invisible strings that were themselves stretched and frayed and in imminent danger of snapping.

But saddest of all, Veronica thought, was that Harry never bought a good book, and thus had yet to experience the actual thrill of literature, the way a fine passage could lift you high above the teeming world, give you focus and a sense of pro portion, allow a small life to expand.

In the years of Saturdays Veronica had spent behind the register, she'd come to divide humanity into those who read good books and those who read bad ones. As for Harry, he topped the list of readers who seemed to have no sense of what a book was for, that it could pull you deeper into life, direct your concentration toward things that really mattered, give voice to longing, prepare you for death. At no time during the ten years of her stewardship had Harry ever bought a hardback book. He had rarely even risen to the level of literature that had at least been briefly housed between hard covers. No, Harry was not only a reader of bad books, he was a reader of paperback originals, a reader of works so entirely without merit, so utterly devoid of any enduring quality of style or story or idea, that even the work's publisher had opted to present it in a form doomed to vanish at the first approach of mold.

"Uh. . ." Harry said tentatively. "Veronica?"

Veronica looked up from her book.

"You don't have the new Bruno Klem, do you?"

Bruno Klem was the author of a decidedly lowbrow series of paperback originals known to its few aficionados as "The Crime Beat Chronicles." From the garish covers, the novels appeared to take place in a neon lit city of strip clubs and after hours bars in which he-man detective Franklin Lord battled the dastardly minions of the Oslo Sinestre, the series' arch villain.

"It hasn't come in yet," Veronica said. She offered a quick smile, then returned her attention to *The Measure of Man*, a book which was, according to the jacket copy, "a beautifully written and philosophically astute meditation on the moral complexity of human life as seen through the eyes of a de-frocked Venezuelan priest."

She turned the page. "We live in the echo of our pain," she read silently.

She glanced up from the book and watched Harry's back, the way his right hand lifted tentatively toward a particular book, then drew away and sank again into the pocket of his frayed coat. He was no doubt preparing to make a selection, and she found herself hoping that something would seize him suddenly, direct his attention to the neighboring shelf where he might find a work of actual merit, one that would enlarge his appreciation of what a book can do, how it can draw you down to previously unplumbed depths of understanding.

But Harry remained in place, and so Veronica returned her attention to the book.

We live in the echo of our pain.

She pondered the phrase, and for some reason, impossible to fathom, found herself seated near her father's hospital bed, the old man stretched out on his back, tubes running here and there, an oxygen mask over his mouth and nose, so that he looked like an astronaut carefully strapped in for the outward voyage.

He had died eight years before, when Veronica had been twenty-one years old, living in her Park Slope, Manhattan being far too expensive, and eking out the same modest living in the same poorly paid trade she still practiced. She'd sat with him each night during the final days of his life, done what she thought required of an only child, the daughter of a divorced father who'd outlived not only her mother, but the two wives he'd later married and divorced, so that by the time of his final illness, there'd been no one who felt the slightest obligation toward him, save Veronica. He had been a wealthy real estate agent until suddenly, at the first onset of middle age, he'd gone completely nuts, sold the agency, and begun spending money hand over fist or losing vast quantities of it in cruelly expensive divorce settlements. Year by year his fortune had dwindled, until the last of it had vanished by the time Veronica had graduated from high school, selected an Ivy League college, made application, been accepted, then learned to her shock and dismay that her father had even squandered the money he had previously set aside for her education, squandered every penny of it on high-roller gambling trips to Las Vegas, extravagant parties at the Pierre, wining and dining an army of fortune-seeking bimbos, and finally on a yacht he'd anchored briefly off Fire Island, then sold at a huge loss to an oil man from Houston. The yacht had been the old man's last costly asset, and he'd used the proceeds of its sale on such stylish perishables as watches and hand-tailored suits, all of which he had later palmed off to various Second Avenue consignment shops, after which, with truly nothing left, he had sunk into absolute penury.

As a result, Veronica had been forced to waitress during the day and at night attending classes at Hunter College, from which she had finally graduated, but with a diploma that could not compete with the Ivy League educated and equally striking coeds who thronged about the great publishing houses of New York. Thus, she had been relegated to the decidedly unglamorous world of freelance editors, living from manuscript to manuscript, and thus from hand to mouth, a condition to which she had adapted quite well. In recent years, she had even concluded that hers was a superior position since she didn't have to kiss anyone's ass and could, with few exceptions, select the titles she wished to edit and avoid the utter trash that salaried employees could not.

We live in the echo of our pain.

She turned the phrase over in her mind, and wondered why it had returned her to her father's bedside during his bleak final days, the smelly hospital ward in which she'd sat night after night, and which she had only left after he'd released his last breath. It was miraculous, really, the way a few words could summon you back to past experiences, illuminate the shadowy corridors of that backward journey, allowing it to resonate within you. Such was the true value of literature, she decided, that it gave life a resounding echo.

"You don't read Bruno Klem?"

Veronica glanced up to see Harry Bentham staring at her, his face barely visible behind the huge black plastic frames of his glasses.

"No, I don't."

Harry nodded slowly and turned back to the shelves, moving his face closer to the individual paperback spines, intently focused on each one, as far as Veronica could tell, as if he were searching for the answer to life among the volumes he found there.

But what answer could he possibly expect to find among the paperback originals, Veronica wondered. Where in any of those inferior volumes could pain's echo rise from the page and in that rising address the great mystery of how we came to be the one we are, how we should proceed, what we should seek in the brevity of our days, and what forgo? In a room filled with mysteries, this seemed the deepest of them all, one Veronica now determined to have answered at least as far as Harry Bentham could answer it.

She closed *The Measure of Man*, and sat back, pressing her spine against the wall behind her. "I have a question," she said.

Harry turned, clearly surprised that she had addressed him.

"Why do read Bruno Klem?"

Harry's thick, eerily purplish lips parted mutely.

"Every Saturday you come in here and buy five or six books," Veronica added. "Always Bruno Klem, or something like it. So, my question is, what do you get out of it? I'd really like to know."

Harry blinked slowly, removed his glasses, wiped them with a handkerchief drawn from his back pocket, and returned them to his face. "They're like a scotch to me," he said.

"A scotch?"

"You know, like when you come home at the end of a bad day, and maybe your wife is waiting for you, and she gives you a scotch."

Veronica knew that Harry Bentham had never been married, that no one waited for him with a drink in hand at the end of the day, but that was not the point.

"A book is a scotch?" she asked. "What does that mean?" She shook her head in exasperation. "Let me try a different direction. When did you start reading?"

"During the war," Harry said.

Judging by Harry's age, Veronica guessed that he meant the Vietnam War, but the precise military conflict to which he had referred was in no sense the issue. "When you were young then?" she asked.

"During the war," Harry repeated.

"Because you were bored?"

"No."

"Why then?"

Harry shrugged silently. He seemed reluctant to go on.

Veronica, however, was in no mood to take silence for an answer.

"Why then?" she repeated.

"We came in from a patrol," Harry answered. "Went to our tents. There was a book on one of the cots."

"What kind of book?"

"A little paperback," Harry said. He nodded toward the wall of paperback originals that rose behind him. "Bruno Klem." He shrugged again, his shoulders rising and falling ponderously. "The sergeant saw me moping around. He tossed me the book. 'Here,' he said, 'it'll take your mind off it.'"

"Off what?" Veronica asked.

"The patrol," Harry answered. "It was a bad patrol."

"Bad in what way?"

Harry drew in a long breath, one that trembled slightly. "We were all around this old man. Asking him questions. He was shaking his head no, he didn't know anything. We kept yelling and he kept shaking his head, you know?"

Veronica imagined the scene, Harry in his raw youth, small and bespeckled, his round shoulders slumped beneath the weight of whatever soldiers carry, canteens and ammo belts and some kind of rifle. He'd probably been the company geek, slow and ineffectual, a burden to the others. More than anything she imagined him naïve and innocent, a kid who'd stumbled into the army the way he might have stumbled into a job at the nearest shoe store and kept it for fifty years.

"It was really hot, and we'd lost some guys," Harry continued. "And the old man just kept shaking his head ad saying he didn't know where the others were, the VC, I mean, the ones who'd killed, you know, some of us."

Now she saw him in a tight circle of other soldiers, all of them wet with sweat, covered in jungle debris, Harry the smallest, the least involved in the interrogation of the old man, wanting only to get away, find a little shade, take a listless snooze.

"Anyway, I started getting mad, you know?"

She could not imagine Harry Bentham mad any more than she could imagine him smart or passionate or good in bed. He was part of the great gray herd, a reader of trash, solitary, a flat-liner, J. Alfred Prufrock anesthetized upon a table.

"Mad?" she asked. "You?"

He seemed hardly to hear her, his eyes now distant, but oddly charged, a strange, unsettling gleam replacing his usual dull stare.

"Something takes you," he said quietly. "It comes and it takes you."

She could feel a wave of heat coming from him, fierce and violent, as if from a raging furnace.

"Takes you," he repeated, almost to himself. "And you're gone."

He jerked his right hand from the pocket of his overcoat and formed it into a fleshy pistol, the index finger as its barrel.

"And so I yelled at him, and he kept saying no, and it was so hot, and I started yelling louder because we'd lost all these guys and so. . ." The index finger curled into a trigger finger and Harry's hand jerked. "So. . . I" He stopped, thought a moment, then added. "The other guys said it could've happened to anybody. War and all. But it was murder. You can't deny it. It was murder, pure and simple."

He sank his hand deep into the pocket of his overcoat, and his voice lowered and its pace slowed to a melancholy crawl. "You think you're one thing, then suddenly, you're something else." His closed his eyes slowly, then opened them again. "Anyway, when I got back to camp, the Sergeant tossed me this book, and said it would take my mind off of it." A small, mournful smile played on his lips, and his eyes glistened. "We all have things we want to forget, don't we?"

Suddenly, Veronica was with her father again, sitting in a chair, staring at him coldly, listening as his breath swept raggedly in and out until suddenly his eyes opened, and in a struggling tone, he called her name.

"Don't we?" Harry asked.

She saw herself rise and walk to the side of his bed, his eyes barely open, his lips moving frantically, repeating her name, *Veronica, Veronica.* She saw in his eyes a strangely desperate pleading, and felt that he was perhaps asking her forgiveness for the hardship to which his reckless self-indulgence had sentenced her. She started to answer him, soothe him, tell him that she loved him, that all was forgiven. But suddenly she considered the wasted fortune, the gray rooms of night school, her long days at a greasy diner, the cramped Brooklyn apartment, and a jolt of consuming anger shot through her, hot and jangling as a vicious electrical charge.

"Things we did, that...you know..."

Now she was staring at the old man sullenly, coldly watching as his eyes closed and his lips parted breathlessly, her hand rising all the while, rising as if drawn into the air by a vast malignant power, furious, demented by rage, rising and rising, until it finally stopped, held an instant, then swept down in blistering fury, and in the echoing horror of the moment, she realized that she had slapped her dead father's face.

"...things...we can't take back."

She drew in a shaky breath and all but shuddered in that remembered rage, all the fuming anger of her lost ambitions, her father's mad indifference, the blighted life that had been his, and which to some degree she had inherited, all of it in full, resounding echo, moving in seething waves over and within and through her.

"Yes," she said. "We do."

Harry nodded. "Anyway, the book worked," he said. "I been reading them ever since."

She thought of Harry now, the echoing violence in which he lived, how it must endlessly swell and eddy in dark and bloody currents, Bruno Klem the wall he raised against them, and behind which he labored to secure a simple, decent life. What had he been before that distant murder, she wondered. What life had he imagined for himself? Had he even remotely guessed that in that single pistol blast he would equally destroy a future wife and children, a life lived in something other than the moral bafflement that now held his heart in thrall, and from which he sought brief escape in the preposterous antics of paperback heroes who shot it out with unreal villains in worlds where the moral lines were never blurred.

She rose, walked over to the shelf behind Harry and drew out the first paperback installment of a new action series. Then she turned and handed him the book, softly, affectionately, as she thought a loving wife might hand him a scotch at the end of a long, bad day. "Try this," she said. "It's by a new author. There'll be lots of books in the series."

Harry took the book. "Thanks," he said, then paid her and left the store, his shoulders hunched against the outer chill, the falling snow.

Veronica returned to her place, retrieved "The Measure of Man" from where she'd placed it on top of the register, and opened it.

We live in the echo of our pain.

The line was still moving through her mind a few minutes later when she placed the book in her bag, turned out the lights, locked the door, and thus secured the merely literary mysteries behind an iron gait.

On the long subway ride to her small, book-stuffed studio in Park Slope, she sat silently, with her hands in her lap. Normally, she would have read her book during the ride home, kept her eyes fixed on the words, turned the pages without ever looking up. But now she took time to consider the other people on the train, wondering what dark, unspoken things might have befallen them, what sorrows they had suffered, witnessed, caused, the varied ways they'd managed to endure the life that followed. In all of that, we were the same, she decided, bent on finding comfort in whatever way we can.

Once she'd peered briefly at each face opposite her, she lifted her eyes to the lighted advertising panel that shone above them. It showed a Christmas tree on a busy corner, a man in uniform holding a red bucket, people dropping change into charity's deep well. She drew her gaze from the photograph, thought of Harry, then of herself, then of the others on the train, in the city, on the planet.

It was the lesson of the season, she supposed, that all of them . . . are you.

Yule Be Sorry

By Lisa Michelle Atkinson

Once the girl in the Santa cap was finally stationed in place outside the bookshop, the proprietor climbed into his display and caroled about on hand and knee, trumpeting so heartily that the windows fogged as he trimmed them with lights and stuffed the stockings with crime novels.

He could have been Saint Nick if he'd only had the belly, for his beard was white as sugar and his smile, warm as the sun. His eyes matched the North Pole sky and, like the heavens above, they twinkled at visions of fresh writing and fresh women.

But his greatest joy was the promise of the yuletide season, when Manhattan's shops were fringed with garlands and zealous readers bought with glee.

This, however, was not a boom season.

In fact, the year had been frightful. Specialty bookshops closed right and left, but the chain stores were sticking like frost. There'd been lawsuits and sickness and debts to pay. He was mortgaged up the wazoo.

The week before, the phone had been cut, but the bookseller tried not to fret. Somehow, things had to improve.

In Christmases past, folks traveled from far and wide to visit the specialty shop. The infamous proprietor was the foremost crime novel expert on the planet. No matter how cozy or puzzling or dreadful a request, the bookseller would nod and inhale and instantaneously advise precisely the right book for the most persnickety collector. He knew every story ever written and had no problem recommending them, no matter how distasteful. (Occasionally, for fans of feline fur-bearers—whom he despised—the distinguished proprietor would even recommend a crime story solved by a cat.)

But the collector of rare and unusual mysteries was in for the best of times, for secreted upstairs in the bookseller's private office were the most curious mysteries in existence, those rare and priceless works that gained value over time, for such manuscripts age like fine wine.

Needless to say, the profits from one rare book alone could have paid his entire month's mortgage, or roughly the proprietor's weight in gold.

If he could find that second novel by Dashiell Hammett, *The Dain Curse*, his snowballing debts could be paid. He already had a buyer. She'd promised any price.

Determined to match the smart jet set crowd, former supermodel Contessa Christie Blitzen demanded nothing but the very finest first editions—complete with signatures, of course, and thanks to The Mysterious Bookshop, she had secured the most comprehensive collection of mysteries in the world. All she needed was *The Dain Curse*.

So, for five years, he'd searched high and low. He'd sent proxy bidders to auction for it. But he had failed to find the book and could not get it no matter how he tried.

The shop lights dimmed and flickered. Soon, the power company would cut him off. He had to do something, and quick. Then hope sprung up like a Rockette's kick. Outside, all bundled and warm with arms piled high with packages that threatened to topple, a flurry of shoppers flooded West 56th Street!

The bookseller rushed to let himself out.

In his haste, he slipped on the ice, but he managed to cry with glee. "Merry Christmas!"

Sadly, the crowd did not hear. They only pushed forward. Without a glance, they scurried past.

The girl in the Santa cap tucked away her paperback novel. "Bummer." She tossed her cigarette down in front of him then snuffed it out with her boot. The girl had the face of an angel, and her long red hair made him weak in the knees.

Exactly one week before, a social worker friend had introduced her to the bookseller. He'd hired her on the spot. Seventeen and down on her luck with no family, education or resume, she'd promised him a week's work in exchange for a letter of reference and a signed copy of the new Stephen King thriller.

"Can I help you with the display?" She rubbed her tiny hands together. "Or should I stand out here in the cold all night?"

He opened the door for her and followed. From behind, the fur-trim on her boots drew the eye to her calves, and they were heavenly. He tripped over a pile of books.

He would have liked to have kept her on permanently, but he was already in the red. There were books to buy, and salaries and the tree-trimming party, the phone bill and last month's mortgage (not to mention this month's mortgage) and the fortune he'd spent on wreaths and jewels for friends the year before.

He sighed. "I hate to say this, but it's been a terrible year. The chain stores have moved in like hyenas, trying to steal our bread and butter business right out from under us." He rolled his moustache and stared into her big green eyes. "It pains me in more ways than you know, but I can't afford to keep you for another week."

"Oh." The corners of her mouth fell into a frown. "Well, that's okay. I didn't expect you to." She removed her Santa cap, letting her long hair fall as she smiled. "I'll just use the john and get my books upstairs."

She climbed the spiral staircase.

Silence fell in the bookshop, quiet as the snowflakes outside.

The proprietor tried not to look morose, but when he saw the look on his cashier's face, he couldn't help himself. Vick Zen (a moonlighting writer with more pen names than Evan Hunter who never failed to sneak under the counter and write like the dickens during work hours) was too sad to type. He hung his head and stared at the register.

A rap on the door startled them both.

"Merry Christmas." A courier held up his clipboard. In seconds, the messenger said, "Hey, you're the owner. Isn't that right?"

"Why?" The bookseller thrust his hands into his pockets. "Is anything due on delivery?"

The courier shuffled a box from one armpit to the other. "Just your signature."

After the proprietor signed, he took the parcel from The Archive Auction House. Heat flushed his face as he carefully unwrapped the parcel and inspected the receipt.

Five years of searching, and his proxy bidder had finally found the book! Insured by its previous owner for a hundred thousand dollars, Dashiell Hammett's second novel, *The Dain Curse*, had fetched twice that amount at auction this afternoon, and the shop's proxy had won on what was once the shop's good credit. Teardrops warmed the bookseller's cheeks.

He stepped under the mistletoe and thought of the Contessa. Fat with cash and eager to collect the prized crime novel, she would surely give him a finder's fee on top of his normal commission. She might even give him a kiss.

The bookseller tightened his grip over the spine.

He placed such items under lock and key in his sculpted mahogany bookcase, the mate of which was on display at The Victoria and Albert Museum. Once the property of Sir Arthur Conan Doyle, the bookcase now housed unique and original manuscripts by Evan Hunter, Robert B. Parker, Nelson De-Mille, Stephen King, Joyce Carol Oates, Elmore Leonard and many more. Every time he scanned the books, many of which were dedicated to him personally, his eyes would water with joy, for the bookseller's list of literary friends had grown so long that nobody could count, not even him.

But the spines of such books could not reveal their true identities, for that would have been too risky. Instead, he disguised the rare old books by dressing them in snappy new jackets. From atop the antique case underneath an authentic human skull, he pulled a Stephen King jacket and slipped it over *The Dain Curse.* The crisp, bright laminate worked magic as camouflage.

"Excuse me." The redhead entered his office with a twinkle in her eye. She tossed her shiny hair over her shoulder and said, "Before I go, I wanted to thank you for everything, especially the books." She held up a paperback. "I can't wait to read Rosamond Smith." She cocked her head and smiled.

He felt awful. "It's nothing. I wish I could do more." It was Christmas, after all. "If you wait a minute, and I'll get your letter of reference from the printer."

She held up a peppermint stick and smiled.

A moment later, as the proprietor rushed back with the letter, his stomach growled. From his tiny kitchen on the floor above his shop, the aroma of pear-stuffed goose had snaked through a vent, and since he hadn't eaten a hot meal all week, the proprietor began to tremble at the crisp shell of crackling and the tender buttered beast.

He held up the letter he'd written on her behalf. "Can you smell that goose cooking? Justin Scott dropped it by from the country. If you'd stay, I'd love to have you for dinner."

She giggled. "Thanks, but I should get going." She folded up the letter and placed it in her bag. "No hard feelings, okay?"

"None whatsoever." He closed the upstairs door, and watching her from behind, he regretted letting her go.

Not a moment later, Vick called from downstairs. "Contessa Blitzen to see you."

The proprietor slipped into his blazer and pressed down his hair before rushing down the spiral staircase.

He took the Contessa's hand and gave it the customary kiss then smiled and looked into her aquamarine eyes. "You sure know how to brighten a guy's day."

"I was in the neighborhood, so I thought I'd have my driver stop." Perfectly coiffed in a blonde chignon and sable coat, the

Contessa oozed prestige, glamour and most importantly, wealth. She waved her gloved hand at the man to her rear. "You've met my valet."

"Of course." Lean and elegant with fawn hair, Rudolph was a dashing young man in a navy cap and a fitted overcoat. "It's a pleasure to see you both, as always." The bookseller corrected his posture and tried to look moneyed. "May I get you a drink? Champagne? Eggnog with brandy?"

"Rudolph?" She turned to her valet and pulled off her gloves.

"No, thank you." He folded his hands in front of him.

"Brandy for me," she purred. "Neat."

"It won't be a minute." The bookseller rushed upstairs and returned with a glass full of brandy.

"I'm sure you know why I came." The Contessa took the glass and surveyed the books on the shelves, the ladders decked with boughs of holly. "I'm simply dying to find that Hammett." She sipped then placed her glass on the counter. "Nobody's answering your phone, so I decided to come in person to inquire. You haven't been able to—"

He nodded, utterly satisfied with himself. "I've got it upstairs. I was just about to call you." He felt like a Christmas elf. "Shall we?"

"Oh, thank goodness." She heaved her Birkin over the shoulder of her sable coat and followed the bookseller up the spiral staircase to his office. "It's the final piece in my collection, and it's come to mean so much."

He stood behind his desk and searched, lifting bills and letters and books, looking under legal papers and stories and binders to find the *The Dain Curse*. "Well, if you'd like to do something in addition to the noir books, I've got several Sherlock Holmes novels." The bookseller sighed. "Perhaps you'd like modern mysteries or British espionage novels or capers set in your favorite cities?" He opened the Conan Doyle bookcase and removed a book in a Stephen King jacket then slipped the old book from its jacket and set it down.

"Perhaps some day, but now I'm late for a date at The Oak Room. You know how dreadful traffic is at this time of year."

He grabbed an album full of letters and asked if she'd like to expand her collection. Inside were original signed letters in longhand by Sir Arthur Conan Doyle, Agatha Christie, Mark Twain and Edgar Allan Poe. But she snorted impatiently, so he re-shelved the album and smiled.

Where was that Hammett? He needed that money. His hands trembled with urgency.

The Contessa stood in protest. "Really, dear. My car is double-parked."

"I'm sorry," he finally said and wiped his brow as he looked up. "I had it a moment ago. I know I left it on my desk." She slipped her hands into her gloves. "I'll call on you again around eleven. That should give you time." She glared. "Please find my Hammett novel."

"Of course." He nodded, and for the next three hours, the bookseller combed his office for the vanished book.

Twice over, he searched every shelf and emptied every box.

At eleven forty-five, he finally gave up. Hopeless, he rested in the leather armchair alongside the Christmas tree, and the treasure-filled tree reminded him of Christmases past, of happier, debt-free days and his childhood home in the Bronx.

Heat flushed his face. He needed some air.

Downstairs, the door buzzed. The Contessa.

He scanned his book-lined office, strewn empty boxes and stacks of books bought on credit and the precious bookcase he would have to sell if he wanted to eat. He remembered the redhead and the books she'd taken, and a knot formed in his throat. Heat bloomed in his chest.

He felt ill.

But he unrolled his sleeves and climbed downstairs to open the door.

The Contessa's valet held his cap to his chest. "I'm terribly sorry. I would have called, but since your phone—"His bloodshot eyes flicked from the ragged rows of books to the empty boxes and dust jackets that were scattered on the floor. "That is, I'm sure you'd like to know that the Contessa won't be needing *The Dain Curse* after all."

"Twenty-four hours. That's all I ask." He tried his best to smile, but nausea was setting in.

"In all seriousness." Rudolph furrowed his brow. "I'm sorry, but the book is no longer required."

Now vertigo accompanied the nausea, and the bookseller was not sure he could contain himself for long. Then he imagined the impossible and said, "Did she get it somewhere else?"

"Of course not, Sir." He took a deep breath. "As I said, I'm terribly sorry to be the one to break the news, but hear me out." He put his hands into his pockets and sighed. "The Contessa is dead."

"What? She was supposed to be at The Oak Room."

"Before they went in, she and her companion decided to have a look at the reindeer in Central Park." He shook his head. "They were hit by a runaway sled." Tears welled in his eyes, and his nose flushed so bright it almost glowed. "The Contessa broke her neck."

"Oh, no." The proprietor stepped forward and put one hand on the valet's shoulder. "Would you like a drink?"

The valet looked down at the threshold and shook his head. "The funeral will be at Saint Bart's."

"Please call on me if I can help."

The valet sniffed and looked up. "Her collection was appraised at over twenty million dollars, thanks to you. She was ever so grateful." He turned to go.

The bookseller scratched his beard. "This may be premature, but I think I know a buyer for that noir collection if you need one."

"My dear Sir." He swung around to face the bookseller. "The Contessa said she was deeply indebted to you for your patient and dedicated service. You made her knowledgeable about the books she loved most." He squinted and searched the bookseller's face. "I thought she would have told you, Sir. She willed you the entire collection."

A chill blew in from the open door, and the bookseller stood speechless as he watched the valet walk to his town car on the street.

And there, in a bright pool of sodium light, the bookseller spotted the redhead who had worked for free.

Alone on a bench, she blew smoke rings and read a Rosamond Smith novel, and on the sidewalk next to her fur-trimmed boot, a Stephen King book peeked out of a bag. The torn jacket exposed *The Dain Curse*.

The Long Winter's Nap

By Rupert Holmes

"I've just checked the display in the front window," reported the fair Jenya Johnson, peering tentatively into the boss's office, "and as you requested, yes, the stockings *were* hung by the chimney with care, but. . .do you really want that creature hunging by the neck right alongside the stockings? I mean, he's not even stirring." She smiled apologetically. "Or is this a bad time to get into that?"

It was our first Christmas on Warren Street and the boss was savoring the holiday season like the world was his oyster stuffing alongside a burnished Alsatian roast goose, accompanied by a 1990 Jean-Louis Hermitage. And why shouldn't he embrace all this comfort and joy? The celebrated shop was now a dream palace, handsome and high, with its head in the clouds even as the spine of each book in our endless procession of murderous volumes kept one foot in the grave. The walls were paneled in wood that an oak tree would have died for—and probably had, I suppose. It was as if the Great Library at Alexandria had dedicated its airiest wing solely to Murders Most Foul or Fictive, ranging from Cain (see *Abel &*) to Cain (see *James M.*) and all stops beyond.

And in a season where the appropriate salutation was "God rest ye merry," I personally didn't know any gentleman who deserved the greeting more. I'd been a freelance staff photographer back in the days when the boss covered sports for the *Daily News*. Our paths had crossed whenever O.P. would be concluding an interview and I'd show up, fresh from photographing the daily jack-knifed tractor trailer on the Long Island Expressway, arriving just in time to snap some jockey or javelin-thrower, then getting to shoot the breeze with the boss for a couple of always edifying minutes.

Since those days, a lot of water had gone under the bridge for me—primarily as chasers to all the bourbon that had gone under the bridge of my mouth for too many years. (It has been rumored that the Jack Daniels Distillery keeps an oil painting of me in their boardroom.) I'd been off the sauce for some time now, but there's nowhere on a job application where you get to check the word "sauceless." However, when O.P. got wind that I'd been out of a job longer than I'd been out of funds, he wrote to me—longhand—as if *he* was the one in need of a favor. So thanks to him, I was gainfully employed this Christmas, in a bright, warm, civilized place, and I'm not just talking about the bookshop.

The boss would have been at home in any New York neighborhood in any era since the Dutch first decided that Manhattan Island was a fixer-upper. He could have sat in the Yankees dugout in 1954, talking shop with The Mick, Moose Skowron and Hank Bauer without batting an average. Yet he'd have been equally comfortable strolling back from Pete's Tavern with O. Henry, listening to the scribe's latest story and not once letting on that he'd already guessed the trick ending. There are lots of tales on the bookshop's crime-ridden shelves about people who travel back in time and palm themselves off as citizens of the past, even while knowing all about the future. Sometimes I suspect the boss is the exact opposite...that he's here via any number of past eras, and walks among us remembering all we've forgotten about chivalry, gallantry, loyalty, duels of wit and duels of honor, and of times when life's pleasures and pains were much more of an unsolved mystery, and better left that way.

I do know that he *loved* his bookshop being so affably en-sconced on the same vintage streets where New York's first greatness began. We were situated, after all, only a minute's carriage ride from the shadows of Boss Tweed's personal bas-tion, and even closer to the site of that windowless debtor's prison called The Bridewell. The very street outside our door (named after Admiral Sir Peter Warren, as if just "Admiral" or "Sir" wasn't enough for one man) had been part of a bold ex-periment to replace the existing cobblestone of the area. In 1833, the city had repaved Warren Street with layers of stone that sandwiched soft wooden blocks of hemlock, the same stuff that Socrates drank as his final libation.

And somewhere beneath us, near the current subway, still existed the lost, sealed tomb of this country's first under-ground railway: The New York Pneumatic Subway of 1870, with a waiting room featuring curtained windows that held no view, and a grand piano and gurgling fountain intended to mask the sounds of the teeming city above. . .boarding station to a twenty-two seat air-driven railroad car, its entrance tun-nel flanked by Grecian statues holding gaslights in shades of red, green and blue. Boss Tweed had blocked its success, but somewhere below The Mysterious Bookshop, the phantom car was still patiently awaiting its next passenger, like the ferry-man Charon patiently awaiting his next lost soul. He would-n't be waiting long.

And Jenya Johnson and I stood waiting in the boss's hand-some office for his response to the creature hanging in our ample display window, but for the moment he was totally ab-sorbed with preparations for the first Christmas party we were to have in that part of New York where "Old" is spelled with an "e."

O.P. was on the phone and not happy about it. "Call your-selves the Salvation Army?" he challenged in as steely a tone as one can use when addressing a charitable organization. "Where are the troops—on permanent leave? I thought Christ-mas was your peak season. Oh please!" He hung up the phone by perfectly tossing it into its cradle several feet away.

"Rough words to say to a person at Christmas," I commented.

"What person?" he snapped back. "I was talking to a recording that's been telling me for twenty minutes how important my call is to them."

He settled into his leather armchair fitfully. He'd been trying all morning to drum up an old-fashioned Salvation Army band to play outside our store that night during our Christmas Eve party. I remembered such things from another time, three or four gray-coated brass musicians playing *Oh Come All Ye Faithful* alongside a hanging pot where passersby would toss their coins. The pot was usually presided over by a Santa who expressed his thanks while the band played on. The biggest problem I had as a kid was understanding how Santa kept jumping around every four or five blocks to team up with yet another musical ensemble. I'd figured he had a real good tour manager.

The boss was still grousing to himself about the Salvation Army's lack of cooperation. "I guarantee them a good night's take, and they tell me brass bands are no longer viable, they have to hire musicians instead of turning to volunteers, and the union is demanding health and welfare—"

Jenya set down the stack of uneven-sized manuscripts in her long, slim arms. "I think Arlan knows some musicians in New Jersey who'd be glad to get the work," she offered. Arlan Page was, like me, one of the boss's Top Ten neediest cases. He'd worked for a book store in Hoboken with the unwieldy name of *It's a Mystery to Me Book Store & Copy Center*. Before their clientele had reached chapter two of any of the books they'd purchased, the store had already arrived at chapter eleven. By repute, Arlan knew his way around collectable crime and so the boss had offered him a part-time job for the holidays, helping catalog some newly arrived semi-precious gems.

"Fine," agreed O.P., "we'll pay them fairly, but we need them by eight tonight, fair weather or foul. What do you have there?"

Jenya was arranging the odd assortment of manuscripts into piles on the side table where the boss occasionally thumbed through unsolicited submissions. "Today's aspiring Sherlock Holmes pastiches," she sighed. "Not too bad for a Friday, only about thirty-five stories, novelettes, graphic novels and haikus all purportedly from the same tin dispatch-box of Doctor Watson at Cox and Company—a bank whose vaults must now be slightly larger in size than the Great Pyramid at Khufu. To think that Conan Doyle only wrote sixty adventures himself. What a slacker!"

"How's today's crop?" asked The Man.

"Oh, the usual team-ups with real people. Holmes assists Albert Einstein." The boss raised an eyebrow and she hastily added, "Young Einstein. Holmes helps him get past square one."

"Very droll."

"And here's 'Sherlock Holmes meets Lara Croft.'"

"Lara Croft?" the boss protested. "Holmes would be a hundred and forty-three today. How does the writer get around that. . .with time travel?"

"No, in the story he makes Holmes a hundred and forty-three."

"Well, that's one way to handle it."

"How about Sherlock solving the adventure of the Red-headed League?"

"But he's *already* solved the adventure of the Red-headed League!"

"According to this story, the first time, he got it wrong." She looked at me. "Did you review the ones written in ink, pencil or Crayola?"

These were clearly expected to be the most amateurish of the lot and so had been assigned to me. I had given them a quick once-over and reached for them now, pocketing a Christmas card that sat on top of them. "Well, the first was kind of interesting—a Sherlock Holmes caper in a Vegas setting, called "The Giant Rat Pack of Sinatra.""

"I think the world is prepared for that one," murmured the boss.

"The others seem to be standard imitations of the Holmes

stories I read as a kid. Here's one called "The Navy Garnet" and another "The Timorous Chimney Sweep—"

"Jenya! What the Hell did you say about a creature hanging in the front window?" blurted the boss, delivering one of the most delayed double takes in the history of modern conversation.

She smiled. "I was being whimsical, as is my wont at this time of year. Arlan thought it would be cute to have one of Santa's elves hanging by the neck alongside the stockings in the window. The elf is supposed to move his arms and legs in circles as if he's struggling in the noose, but it's not working and I'm not sure it's in the best of taste for the bookstore that offers *la crème de la* crime."

The boss concurred and dispatched us both to prepare for the evening's festivities.

As a freelance photographer, I'd staked-out many a private party, but this one turned out to be the way I'd always thought a *real* New York party would be, and so seldom was. Maybe it was because the boss loved real people who cared about books and the words inside them. Maybe it was because he couldn't stand phonies, so the only way a phony got into one of his parties was if that phony was a friend of a real person.

I suppose what distinguished a Mysterious Bookshop party from others is that every once in a while, during a break in the conversation, you'd hear someone pipe up with, "The murder's been committed but I have no idea where to hide the body"—and all conversation would then calmly resume as usual.

For background music, the boss had opted for Corelli's "Christmas Concerto." I only know this because he told me. I can't Telemann from a woman in a crowd of Baroque composers and I spent much of my life thinking Rococco was a powder made by Nestles.

The boss, at ease in his tux, quipped adroitly with many of his dearest friends, clinking his glass of Veuve Clicquot in so many toasts that he could have gone into the crouton trade. He'd subtly scan the room to see who was standing alone or seemed ill at ease and make them his next port of call. It was a treat to watch him thread together the various personalities in attendance, weaving his invited cast of characters into a crazy quilt that was eye-catching and diverse even as it was warm and inviting.

I was seated at a small table checking off guests' names. Arlan Page, who seemed aggressively underdressed for the evening in ratty jeans and a tee shirt he'd outgrown in both its size and the wit of its emblazoned slogan, looked enviously at the gathering. "We never did anything like this in Hoboken," he said. He'd been miffed since Jenya had advised him to remove his throttled dwarf from the window, and he now held in his arms both the figurine and an armful of old bindings. He wasn't the biggest of men and he seemed a bit overburdened. "What are the books?"

"First editions of classic Christmas mysteries," he answered. "They were on display on the front shelves, but they're a little too valuable to let them be so available at a crowded party. Thought I'd put them away in the storage room. Got the key?"

It sounded like a sensible idea to me and I reached into the breast pocket of my corduroy sports coat and handed him the keys I'd been entrusted with, owing to my having worked at the bookshop eight days longer than Arlan. He took the key and mazed his way through the crowd over to the stairs leading down to the bookshop's lower level.

In reaching for the keys, I found a small Christmas card-sized envelope addressed to O.P. and labeled "Urgent." Damn. I remembered pocketing it in the boss's office when we were going over the Sherlock Holmes manuscripts.

I looked across the room and saw O.P. laughing richly at something the goodly and entrancing Lady Boss had just whispered to him. Should I interrupt him when he was so clearly enjoying himself? I was in need of tactical advice from someone who was far more savvy and diplomatically adept than I. Someone whose opinion I could trust.

"Merry Christmas," said Santa Claus in the low gruff voice of every Santa that ever was. He was dressed in the regalia you would expect, including snowy white beard and moustache.

"Evening, Santa," I said, looking at the wall clock. "Thought you'd be somewhere over Akron, Ohio by now."

He was a rotund but broad-chested Kris Kringle. Leaning forward, he confided, still employing his trademark voice, "I'm with the band outside. We're about to start and I'm all suited up when suddenly, it's 'Ho-ho-ho, I gotta go' if you catch my snow drift." His arms were crisscrossed across the waist in the timeless symbol for nature calling.

"Sure, go ahead," I said. "You might want to use the one downstairs, it's more private if you have to take off the costume—" Away he flew like the down of a thistle, dashing and half-dancing toward the stairs. I turned my attention back to the card in my hand.

"What's that?" asked Jenya, indicating the object of my inspection. She had, by my count, her third glass of champagne in hand and I hadn't been watching her all that carefully. I explained to her about the card and asked her if I should show it to O.P. now.

She shook her head much longer and slower than she would have earlier in the evening. "Not if it means he might ask me to do something about it. I'm off-duty. In fact, I'm almost off the chart."

"You okay?" I inquired.

She smiled wistfully. "I remember the first time I came home in this state. My father took one look at me and said, 'Jenya, you must be drunk.'" She finished her glass. "And I've been following his orders ever since." She stepped away from me in a path so crooked that a kindhearted cop would have bought her coffee. I sighed and put the envelope away. If the matter had been *really* urgent, surely someone would have called us by phone.

The festivities were rapidly approaching Fezziwig 101 on the Fa-la-la-la-la Scale of Measurement and not only was the evening becoming merry and bright, but it seemed as if this particular Christmas would be white. Snow had begun falling as if paratroopers with billowing bed sheets were invading Manhattan by the thousands. The street quickly was rendered timeless, for under the thick cake frosting that was rapidly accumulating, there was no way to determine the vintage of cars parked along the curb. Each snow flake had its moment in the artificial sun of the street lamps, a billion falling reflections serving as microscopic mirrors, giving Warren Street the luster of midday, while the red neon sign for The Raccoon Lodge across the way beckoned like an invitation back to the thirties or forties, promising the real thing rather than an homage.

Those of us who lived near any subway stop in the five boroughs grew all the merrier in the knowledge that The (increasingly) Mysterious Bookshop was only a few steps from almost every underground line in the city. We'd all get home when we wanted, but for the moment, with refreshments and food and delightful company close at hand, we wanted for nothing.

Every now and then, during a lull in the recorded music over the speakers inside, I'd hear the sound of our ersatz Salvation soldiers leaking in from the street. After the first fifteen or twenty minutes, a lanky fellow in a belted trench coat entered through the front door. He cradled a tuba in his lengthy arms as if he were carrying an orphan in from a storm.

"You work here?" he asked, setting the tuba down by my table. I acknowledged the same and he smiled cheerily enough. "Look, we have no objection to playing in the snow — we found ourselves a little canopy to stand underneath and it's not really all that cold, but we'll need to step inside every twenty minutes or so. We told the woman that hired us. . ." He looked around for Jenya, but she was nowhere to be found.

"Sure, of course," I nodded. I couldn't have them play Little Match Girl all night, staring outside the windows at the warm surroundings within.

He asked me if he could wash his hands somewhere and I smiled at the euphemism. He smiled right back. "When I say I need to go wash my hands, that's what I mean. I just need to run some hot water over them for a few minutes. The metal gets like ice after a while." He hefted the tuba around in his hands. "The name is Doug, by the way."

I introduced myself and told him I'd show him the way to the washroom downstairs. He had a little difficulty negotiating the steps with the instrument in his hand, although it wasn't as big as I expected a tuba to be, and I said as much.

His reply seemed a bit defensive. "Okay, okay, so it's not a tuba, it's a euphonium! but it plays the same. I use it for this kind of work. It goes "oom".. .it just doesn't go "pah.""

"Wouldn't a Sousaphone be closer to the real thing?" I asked, referring to the instrument that wraps like a boa constrictor around the player's shoulders and torso. I'd played one myself in high school.

He snapped back, "There's a reason why tubas are played at Carnegie Hall and Sousaphones are played at halftime shows." He spoke with the kind of fierce pride for which there was little argument.

We reached the bottom of the stairs, passing O.P.'s office and reaching a storage room within which was also the staff rest room. "Funny," I said, suddenly realizing. "The guy playing your Santa came down here to use the john and I don't remember him coming back."

Doug answered with some very innocuous words, and the moment he pronounced them, I was woefully uneasy.

He said, "What Santa do you mean?"

I opened the door to the storage room.

The white-bearded man looked like he'd come straight down a chimney and landed head first in an empty hearth. Only it wasn't a hearth, but a chimneyless and otherwise empty corner of a stock room filled with stacks of cardboard boxes.

For a ghastly moment I thought I heard his blood dripping, but it was just one of the pistons on Doug's horn leaking black drops of valve oil onto the linoleum floor. "What's that?" he asked, transfixed.

"That" was a man in the same Santa suit I'd seen him wearing upstairs. His eyes, how they twinkled as they continued not to blink. His cheeks were like roses (or rather the blood drying upon his cheeks was) and his nose was like a cherry. . .a large, crushed black cherry. A twist of his head—more specifically the odd angle at which it lay against his shoulders — soon gave me to know St. Nick had nothing to dread. Not this Christmas Eve, not the next. He was as dead as the toy department of Macy's on Christmas morning.

♣♣♣

"Jesus," swore the boss, commendably putting Christ back into Christmas.

He'd seen murder before, and he knew he was seeing it again.

The party was still going on above us. I'd rushed upstairs to inform the boss of the grim tidings. The rumors that O.P. had a great poker face proved true. He publicly reacted to my whispered aside as casually as if I'd told him we were running low on ice cubes. He directed Sally, who knew the guests as well as anyone there, to keep the guests happy, on the premises, and in the dark about Santa's death until the police arrived. He asked Dan to call 911.

I brought Jenya down the stairs with me, and it was surprising how quickly the sight of a corpse in an oversized Santa outfit can knock the champagne buzz out of someone's head. O.P. turned on the overhead fluorescents with his handkerchief.

"It's Arlan," Jenya muttered. With the white wig and beard askew, I could now recognize the mystery connoisseur from Hoboken, New Jersey. I kicked myself for not recognizing him when he first appeared and said as much to the others. Jenya quickly began to murmur some words to herself. Until that moment, I had not known she was Catholic.

"Oh god, what's that coming out of his coat?" I asked in a greenish voice as I noticed something spilling from the folds of his roomy red jacket.

The boss crouched near him. "I can't touch anything but it looks like his shirt is stuffed with paperbacks, maybe twenty, thirty copies of. . ." he peered about in the light and allowed himself as much of a dry chuckle as he could, given the circumstances.

"Copies of what?" I asked.

"*The Da Vinci Carb Diet*," he said with a wince. "A recent trade paperback about a high carb, low protein weight reduction program, based solely on foods mentioned in the Bible, or depicted in paintings by guess who. It relied heavily on grains like yellow millet."

"How'd it sell?"

The boss rose to his feet. "Like yellow millet. We were returning our entire stock. Who's this?" He had stepped out to the hallway, where Doug sat numbly on the floor alongside his mini-tuba. I explained who he was and why he now was here, and how I had last seen Arlan heading downstairs with some valuable first editions before he'd reappeared in a Santa costume with his head caved in.

We headed back upstairs, where O.P. had Sally bring the two other musicians in from out of the snow. Rob, the boss's assistant, brought them down to O.P.'s office to join Doug for some food and Irish coffee.

"What do we do now?" I asked the boss.

He frowned. "Believe it or not, I think now it's time we play a party game." And with that, he flipped a switch on the PA system, bringing an abrupt ceasefire to the festive Christmas music. The guests looked about as the boss called for their attention.

"Ladies and gentlemen, thank you for sharing your Christmas Eve with us here at The Mysterious Bookshop, and for making possible such a murderously eventful evening." If anyone in the crowd knew what had happened downstairs, their pattering applause and light laughter was no indication. "Now before we turn you over to the good graces of your limousines, the MTA, or your own two feet, we have a quick game to play, with the prize being an autographed copy of *The Maltese Falcon*."

Peas-And-Carrots-Peas-And-Carrots went the crowd in pleasant surprise.

"I've decided to revive," he continued, "a streamlined mainstay of the New York party scene during the detective story's golden age: I refer to The Scavenger Hunt! There will be a five minute time limit, and you will be divided up into five teams, each to be supervised by one of my trusted associates—Ian, Sally, Rob, Hillary, Dan, this means you — and the rules are that while you may look, you must not touch or move anything in the store. The prize goes to the first team who finds one of the following items: a beach ball. . ."

"At Christmas?" someone inquired.

"Yes, inflated or deflated will do, or any similar inflatable object. Or a towel, blanket, or other such swaddling that can't be accounted for. Or pillows. Foam rubber cushions. Anything that one might use to stuff a beanbag chair the size of an ottoman, as long as it is reasonably soft and has never been on these premises before this evening—my associates will help you in determining that. We'll regroup here in five minutes and may the best team win!"

As the bookshop's staff began divvying up the guests into hunting parties, O.P. asked me to come down with him to his office. On the way, I asked, "We can afford to give away an autographed copy of *The Maltese Falcon*?"

"I said it was autographed. I didn't say by whom. Anyway, I won several penmanship awards in elementary school."

We joined Doug and his two musical compatriots, a cornet player and a trombonist, who were comfortably seated on the couch, gratefully devouring a tray full of finger sandwiches and steaming mugs of Irish coffee minus the whipped cream. As I noticed the manuscripts stacked on the side table near his desk, I thought now might be the best time to show my boss the letter I'd neglected to give him. After all, how bad could my mistake be compared to a dead body in the storage room?

He took my news in stride and tore open the envelope I'd handed him. "Damn," he muttered, and quickly started riffling through the various Holmesian manuscripts laid out on the table.

"Do you know what you're looking for? And have you found it?"

He put down the last manuscript. "I can't find it. Which of course tells me it's exactly what I'm looking for." He moved to the desk and his checkbook and asked Doug how much Jenya had agreed to pay the trio. Doug mentioned what I thought was a fair figure and O.P. began writing, when there was a courtesy rap on the door and Jenya entered.

"We have no winner in the scavenger hunt, O.P. More than fifty people looking everywhere. You'd think they'd have found something."

My boss nodded patiently. "Yes, you'd have thought that, wouldn't you? Just wanted to make sure before the police arrive." He indicated that she should sit with the rest of us. "Where *are* the police, by the way?"

Jenya dropped herself into a straight-backed chair near mine. "911 says the heavy snow places us several notches down among those who need help from the police right now. There should be a small team getting here in the next half hour."

I had to speak up. "Okay, what's with the scavenger hunt? What were you looking for?"

O.P. undid his bow tie and unloosed the top button of his tuxedo shirt. "That commodity served at every Christmas dinner. Stuffing." He saw our blank expressions. "Padding. Whatever it was that Santa wore to fill him out when he walked into the bookshop."

I was surprised by this waste of everyone's effort. "But we saw his jacket was padded with a few dozen copies of *The Da Vinci Workout*, or whatever that was."

O.P. smiled. "Do you really think thirty large paperbacks under your shirt would look like a bowlful of jelly? Those books were a last minute improvisation to throw us off the track. Please, follow the series of events: Arlan goes to the stock room with some valuable first editions. Then a big old Santa enters the bookshop and heads down to the staff washroom. You and Doug then go downstairs and find Arlan dead wearing the same Santa outfit. But what makes you think that the Santa who walked in the store was Arlan? You told me you felt foolish that you didn't recognize his face or voice when he first showed up. That's because it wasn't him."

Jen and I processed this, as the cornet player asked Doug, "Who's Arlan?"

Doug murmured, "Just make sure he isn't the one who signs our check."

"And where were *you* during all this, Jen?" asked the boss.

"Mingling," she shrugged. "Flirting, getting polluted, constructive stuff like that. But if Arlan wasn't Santa — where's Santa now?" Her excesses that evening had left her as white as an albino mime.

"He isn't anywhere."

"You mean — ?"

"Yes, fair Jenya, there is no Santa Claus. Although he did exist for a brief minute or so. Entered the bookshop pretending to be one of Doug's fellow fundraisers. Was allowed to go downstairs, where Arlan was waiting with the valuable first editions, which Santa was supposed to smuggle out of the bookstore via the emergency exit at the back of the lower level."

"An alarm goes off — " I began.

"Arlan had the key to the alarm, to my office, to everything, remember? You gave him the keys. But Santa might just as easily have gone out the front door with the first editions, considering how well they'd be hidden. He was supposed to give Arlan a little bump on the head for credibility, and we'd have to tell the police that the suspect was a man dressed like Santa Claus in New York City on Christmas Eve. Some hot tip that would have been."

I could understand what he was saying, but still. . . "Those may have been nice first editions, but how much were they worth? Enough to commit murder?"

O.P. walked over to the stack of amateur Sherlock Holmes stories. "No. But one of the manuscripts that arrived in today's mail might have been reason enough. The one that's currently missing." He took out the card I'd neglected to deliver and read aloud. *"If your astute eye and your own team of experts verify that this is the real thing, your commission on this manuscript should easily be worth no less than. . ."* He stopped himself, no doubt thinking that the IRS might someday read an account of this. "Arlan had seen this priceless manuscript, one I hadn't seen or known about, sitting unguarded in my office. He made the fatal mistake of mentioning it to his accomplice.

"Santa told Arlan that if a Christmas gift had fallen from the heavens, they had to take it. Arlan countered that he wanted no part of grand theft. Enraged, instead of giving Arlan the light tap on the head as promised, Santa hit him hard, once, twice, then grabbed the manuscript as well as the first editions, and fled out the emergency exit, only to return to the party because their absence would have drawn far more attention than their presence."

As if trying to change the subject, Jenya protested, "But I still don't understand about Santa's padding. If it isn't here—"

"No, it's here, Jen. Santa couldn't throw it away without clearly betraying his identity. And wrapped in his own trench coat, it not only provided Santa's bulk under his oversized shirt, but the hiding place for the stolen books and manuscript. Not to mention being the murder weapon. What we call the blunt instrument."

He turned toward the couch.

"Doug—where's your tuba?"

Doug raced out the door and into the tender embrace of Lieutenant D'Alessandro and Detective McTeague of the NYPD, City Hall Division, who'd arrived a little early for Christmas this year.

🎄🎄🎄

My boss loved the entire spectrum of the crime field, not just a certain Mr. Holmes of Baker Street. Still, the next day, Christmas Day to be sure, his voice rang with authority and even a smidgen of passion as he read aloud for his beloved wife Lisa, the staff, and assembled members of the press, employing a British accent that would never rob Kenneth Branagh of a single night's sleep: "*Holmes said, 'The goose laid an egg after it was dead, the bonniest, brightest-colored navy blue jewelry egg that ever was seen. I have it here in my museum.' He unlocked the strong-box and held up the navy garnet, which shone out like a star, with a cold radiance at its center. 'The game's up, Ryder,' said Holmes quietly.*"

He allowed himself a small bow of the head to our perhaps anticipated applause. "And there you have it, the stuff that one murderer's dream was made of. The first draft of *The Adventure of the Navy Garnet*, apparently to be re-titled in its next revision *The Adventure of the Blue Carbuncle*. One of the earliest Sherlock Holmes stories and the only one set at Christmas."

"How much is it worth, do you think?" a reporter for the Sun asked.

My boss frowned. "To Arlan Page, his life. For his killer, several decades in prison. For me, as the first mystery solved at 58 Warren Street, home to The Mysterious Bookshop, its value is inestimable."

The reporter followed up, "But how much in dollars and cents, would you say? More than, say. . .I mean, would it be a million?"

"As a literary curiosity, I'd say closer to a hundred."

"A hundred million?" I croaked.

"A hundred dollars. That is unless you can find evidence that Sir Arthur Conan Doyle had a habit of spelling *coloured* without the 'u,' *jewellery* without the extra 'l' and 'e,' and *centre* as 'center.'" My boss sighed a manly and understandable sigh. "I'm afraid this fake document was drafted by an American, not a Knight of the Realm."

An hour later, he and Lisa, Jenya, and I were locking up the bookshop. I asked the question that had troubled me all morning. "Once he'd murdered Arlan and had the manuscript hidden in the tuba's bell, why the hell did Doug come back inside the bookshop?"

O.P. explained, "After he left by the rear exit, he noticed his tuba had a leaky piston. It might have left musician's valve oil at the murder scene. He had no choice but to return with his tuba, and let the instrument drip oil on the floor as you discovered the body, to account for how and particularly *when* the traces got there."

"Well, Otto," soothed Lisa, "it's not often you solve a murder mystery in ten minutes, and go through a million dollars faster than you can spell-check a book review." She offered this as consolation, but he was in need of none.

As so often happens on December 25th, the sun was in full array, reflecting brightly on the heaps of clean, crusted snow from the night before.

"That fraudulent document may not have been the real Holmes," he observed, removing his key from the lock and taking the cold afternoon deep into his lungs. "But our bookshop, this street, this part of old New York. . .these are my real homes, as much as anywhere on Earth, I suppose. Come on. Lunch at Bouley?"

"Aren't they closed for Christmas?" I asked.

"Only for those who haven't a clue," he laughed, and we rounded the corner onto West Broadway.

Cold Reading

By Charles Ardai

It wasn't Christmas yet, not for two days still, but it might as well have been. Every store but ours had the same music playing on an endless loop—happy this, jolly that. Every window was trimmed in red and green, every tree in twinkling lights. The air smelled of pine needles and was so cold it hurt to breathe.

Down on Warren Street, we had an odd mix of holiday shoppers and professionals brushing past each other on the sidewalks—odd because the shoppers were mostly Tribeca hipster types while the professionals were working stiffs from the courthouses over on Centre Street. Some of each group would come into the store, the hipsters to check out the avant garde stuff—Paul Auster, James Sallis, Jonathan Lethem—while the working stiffs would generally go for legal thrillers: Grisham, Turow, that lot. I'd have thought they had plenty of courtroom drama from nine to five and wouldn't want to read about it on their days off, but there you go.

I could generally tell, when a person walked through the door, what they'd be interested in. It was a little game I played with myself, a bit of Sherlock Holmes to pass the time. The silver-haired gent with mud stains on the cuffs of his chinos and a touch of sunburn on his cheeks and forehead? A John D. MacDonald man if I'd ever seen one; I directed him to the shelf where we had a batch of Gold Medal first editions. The portly fellow whose down parka didn't quite conceal his clerical collar? It would have been too easy to peg him as a Chesterton reader, but I figured it was a safe bet he'd rather pick up a Father Brown than a Dan Brown. I wasn't surprised when he headed for the 'M's and tugged a Ralph McInerny title off the shelf.

But my powers of observation and intuition weren't always 100 percent, a fact of which I was forcibly reminded when our next customer walked in.

She was dressed not nearly warmly enough for the season, just a black sweatshirt and a denim skirt over candy-striped leggings. The knit muffler wrapped around her throat was her sole concession to the falling mercury. She had short hair, cut close to her head in a ragged little gamine style and dyed a fiery orange. She was small, maybe five-two, and had enormous green eyes. It's a good thing she hadn't decided to go shopping in Herald Square instead—I'm sure someone from Macy's would've spotted her, dragged her off to the eighth floor, and put her to work as one of Santa Land's elves. Assuming they didn't have a prohibition against bosomy elves.

All of which I mention by way of excuse. When she came up to me at the register, I thought I'd impress her by guessing her favorite author. Cute, maybe five years younger than me, orange hair, striped tights. "Janet Evanovich?" I said.

She seemed baffled for a moment. "No," she said, "Madeline Kirk."

I was startled. I knew my mid-century paperback writers—I do this for a living after all—but what in the world would a twenty-something like this know about the author of 1952's *Death On a Dare*, 1954's *Kill—Or Be Killed!* and not a damn thing else? Both books had been award winners, sure, but that was half a century ago; Madeline Kirk had been dead thirty years before this lovely little elf had been born. Besides which, she'd written her two award-winning novels under a male pseudonym, Kirk Masters, because what he-man wanted to read two-fisted action written by a dame? Scholars in the field knew Kirk's real name, but even knowledgeable mystery readers generally did not. I was impressed, to say the least.

"Well," I said, "you're in luck. Copies of *Kill — Or Be Killed!* are almost impossible to come by, but Otto's got one downstairs — "

She blushed — actually blushed. "No, no — that's my name. I'm Madeline Kirk."

"Oh," I said.

"You thought I was someone named Janet, so I. . ." She stuck out a hand. "Let's start over. Pleased to meet you. I'm Madeline."

I shook the hand. "Roger," I said. "That's *my* name; I'm not saying 'yes' in military fashion."

She smiled. "Roger," she said. "By which I mean yes. In military fashion."

"Tell me, Ms. Kirk," I said, "are you aware that back in the 1950s there was a writer with your name?"

"I am," she said. "That's why I'm here. You deal in rare books, right?"

"We deal in books of all vintages and degrees of scarcity," I said, "rare ones included."

"Well," she said. "I've got something pretty rare I'd like your opinion on. You see, the author Madeline Kirk was my grandmother. On my father's side. He died last month — "

"I'm sorry," I said.

"Thanks. I was going through his things, and I found some copies of my grandmother's books."

"Really?" I said. "Well, we can certainly let you know what they'd be worth, if you want to bring them in. A copy of *Death On a Dare* in the first paperback printing can go for anywhere from $175 to upwards of a thousand dollars, depending on condition, and *Kill — Or Be Killed!* is even rarer."

"What about *Murder Takes a Bride*?"

"By Madeline Kirk? There's no such book."

"But I was reading it just this morning," she said. "It's about this carnival strongman who's in love with the ticket booth girl — "

"Hold on," I said. "Who published this? Popular Library?"

"I don't know if it ever was published," she said. "All I have is a manuscript. It's not even typed, it's written out by hand. It's got to be at least two hundred pages." She looked hopefully at me. "Do you think it might be worth anything?"

I didn't mean to torture the poor girl by making her wait for an answer. I just needed to get my breath back. "Yes," I said. "I think it might be worth something."

"I wonder what," she said. Then she smiled at me winningly and turned those great big eyes on. I got the impression I wasn't the first man she'd ever tried to charm. Knowing that didn't make it any less effective. "Do you think you could come take a look at it? I'd bring it here, but I don't want to carry it around on the street—the paper's a bit fragile, and it's supposed to start snowing later. . ."

I looked at the clock on the wall. I was by myself in the store right now.

"I'm just a few blocks away," she said, "over on Barclay, near Church?"

What the hell. Dan would be back from lunch any minute and he could cover for me; I'd covered for him often enough. "Give me half an hour," I said.

"Oh, thank you!" she said, and gave a little leap, clapping her hands together. "I really appreciate it, Roger."

"I'll need the address," I said.

"Of course," she said, and she wrote it down for me.

Then she was gone, out into the cold. I thought about what she was offering to show me. A lost novel by Kirk Masters! If it was real (and what else would it be? did I think young Ms. Kirk had forged a two hundred-page manuscript in her grandmother's handwriting?) collectors would climb all over each other to own the thing, not to mention publishers. Hell, Hard Case Crime would probably buy it sight unseen. They lived for this old pulp stuff.

Assuming Otto didn't want it for himself.

I heard the door swing open and looked up, hoping to see Dan walk in, but instead I saw Mr. Chinos-and-Sunburn heading out. "Didn't see anything you liked?" I asked.

"Never cared much for his early stuff," he said, in a syrupy Southern drawl. And walked out.

Which just goes to show, some days you bat 1.000, some days you just can't get any wood on the ball.

♣♣♣

Dan showed twenty minutes later. I told him I had an errand to run. I didn't say what it was. Was this because I didn't want to get his hopes up until I knew the book was for real or because I wanted to keep this bit of exciting news all to myself a while longer? Or perhaps because I was embarrassed to admit that half the attraction was Ms. Kirk herself? Who knows? A bit of each, perhaps.

I bundled into my heavy winter coat; slipped on a knit cap and scarf and gloves, and even so I hadn't gone half a block before I felt I'd been transported to the Russian tundra. How Madeline could stand it in a skirt I couldn't comprehend.

I took West Broadway to Murray, then walked east till Church, past the neighborhood's other mystery landmarks. There was a pub called Baker Street, whose sandwich board menu advertised the soup of the day (potato leek with bacon) beneath a silhouette of a long-nosed gent with a pipe and deerstalker cap, and on Church there was a neon sign in a second-story window advertising plumbing services under the name "Busted Flush." You had to wonder if the owner knew about Travis McGee's boat or was just a poker player with a witty streak.

Madeline Kirk's building was a walk-up and not the charming, recently renovated kind, either. Some anonymous turn-of-the-century city architect had given it a handsome rusticated doorway but it had long since been defaced by enough marker scrawls and spray-paint tags that you could hardly see the stone underneath. The glass panels of the door were clouded and scratched and if there had once been nameplates beside the buzzer for each apartment you wouldn't know it now. Fortunately, the front door was propped open with a brick. Fortunately for me; I couldn't imagine it did wonders for the tenants' security.

I pulled the door open and went inside, peered up the central well of the building's narrow staircase. The apartment number she'd given me was 3-RW, which I assumed meant there were four apartments per floor—rear and front, east and west. I climbed to the third floor and knocked on the rear, west door.

It swung open as my knuckles struck. It hadn't been closed, I realized.

And when I stepped over the threshold, I realized something else: The place had been ransacked. Either that or Madeline Kirk normally kept her clothing on the floor in front of her closet and the contents of her dresser strewn across her bed. It didn't seem very likely.

The window on the far wall was open, curtains flapping in the wind. I walked to it, looked out. A rusted fire escape led up and down. Beside the window, an overturned glass of water lay at the foot of a splintered night table.

Could this all have happened in the half hour since Madeline and I had spoken in the store? Had Madeline come home to a burglary in progress? She was a tiny thing, not up to fighting off the sort of brute who (as I pictured it in my mind) had smashed her night table with one blow of a meaty fist. I hoped she was all right.

I looked in the small bathroom, opened the medicine cabinet, pulled back the shower curtain. Nothing leaped out at me, literally or otherwise. Madeline wasn't there, cowering in the tub, nor were two hundred handwritten pages tucked in among the cotton balls and Q-tips.

There was only one other room, and it barely qualified as such. It was what artful real estate agents called a "kitchenette," the *-ette* meaning that the stove had only two burners and the fridge only came up to my chest. I opened both. Nothing out of the ordinary in the oven, but I found a tidy pile of twenty dollar bills in the refrigerator's butter compartment. Next month's rent money, I imagined, and only an incompetent burglar would have missed it. Or one who'd been looking for something other than cash.

I was startled, suddenly, by the ringing of a telephone. I went back to the main room and glanced around, trying to isolate the sound. It was coming from under the heap of clothes by the closet. I dug to the bottom, unearthing an old black dial phone, the sort you'd have found in every apartment in New York back around the time of the Bicentennial. Maybe Madeline had found that relic among her dad's things as well. Or maybe it was a sign that she shared my taste for things from the past.

Meanwhile, the phone had continued to ring. After seven rings I stopped counting, but it didn't stop ringing. I was tempted to pick it up, but when my fingers brushed the handset I hesitated. It wasn't my apartment, or my phone, or my call, and it wasn't my place to answer it. But the thing kept ringing and finally I picked it up just to put an end to the noise.

A high-pitched voice sprang out of the earpiece. "Hello? Hello? Roger is that you?"

"Madeline?" I said. "Where are you? Are you okay?"

"Thank god!" Madeline said. She sounded out of breath. "I was hoping you'd be there. I don't know how long I have. There's a man—"

"What man? What happened?"

"He followed me home," she said. "From the store. Maybe a minute after I got home, he knocked on my door, said he'd overheard us talking about my grandmother's book and could he see it? Hold on." I heard some clattering on the other end, like she'd moved the phone from one hand to the other. "Sorry, I thought someone was coming."

"What does he look like?"

"I don't know! I only heard his voice through the door, I didn't see him."

"What's his voice like?"

"He's got this southern accent," she said. "Really thick." Instantly I had a vision of my putative John D. MacDonald fan, and I remembered how he'd walked out the door just moments after Madeline had left. "Like maybe he's from Tennessee or Kentucky, you know what I mean?"

"Yes," I said. "I know."

"There was something about him. Something. . .I don't know, I just didn't feel comfortable. So I said no, I'd promised it to you. And he started hammering on the door."

"Why didn't you call the police?"

"You've seen my building," she said. "No way would my door hold up long enough for the police to get there."

"So you went out the window," I said, "and down the fire escape." I pictured her struggling to open the window; in my imagination it was painted shut and she had to wrestle with it while Max Cady out in the hallway rained blows on the door, forcing it open by inches. Clearly I've read too many thrillers.

"That's right," she said. "I grabbed the manuscript and got out of there."

"Where are you now?"

"It's a Citibank," she said. "I'm in with the ATMs. Hang on, someone's coming in." For a moment she sounded tense, then I heard her relax again. "It's okay, it's an older guy, white hair—"

My blood froze. "Madeline, that's him. You've got to get out of there. Madeline? Madeline!"

I heard her scream. The muffled sounds of a struggle. Then a crash and the call went dead. I jiggled the hang-up buttons uselessly. After a second, a dial tone buzzed in my ear. I dropped the receiver.

Citibank. There was only one in the area, back on Warren Street, right near the park. I briefly considered calling the police, but how quickly could they get someone over here? I ran out of the apartment and pounded down the stairs, going as fast as my heavy winter coat permitted. It wouldn't do Madeline any good if I fell and broke my neck.

Not that it was at all clear I could do her much good even if I didn't.

Who was this guy? As I ran toward Broadway, I thought

back to my impressions of him from the store. Sturdy, in good shape, probably in his early fifties. Definitely an outdoors type—the touch of red on his cheeks and forehead were a ski-goggle tan. Did I remember muscular forearms showing under his shirtsleeves, or was I just imagining it after the fact?

I ran. In the freezing air, the sweat pouring out of me turned clammy against my skin. The air sawed my lungs like a blade—in and out, in and out—and I felt the strain in my chest. I wished, suddenly, that I'd actually used the treadmill at my gym rather than just nodding at it familiarly each time I passed it. Hell, forget being in better shape, I just wished I'd worn sneakers today—as I ran, I could feel each step hammering my shins.

I passed Park Place, came up on Murray Street. I was dodging between pairs of pedestrians, drawing irritated glances and shocked intakes of breath. "Watch it!" one woman shouted. I mumbled an apology she couldn't hear. In the distance I saw the bank, saw the floor-to-ceiling plate glass, saw the ATMs behind it, saw no one in there—not Madeline, not the man, no one.

I reached the door, yanked my wallet out of my pocket, fumbled in it for my bankcard. I had to swipe it twice before the green light went on and the mechanism buzzed me through. Inside, I took a second to recover my breath, praying that the stitch in my side would go away quickly. I looked around. At the foot of the counter, next to a crumpled deposit slip, was an open cell phone. I picked it up, pocketed it. She'd been here. She'd been here with her grandmother's book and this guy, this lunatic, had. . .what, kidnapped her? What the hell could he have been thinking? I knew book collectors could be passionate sometimes, even zealous, but this was taking things too far. A lost Kirk Masters manuscript was exciting—for some collectors, it might be up there with a lost Chandler—but even if it had been a newly discovered Salinger, for crying out loud, there were things you just didn't do.

I racked my brain, trying to think where he might have taken her. In any other part of the country, you'd have figured he'd cram her into a car and drive off, but in Manhattan that was just out of the question—no one had a car, for one thing, and even if someone had, downtown traffic at the height of the Christmas season didn't make for a high-speed getaway. So that left them on foot, and there was only so far you could walk an unwilling young woman in broad daylight, even if you cowed her with a gun pointed at her back or some other threat of violence. Keep walking long enough and she'd find some way to break away, to get someone's attention, to flag down a passing cop. There was certainly no shortage of cops around Centre Street.

At minimum, then, he'd walk her away from Centre. Presumably he had a place somewhere nearby—that way he could get her off the street quickly. I closed my eyes, thought about the man, tried to catalogue what I knew about him. There wasn't much. He was of an age to remember Madeline Kirk's books and get excited by the prospect of a new one. He had a Southern accent. He liked to ski, or didn't like to but did it anyway. He had stains on his pant cuffs. Maybe he had muscular forearms, maybe not. He was picky about which John D. MacDonald books he read. What could I make of all that?

And it came to me that I could actually make quite a lot of it.

I headed back out into the cold.

☘☘☘

The stitch in my side hadn't gone away, so I had no choice but to walk rather than run. As I made my way impatiently, trying to breathe steadily, slowly, trying to make the pain fade, I felt a snowflake strike my cheek. Then another. So we were going to have a white Christmas. Smashing. I just hoped Madeline would live to see it.

I reached Murray Street and turned west. Halfway down the block, I looked up at the orange neon letters. *Plumbing And Repairs*, it said. *24 Hours, 7 Days*. There was a printed sign next to the neon showing a cartoon of a man in bib overalls and a painter's cap, holding an enormous monkey wrench and leaping into action with a big smile on his face. There were no stains on his pants, but what do you want, it was a cartoon. And next to the cartoon, more neon letters, spelling out *Busted Flush*.

As I watched, a man came into view in the window, reached up, and pulled down a shade. I only saw his face for a second. It was enough.

Sometimes you bat 1.000, sometimes you whiff. I'd figured I'd whiffed. But I hadn't. The guy *had* been a MacDonald fan— he just preferred the Travis McGees to *The Empty Trap* and *A Bullet for Cinderella*. And apparently he'd internalized the wrong lessons from the books, since he was behaving less like McGee than like the guys McGee regularly dispatched.

I had twenty years on him, and probably twenty pounds, but I also had a stitch in my side and no talent for violence. I worked in a bookstore, for god's sake. I wasn't going to be able to take him in a fair fight. What I could hope to do was to keep him occupied longer than the door to Madeline's apartment had. I took out Madeline's cell phone and dialed 911.

I told the operator where I was and quickly related the bare bones of what had happened. I could tell she found it confusing. I found it confusing myself. But abduction's abduction and she said they'd send a car over. I flipped the phone shut.

Then I pressed all the buzzers on the building's intercom panel, except for the one for the second floor. There were eight floors in all and someone buzzed me in by the time I got to the fifth button.

There was an elevator, but I took the stairs.

One flight up, I listened at the stairway door, then slowly eased it open. There was a chest-high counter and, past it, a pair of desks. A wall calendar from a plumbing supply company showed a busty model holding an enormous valve of some sort. Every industry has its own version of Miss December, I suppose.

There was no one in sight, but from behind a closed door marked "Employees Only" came muffled sounds, as of a heavy object being dragged along the floor.

Then the door opened and my friend came out, holding a sheaf of yellowed pages in his hands. Even from where I was standing I could see the strokes of ink running in neatly penned rows across the top sheet.

He stopped when he saw me.

"You," he said.

"The funny thing is, I wouldn't have figured you for a Kirk Masters reader," I said. "What were you, two when she died? Three? But I guess her books do have something in common with MacDonald. The crane operator in *Death On a Dare* could've been a MacDonald character."

He shook his head. "You don't know what you're talking about. She was nothing like MacDonald. She was one of a kind." He set the pages down on the counter, weighted them down with a length of lead pipe. "If she'd lived, she'd have been bigger than MacDonald. *If* she'd lived. But she didn't. You know how she died? She got drunk and ran in front of a streetcar."

"I thought it was a bus," I said.

"No, sir. A streetcar. I went to Baltimore once and saw it. The very car." He walked slowly toward me as he spoke, his drawl soft and thick. "What are the odds? An hour ago, I'm standing in your bookstore, looking at nothing much, and now here I am with Kirk Masters' unpublished third novel in my hands. You tell me that—what are the odds?"

"Low," I said. "But so are the odds that you'll get away with kidnapping Kirk Masters' granddaughter."

But he wasn't done marveling over his good fortune. "I could've come to the store yesterday. I could have come to-morrow. I could have come an hour later or an hour earlier. But I came when I came and she came when she came, and she piped up with me there listening. Put a coincidence like that in a book and a reader will howl bloody murder—but in real life. . . ?"

"It's a hell of a coincidence," I agreed, though privately I was thinking, *It is The Mysterious Bookshop, after all. It'd be more of a coincidence if you'd both shown up at Home Depot.*

"I couldn't pass the opportunity up," he said, and he spread his hands as if to say, See? See how reasonable I am? "But she wouldn't open the door. She wouldn't let me see it. Remember what she said to you? 'Do you think it might be worth anything?' She didn't even know what she had. She didn't deserve to have it."

"But she deserved this," I said. "What you've done to her."

"I haven't done all that much, not yet. Just a little tap on the head." He nodded toward the length of pipe and I shivered, as much from relief as from horror. At least she was still alive.

"And what do you plan to do when she wakes up? Another tap on the head?"

"No, no," he murmured, "nothing like that. We're working a construction site out in Canarsie. Figured I'd bury her there. No one'll find her."

"You're crazy," I said. "You can't kill someone over a book!"

"Name me a better reason," he said.

"What about me? You going to kill me, too?"

He shrugged. "There's room for two."

I lunged for the pipe. We reached it at the same time, each grabbing one end. He wrenched it out of my hand, scattering the pages of *Murder Takes a Bride* all over. He swung at me but I ducked and grabbed a handful of pages off the floor. I held them up. "One step and I'll shred them!"

That stopped him. "Don't," he said.

"Put it down," I said.

We stood there in a sort of Mexican standoff, he with his length of pipe, me with the manuscript pages gripped tightly in two hands. Then we heard two sounds. From behind the "Employees Only" door came a clatter followed by a muffled groan. And from the street outside came the sound of a police siren.

"You didn't," he said. "You didn't call the police."

"Of course I called the police," I said. "You think I'm crazy enough to come up here all on my own?"

He stood there, letting it sink in. Finally, he slapped the pipe down on the counter. "Well, fine," he said, and went to one of the desks. From the top drawer he pulled out a gun, a long-barreled automatic pistol that he slapped a magazine into. Then he leveled the thing at me.

Simultaneously, two doors burst open. The door to what turned out to be the employee restroom slammed loudly against the wall as Madeline staggered out. Her legs were free, but her hands were trussed behind her. And on the opposite side, the door to the stairwell opened and a pair of cops spilled through, guns drawn. For a moment I thought he might pull the trigger anyway, just out of sheer vindictiveness. But the moment passed, and then he lowered his gun.

🌲🌲🌲

We were back at the store, downstairs in Otto's office. Floor-to-ceiling bookshelves lined the walls and a rich Oriental carpet covered the floor. It made what had formerly been industrial space look like the set of a Sydney Greenstreet movie. He had the first dozen or so pages of *Murder Takes a Bride* laid out side by side along the surface of his desk. A few of them still bore the marks of the rough handling I'd given them.

Madeline was in one of the room's plump leather armchairs, nursing a glass of wine from Otto's personal collection. The bandage wrapped around her head peeked out from under a 1920s cloche hat. Telephones, hats, manuscripts—the woman liked her vintage things. A woman after my own heart.

"This is truly an extraordinary find, Ms. Kirk," he said. "I'm certain we'll want to publish it. But the original manuscript itself—yes, there are collectors who would pay quite a lot for it, but are you sure you want to part with it?"

She looked up at me with those big eyes of hers, and smiled, and my heart started to race as if I'd just run three blocks and faced down a murderous madman for her all over again.

She took my hand and nodded to Otto.

"Roger," she said.

The Killer Christian

By Andrew Klavan

A certain portion of my misspent youth was misspent in the profession of journalism. I'm not proud of it, but a man has to make a living and there it is. And, in fact, I learned a great many things working as a reporter. Most importantly, I learned how to be painstakingly honest and lie at the same time. That's how the news business works. It's not that anyone goes around making up facts or anything—not on a regular basis anyway. No, most of the time, newspeople simply learn how to pick and choose which facts to tell, which will heighten your sense that their gormless opinions are reality or at least delay your discovery that everything they believe is provably false. If ever you see a man put his fingers in his ears and whistle Dixie to keep from hearing the truth, you may assume he's a fool, but if he puts his fingers in *your* ears and starts whistling, then you know you are dealing with a journalist.

As an example of what I mean, consider the famous shootout above The Mysterious Bookshop in the downtown section of Manhattan known as Tribeca. Because of the drama of the violence, the personalities involved and the high level arrests that followed, the newspaper and television coverage of the incident ran for weeks on end. Every crime expert in the country seems to have had his moment on the talk shows.

Two separate non-fiction books were written about it not to mention the one novel. And along with several movies and TV shows featuring gunfights reminiscent of the actual event, there was a docu-drama scripted by a Pulitzer Prize winning newspaperman who covered the story, though it was never released theatrically and went straight to DVD.

There was all that—and no one got the story right. Oh, they got some of the facts down well enough, but the truth? So help me, they did not come nigh it. Why? Because they were journalists and because the truth offended their sensibilities and contradicted their notions of what the world is like.

So they talked about how La Cosa Nostra had been hobbled by the trials of the 80s and 90s and how new gangs were moving in to divide the spoils left behind. They focused on what they called Sarkesian's "betrayal" of Picarone and speculated about the underworld's realigning loyalties and racial tensions. They even unearthed some evidence for a sort of professional rivalry between Sarkesian and the man known as "The Death."

But the truth is, from the very start, this was really a story about faith and redemption—quite a mysterious story too, by the end of it. And that was too much for them—the journalists. They could not—they would not—see it that way. And because they couldn't see it, they put forward the facts in such a fashion as to insure that you would fail to see it too.

It falls upon me, then, to tell it as it actually happened.

Sarkesian, to begin with, was a Christian, a Catholic, very devout. He took communion as often as he could, daily when he could, and went to confession no less frequently than once a week. What he said in those confessions of course I wouldn't know, but it must've been pretty interesting because, along with being a Christian, Sarkesian was also an enforcer—a killer when he had to be—for Raymond Picarone. How Sarkesian reconciled these two facets of his life can be explained simply enough: he was stupid. Some people just are—a lot of people are, if you ask me—and he was one of them: dumb as dirt.

So on a given day, Sarkesian might kneel before the Prince of Peace asking that he be forgiven as he himself forgave; he might listen attentively to a sermon about charity and compassion, lift his eyes with child–like expectation to the priest who handed him the body of his Lord—and then toodle off to smash his knuckles into the mouth of one of Picarone's debtors until the man's teeth went pitter-pattering across the floor like a handful of pebbles. Virtually every journalist who reported the story discounted the sincerity of Sarkesian's beliefs because of the nature of his actions, but they were mistaken in this. Indeed, if it seems strange to you that a man might hold his faith in one part of his mind and his deeds in another and never fully examine the latter in the light of the former . . . well, congratulations, you may be qualified to become a journalist yourself.

No. Sarkesian prayed with a committed heart and did his job with a committed heart and that his job included murder everyone who knew him knew. That he did that murder efficiently and without apparent compunction made him much feared by his employer's enemies. It also made him much appreciated by his employer.

"Sarkesian," Raymond Picarone used to say with an approving smile, "is not the sharpest razor at the barber shop, but when you tell him you need the thing done, it gets done."

Now it happened one day that the thing Picarone needed done was the killing of a young man named Steven Bean. Bean was a minor functionary in Picarone's organization and a sleazy weasel of a boy even for that company. For the third time in six months, Picarone had caught Bean skimming from his profits. He had decided to make an example of him.

So he summoned Sarkesian to his gentlemen's club on West 45th Street by the river and he said to him, "Sarkesian . . . Stevie B . . . it's no good . . . we have to make, you know, a new arrangement." Picarone had taken to talking in this elliptical fashion in order to baffle any law enforcement personnel who might be eavesdropping electronically on his conversations.

Unfortunately, Sarkesian, being not very intelligent as I

said, was frequently also baffled. "Arrangement," he said slowly, chewing on the word as if it were a solid mass and blinking his heavily lidded eyes.

"Yeah," said Picarone impatiently. "Bean and us . . . I think we're done . . . you see what I'm saying? It's no good . . . we've come to a parting of the ways."

Sarkesian blinked again and licked his thick lips uncertainly.

"Kill him!" said Picarone. "Would you just kill him? Christ, what an idiot."

Sarkesian brightened, delighted to understand what was expected of him, and set off on his way.

It was mid-December and the city was done up for Christmas. The great snowflake was hung over Fifth Avenue and 57th Street and the great tree was sparkling by the skating rink just downtown. Gigantic ribbons decorated the sides of some buildings. Sprays of colored lights bedecked the fronts of others. And early flurries of snow had been blowing in from the north all week, enough to give the streets a festive wintry air but not so much as to be a pain in the neck and tie up traffic.

So when Steven Bean awoke one early evening in his cramped studio apartment on the upper west side, he staggered to the window and looked out at a cheery Yuletide scene. There was snow in the air and lights in the windows of the brownstones across the way. There were green wreaths on the doors and the sound of a tinkling bell drifting from where Santa Claus was standing on the corner.

Unfortunately, there was also Sarkesian, trudging over the sidewalk on his way to kill him.

Steven had full awareness of his guilt, as do we all, though he'd managed to push that awareness to one side of his consciousness, as likewise do we all. But seeing Sarkesian plodding along with his great shoulders hunched and his big, murdering hands stuffed deep into the pockets of his overcoat, the guilt awareness snapped back front and center and Steven understood exactly what the killer was here for.

He leapt off the sofa and jammed his scrawny legs into his

jeans, his scrawny feet into his sneakers. He already had a sweatshirt on and was pulling a blue ski jacket over it as he rushed out of the apartment. He could hear the front door closing three floors below as he raced up the stairs. He could hear Sarkesian's heavy footsteps rising toward him as he reached the next landing. There was a ladder there leading up to a trapdoor. Steven climbed quickly and pushed through the trap and up to the roof.

Here, the white sky opened above him and the swirling flakes fell cold upon his face. Steven dashed through the chill air, across the shadow of the water tower. He reached the parapet at the roof's edge and leapt over it, flying across a narrow airshaft to land on the roof of the building next door. From there, he found his way to another trap, down another ladder, to the stairs of the neighboring building. In moments, he was on the street, running along the damp-darkened pavement, dodging the homecoming pedestrians. The streetlamps were just coming on above him as he passed, making the falling snow glisten against the night.

At first, as he ran, he asked himself where he would go, but it was really a rhetorical question. There was only one place he could go: to the downtown theater where he knew he would find his younger sister.

Hailey Bean was in her mid-twenties, and was just beginning to realize she was not going to be a successful actress. She was a sweet girl, kind and gentle and loving; practical, down-to-earth and sane. Which is to say she was completely unsuited for a life in show business.

At the moment, however, she was rehearsing a very small part in a once-popular drama that was to be revived off-off— not to mention off—Broadway. Hailey's role was that of an angel. At the end of the first act, she was to be lowered toward the stage in a harness-and-wire contraption. Hanging in midair, she would then deliver words of prophecy as the first act curtain fell. It was only a 45-second scene, with another scene about the same length in the second act but it was pivotal. An elaborately beautiful costume, a white robe with gold trimming and two enormous feathery wings, had been designed to make Hailey's attractive but not very imposing figure more impressive, and electronic enhancements and echoes were going to be added to her pleasing but less than awe-inspiring voice.

She was in the back of the small theater discussing these embellishments with the stage manager when Steven Bean burst through a rear door. Trying to keep a low profile, he planted himself in a dark corner, where he proceeded to make himself ridiculously conspicuous by gaping and whispering and waving frantically in an attempt to get his sister's attention.

The differences in character between Hailey and her brother can probably be at least partially explained by the fact that they were, in fact, only half-siblings. Steven had endured his parents' vituperative divorce, whereas Hailey had grown up in their mother's second, more stable and loving household. Hailey was aware of her advantages and she felt compassion for her brother. But she also knew he was corrupt and reckless and dangerous, incapable of feeling anything more for her than a sort of puling, hissing envy and a fear of her decency which could shade over into hatred whenever she refused to give him whatever it was he was trying to get out of her at the time.

Still, he was family. So, as soon as she politely could, she excused herself to the stage manager and went over to see what he wanted now.

"He's after me," were the first words he gasped at her.

"Calm down." Hailey touched his arm gently. "Who's after you?"

"Sarkesian. He's coming to kill me."

The sister caught her breath and straightened. She didn't bother with any expressions of disbelief. She believed him well enough. "What do you want me to do?"

"Hide me!" Steven whined.

"Steven, where can I hide you? My apartment is the first place he'll look."

"You must have friends!"

"Oh, Steven, I can't send you to my friends with some thug coming after you."

"Well, give me some money at least so I can get away!"

"I don't have any more money."

"I'm your brother and I'm going to be murdered in cold blood and everything's fine for you and you won't do anything for me," Steven said.

Hailey sighed. She knew he was just trying to make her feel guilty but it didn't matter that she knew: she felt guilty anyway. Especially because, as she was forced to admit to herself, she wasn't being completely honest with him about the money.

Hailey was a clerk during the day at The Mysterious Bookshop, a store specializing in crime fiction located on Warren Street downtown. Because Hailey was pretty and efficient and meltingly feminine, she had become a favorite of the avuncular gentleman who ran the place. Sympathetic to her situation, he'd supplied her with an apartment in the brownstone over the shop and so her rent and expenses were fairly cheap. Thus, while it was true that Steven had all but cleaned out her savings six months ago when he'd gotten himself in trouble with Picarone's bookies, Hailey, by working overtime and scrimping on luxuries, had actually managed to save up a little more since then. The trouble was, she had a strong feeling she was going to need that money pretty soon. In a sort of semi-subconscious way, she had begun making plans to give up her acting career and go back to school.

She hesitated another few seconds, but she couldn't stand up to Steven's terrified eyes and his accusatory wheedling and her own guilt. Finally she said, "All right. I can't leave now. But come back at nine when the rehearsal is over and we'll go to the bank and I'll give you whatever I have."

Steven whined and pleaded a little more, hoping to convince her to go with him right away or even to let him use her bankcard, but she stood firm and at last he slunk back out into the snow.

On some other evening, he might well have persuaded her to

come with him. But as it happened, this was the night of a special technical rehearsal dedicated almost entirely to her character. An hour after their conversation, Hailey was dressed in her winged robe of white and gold, trussed up in her harness and dangling in mid-air about ten feet off the stage.

She was alone. The other actors had gone home for the night. Only the director and the stage manager were left and they were shut away in the booth at the back of the balcony. They had finished perfecting the echo effect for Hailey's voice and were now discussing their various lighting options, but where Hailey was their conversation was inaudible. The theater was silent around her. For long periods, it was dark as well. Then, every so often, a spotlight would appear and catch Hailey dangling there in her magnificent winged costume. It would hold her in its glow for a moment as the director judged the effectiveness of the light's color and intensity. Then it would go off again as he and the technician fell to discussing their options once more.

For Hailey, it was a boring process. And since the harness dug into the flesh under her arms, it was kind of uncomfortable too. To distract herself, she tried going over her part in her mind but as she only had four lines, her thoughts soon began to wander. She thought about Steven, of course, about the danger he was in and the troubles he had had as a child and the sad mess he had made of his adulthood. She thought about the money she was going to give him and how hard she had worked to save it and how long it would take her to save some more. She fretted that she would never find a way to improve her life. Ironically, if she could have peered only a little more than a decade into the future, she would have seen herself the mistress of a large house in the northwestern corner of Connecticut, the cheerful mother of no less than five children and the wife of a man who felt more love and gratitude to her than I can rightly say. But for the present, all this lay obscured within the mists of time, and she hung in the darkness anxious and troubled.

Then, as she hung, she saw a pale slanting beam of light fall at the head of one of the theater's aisles. Someone—a man—had opened the door from the foyer. Now his enormous shadow fell into the light and now he himself was there. He came forward a few steps but as the foyer door swung shut behind him the theater was plunged into a nearly impenetrable blackness and he paused uncertainly.

Hailey felt her pulse speed up. She had caught a glimpse of the man as he entered and there was no doubt in her mind who he was. A hoodlum that size with a face that low surely, this was the very Sarkesian her brother had told her about, the one who was coming to kill him.

Hailey dangled in the air and watched as the man began slowly advancing again down the aisle, hunting, no doubt, for Steven. She held her breath. Her heart pounded against her chest. The killer came nearly to the foot of the stage. He stopped almost directly beneath her. Sarkesian took a long slow look from one side of the proscenium to the other. Hailey shuddered with fear that he would now lift his eyes and see her.

And then the spotlight came on.

Suddenly, to Hailey's horror, she was fully exposed, hanging there helpless and ridiculous in her white and golden robe with the feathery wings outstretched on either side of her.

Sarkesian looked up, and Hailey was surprised to see he seemed even more horrified than she was. He cried out. He threw his scaly ham-sized hands up beside his face. He leaned back as if afraid Hailey would strike him down on the spot. Frozen there, trembling, he stared up at her with a mixture of terror and awe.

Hailey understood at once what had happened, understood what Sarkesian must've thought she was, and understood too the incredible piety and even more incredible stupidity of a man capable of believing such a thing. Acting almost as quickly as she thought, she stretched out her arm and pointed her finger at him sternly.

"Sarkesian!" she thundered, and the echo effect, which the director had left on for further testing, magnified her voice so that it vibrated from floor to rafters. "Sarkesian, repent!"

At that, as if the timing had been arranged by a power higher even than the director, the spotlight went out again.

Hailey couldn't see what happened next. The light had temporarily blinded her. But she heard Sarkesian send up a high-pitched wail—and the next instant, she could hear his enormous body fumbling and bumping into seats as he made his panicked way back up the aisle.

The door at the rear of the theater flew open. Sarkesian's massive silhouette filled the lighted frame. Then he was gone. There was the light alone. The door swung shut. There was darkness.

Sarkesian didn't look back. He didn't even look left or right. He ran out of the theater and into the street and was nearly struck down by an oncoming taxi. He found himself bent over the cab's hood, both hands braced against the wet metal as he gaped through the windshield at the frightened driver. Waving his arm wildly to make the cabbie stay, he rushed around to the car's side door and tumbled into the back seat. He gasped out his address to the driver. He sat huddled in a corner, shivering and whimpering, all the way home.

Now, all right, you may laugh at Sarkesian. But even outside of journalism, truth and fiction are sometimes impossibly intertwined. A figment of imagination, a myth, even a fraud may lead us to powerful revelations. Come to think of it, do we ever find revelations in any other way? If Sarkesian was fooled by Hailey's quick-witted improvisation, if it caused him to stagger into his apartment and fall to his knees, if it made him pray and weep in the searing realization that he had lived a life of wretched wickedness in complete contravention to the commandments of his God—was that realization any less true for the way it came to him?

In any case, the fact is: he remained on his knees all night long. And when the gray day dawned, he knew exactly what he had to do.

He went to see Picarone. He found his boss eating breakfast with his wife on the terrace of their penthouse. The presence of the glamorous and somewhat regal Mrs. P. cowed Sarkesian and he spoke with his chin on his chest, gazing down at his own titanic feet.

"I can't do that thing we talked about," he said in his slow, dull voice. "I can't do any of that anymore. The bad stuff. I gotta do, I don't know, good stuff now, from now on. Like the Bible says."

"O-o-oh," said Picarone, lifting his chin. "Yeah. The Bible. Sure. Sure, Sarkesian, I get it. We'll only give you the good stuff from now on. Like the Bible says, sure."

It was touching, Mrs. Picarone later told her friends, to see Sarkesian's great, granite face wreathed in childlike smiles as he floated dreamily out of the room.

When he was gone, Picarone picked up the phone. "Hey," he said, "I need you to take care of a little weasel named Steven Bean for me. And while you're at it, you can do me Sarkesian too."

The call had gone out to a man named Billy Shine. He was known to all who feared him as "The Death." There was no one who didn't fear him. He was a lean, sinewy man with a long, rat-like face. He moved like smoke and half the terror he inspired was due to the way he could appear beside you suddenly, as if out of thin air. He could find anyone anywhere and reach them no matter what. And when he did find them, when he did reach them, they were shortly thereafter dead.

Sarkesian would never have seen him coming. But he was tipped off, warned that The Death was on his trail. Mrs. Picarone had been sincere when she told her friends she'd been moved by Sarkesian's simple faith. She was, in fact, a regular church-goer herself. Sometimes, she lay awake in a cold sweat, painfully aware of the contrast between the dictates of her religion and the source of her wealth. Normally, a quarter of an hour spent running her fingers over the contents of her jewelry box soothed her until she could sleep again. But that night, somehow, this was not enough. Exhausted, she made a stealthy phone call to a manicurist with whom Sarkesian sometimes shared a bed.

Steven Bean, meanwhile, was sleeping just fine, curled up

on the sofa in his apartment. I know: you'd think he'd be just about anywhere else *doing* anything else. But after scrounging money from his sister to fund his escape, he had hit on the brilliant idea of increasing the stash by joining a 24-hour poker game he knew of. By the time he wandered out into the streets the next evening, he was all but broke again, and so tired that he convinced himself it would surely be safe at his apartment by now. Sarkesian had probably only been sent to scare him anyway. He might even have been in the neighborhood to see someone else. Maybe it was Steven's own guilty conscience that had made him jump to conclusions and panic when he saw the killer approaching. What he really needed, he thought, was to be home and snug on his own little sofa. And so that's where he went and, after a few more drinks and a joint or two, he was out like a light.

It's amazing people do these things but they do. It's amazing what a little distance there needs to be between our actions and their consequences before the consequences seem to us to disappear entirely. One a.m. rolled around and there was Steven, snoring away with his hands tucked under his head, so deeply unconscious that even the entry buzzer couldn't wake him.

But the door woke him when it crashed open, when its wooden frame splintered and fragments of it went flying across the room. That made him sit bolt upright, his jaw dangling, his eyes spiraling crazily. Before he could speak—before he could even think—someone grabbed him by the shirt–front.

It was Sarkesian.

"The Death is coming," the big man said. "Get up. Let's go."

What had happened: Sarkesian had become a new man since his encounter with the Angel of the Lord and he was determined to stay that way. After getting the warning call from the manicurist, he understood that it was not enough to just save himself. Knowing that The Death would come after Steven first, he saw he was responsible for protecting him as well. A sterner moralist than I am might wonder why he didn't call the police. But others had called the police in an attempt to avoid The Death and they were dead. No, Sarkesian knew Steven's safety was in his own hands. So here he was, shaking him awake

At the first mention of The Death's terrible name, whatever was left of Steven's drunken complacency vanished like an ace of spades at a magician's finger snap. He didn't know why Sarkesian had come to help him. At the moment, he hardly knew where he was. But he did understand that he had to run, and that there was nowhere to run from the likes of Billy Shine.

Sarkesian didn't wait for him to figure this out, or for anything else. He grabbed him by the arm, got him dressed and dragged him out the door. They were halfway down the second flight of stairs, Sarkesian in the lead, before he spoke again.

"Where can you go?" he asked Steven over his shoulder.

And Steven, still stupid with sleep, gave the only answer he could think of. "Tribeca. Above the bookshop. My sister's there."

They took three cabs to avoid being followed. They traveled the last few blocks on foot. Soon they were running together through the severe, slanting shadows falling across the downtown boulevard from the line of brownstone buildings to their right. Tinsel and colored Christmas lights hung from the windows above them. And snow fell, a thin layer of it muffling their footsteps as they ran.

As they approached The Mysterious Bookshop itself, they saw warm yellow light spilling through its storefront to lay in an oblong pool on the snowy sidewalk. Shadows moved behind the storefront's display of brightly jacketed books. Murmuring voices and laughter trailed out from within and a Christmas carol was playing, "O Holy Night."

With a silent curse, Sarkesian understood: there was a Christmas party going on inside.

A moment later, the voices and music grew louder. The bookshop door was coming open. A man and woman were leaving the party, waving over their shoulders as they stepped laughing into the night.

Suddenly Steven found himself shoved hard into an alcove, Sarkesian's massive body pressed against him, pinning him, hiding him. They huddled there together, still, as the couple walked away from them toward West Broadway.

When Sarkesian's body relaxed, Steven was able to move his arm, to lift his finger to point out his sister's name above a mailbox in the alcove. Sarkesian nodded. But Steven didn't press the buzzer button below Hailey's name. He was afraid she would turn them away. Instead, he went to work on the lock of the outside door. His fingers were trembling with cold and fear, but it wasn't much of a lock to speak of. In a second or two, he had worked it and they were inside.

The talk and music from the bookshop came through the walls inside. "O, Little Town of Bethlehem" followed them up the stairway as Sarkesian and Steven raced to the fourth floor landing. They made their way down the long hallway to the last door. Steven pounded on it with his fist. He shouted, "Hailey! It's me! Open up!"

There was a pause. Steven was gripped by the fear that Hailey herself might be at the party in the bookshop downstairs. But then, her sleepy voice came muffled from within, "Steven?"

"Hailey, please! It's life or death!"

There was the sound of a chain sliding back. The door started to open.

And at that moment, Sarkesian, waiting at Steven's side, felt a chill on his neck and looked to his left.

There was The Death standing at the other end of the hall.

He had materialized there in his trademark fashion, without warning, silent as smoke. Now, like smoke, he began drifting toward them.

Sarkesian reacted quickly. With one hand, he shoved Steven in the back, pushing him through Hailey's door. With the other, he drew his gun.

The Death also had a gun. He was lifting it, pointing it at Sarkesian.

"Don't you do it, Billy Shine!" Sarkesian shouted.

He heard a loud *clap*: the terrified Steven had shut Hailey's door, hoping Sarkesian would kill The Death while he cowered inside. But that changed nothing for Sarkesian. He was already moving down the hall toward Shine.

The two killers walked toward each other, their guns upraised. They were 50 yards apart, then 40, then 35. Sarkesian called out again: "Don't do it!" The Death answered him with a gunshot. Sarkesian fired back. The men began pulling the triggers of their guns again and again in rapid succession. One blast blended with another, deafening in the narrow corridor. The two kept firing and walking toward each other as steadily as if hot metal were not ripping into them, were not tearing their insides apart.

At last, their bullets were exhausted. Each heard the snap of an empty chamber. They stopped where they were, not ten yards between them. Shine lowered his arm and Sarkesian lowered his. Shine smiled. Then he pitched forward to the floor and The Death lay dead at Sarkesian's feet.

Sarkesian barely looked at him. He simply started walking again, stepping over the body without a pause. He let the gun slip from his fingers. It fell with a thud to the hall carpet. Only when he reached the stairway did he stagger for a moment. He held onto the banister until he was steady again. Then he started down the stairs.

All this time, no one on the fourth floor had ventured out of his apartment. People heard the gunfire. They guessed what it was. They called the police and just hunkered down. But on the floors below there were doors opening, faces peeking out. The sound of choral music from the bookshop grew louder. "Silent Night."

As the moments passed with no more shots, people on the fourth floor looked out too. Hailey looked out and Steven peeked over her shoulder, hiding behind her.

"Yes!" he said, pumping his fist when he saw that The Death had fallen.

But Hailey said, "What happened to Sarkesian?"

Steven had told her in a single sentence about his rescue.

She had guessed the rest, guessed what had happened to Sarkesian as a result of their encounter in the theater. Tender soul that she was, she felt bad for the thug. She felt any injuries he might have suffered were in part her responsibility.

She came out of her apartment into the hall.

"Sis! Sis!" Steven hissed after her, frantically waving her back.

But she kept moving forward cautiously until she reached the stairway. She saw the trail of blood on the risers. With a soft cry of distress, she started down the stairs.

She found Sarkesian lying on his back in front of the building, his blood running out into the snow. The partygoers in The Mysterious Bookshop had poured out of the store to investigate the noise and now stood gathered around him. The sound of sirens was growing louder as the police drew near. The bookshop door was propped open so that "Silent Night" drifted out.

No one came near Sarkesian. He lay alone in the center of the crowd. He blinked up at the falling snow, his breathing labored.

Then Hailey came toward him, her long white flannel nightgown trailing behind her. Many people saw and heard what happened next. Many of them talked about it to the journalists who soon flooded the scene. And yet it was never reported in a single newspaper, never mentioned on radio or television even once. This is the first time it's ever been told.

Hailey knelt down in the snow beside Sarkesian. She leaned over him. He stirred, turning his eyes toward her. He tried to speak. He couldn't. He licked his lips and tried again.

"I see," he whispered hoarsely. "I see an angel."

"Oh, Sarkesian," said Hailey miserably. "I'm really not."

Sarkesian blinked slowly and shook his head. "No," he whispered. "There." And with a terrible effort, he lifted his enormous hand and pointed over her shoulder at the sky.

Then his hand dropped back into the snow and he was dead.

The 74th Tale

By Jonathan Santlofer

I swear it wouldn't have happened if it were not for the book. Really, I didn't plan it. It's just that I'm impressionable you know, sensitive to others and to suggestion. It's the way I'm made, the way my brain works and I've come to accept that.

The book was a gift to myself. For Christmas. I knew I wasn't going to get any and was feeling a little bad, like I deserved something, you know, at least one, and it was just a paperback, no big deal, though you could say it changed my life; two lives, really.

I got it at this place called The Mysterious Bookshop. Woo, woo, right? Like it should have been Halloween, not Christmas. What lured me in were the books in the window, all those titles with death and murder and blood, which is not something I think about all the time, just on occasion like most people. Someone had tied black and red ribbons around some of the books which is what got me thinking about a present, plus the little lights, black and orange ones, again more Halloween than Christmas, and funny.

Inside, the store was old and new at the same time, lots of wood and stuff but airy and nice, with books everywhere, floor-to-ceiling, on tables, stacked on the floor; I'd never seen so many in one space. There was even one of those ladders you have to climb to get at the books on the top rows, which I couldn't do for "insurance reasons" I was told by this woman, from England I think, with a fancy accent, who smiled when she told me I couldn't use the ladder, that she'd get the higher up books for me. I said I'd make do with the ones I could reach which was more than enough.

They were in alphabetical order, which appealed to my mind. I may not have leadership qualities but I'm organized and methodical, just as important, if you ask me, and why I was so good in my job at the post office.

I spent a long time going from A to Z but of course there were big gaps, like I missed half of D and more of H and other letters as they were in the top rows, but it didn't matter because I was just choosing books with titles that appealed to me. I wasn't looking for anything special. That's always the way, isn't it, the important things just sort of coming to you when you least expect it?

After a while my eyes were starting to blur from all the books and the English lady came over and asked if she could help me. I told her I was okay and then this white-haired guy came out of a back room and the English lady went and talked to him and I could see they were eying me and then he came over and asked exactly what the English lady had asked: if he could help me, which was annoying because I could tell they thought I was going to shoplift, which I'd never do, I'm not that kind of guy.

I told him I was making up my mind and he said that was fine but they were closing in a few minutes so I had to hurry, which sort of annoyed me, I mean the pressure of making a decision like that when I could buy only one book and I had pulled out about twenty. Like I said I was feeling bad because I knew I wasn't going to get any Christmas presents, not from my mother who I hadn't spoken to in like five years and my father was long dead and my brother, hell, he hated me because I'd mouthed off to his wife last time I saw him which was at Thanksgiving two years ago, a holiday I haven't celebrated since, but she deserved it, and to be honest I don't miss my brother or his wife or his two bratty kids or their stupid split-level house out in Levittown or wherever. He, my brother, is six years older than me and never really gave a crap about me and told me I was crazy, like I'm crazy and he isn't? and I'm not going to patch it up unless he calls me and makes like a huge apology and I don't see that happening because I read in the newspaper that some reporter called him and he said *I have nothing to say*, which proves he never really cared about me, right? I mean, wouldn't you say something nice about your brother at a time like this?

The white-haired guy was going around the store adjusting books but keeping an eye on me, which made me want to leave but I wasn't ready to go back to my one room above the Korean deli because the thought of seeing the owner with his creepy bent finger and the way he was always looking at me, squinting, was just too much, too much, so I went through the twenty books and decided to buy the one that had seventy-three stories, which seemed like the best deal, all those stories for the price of one book. It was a paperback, like I said, but really fat with poems in it too, which I didn't think I'd read but it was still a good deal.

The white-haired guy came over while I looking through it and said it was a *classic* and how I'd made the right choice and that made me feel good and he smiled and patted me on the arm and called me *son*, which was nice even though I'm not crazy about being touched and he said, You'll learn a lot from that book.

I asked him what he meant and he said I'd have to read the book to find out, which was pretty cagey, like he was pressing me to buy it and that's when I saw it was fifteen dollars so I said no way I could afford it being out of work and all and he asked how much I could spend and I told him I had seven bucks on me, a lie, I had twenty-two but wasn't going to admit that. He sort of rocked back on his heels and tilted his head with his face screwed up like he was making a decision and finally said, Okay, it's yours for seven dollars, Merry Christmas, which kind of blew me away.

If I'd known then that the book was going to change everything I wouldn't have felt so good, but when someone does
something nice like that you just want to believe in the goodness of people, don't you?

Funny thing is I hadn't planned to buy a book. I'm not
much of reader; I haven't read much my whole life except for
comic books, lately *Bloody Skull* and *Blade* and *Hack/Slash*,
before that *X-Men* and *Fantastic Four,* which are more for
kids but when I turned twenty-one, my brother, this was before we had our fight, said I needed to improve my mind
which sort of irritated me but my friend Larry who worked
with me at the Post Office before I got laid off said the same
thing when he saw me reading *Fantastic Four* and he meant
it as a good thing because he knows how smart I am and he's
the one who turned me on to horror comics, so I figured I
could learn a lot from a book with seventy-three stories and
that was true, though some people don't agree it was such a
good thing.

By the time I left the store it was dark and drizzling with
little icy puddles that looked like frozen lemonade because of
the yellow light cast from street lamps, no one around and I
was glad. I liked the feeling that I was alone in the world,
which I guess I am but don't start feeling sorry for me because
I could have lots of friends and a girlfriend if I wanted one.
I've had plenty, and most girls say I'm good looking which
doesn't mean anything to me though I wouldn't say it's a bad
thing. My last girlfriend, who I met in a bar and went home to
her apartment in Murray Hill decorated all modern with girly
touches like a ruffled bedspread and such, said my mouth was
pouty. I wasn't totally sure what she meant but didn't want to
ask and appear uneducated so I looked it up in her dictionary.
It said: To protrude the lips in an expression of displeasure or
sulkiness. That didn't sound so good to me though I was pretty
sure Loretta, that was her name, meant it as a good thing since
she liked running her finger over my lips, but we didn't last
too long so it didn't matter if my lips were pouty or not.

I live only five blocks from the book store so it was weird

that I'd never seen it. I guess you could say it was fate or evil forces, as they say in *X-Men*, that drew me to it.

When I got to my apartment building I stopped into the deli downstairs and bought a six-pack of beer and a family-size bag of potato chips and a Snickers bar. I tried not to look at the owner's bent finger. I carefully laid my money on the counter so I wouldn't have to touch him, but when he gave me the change he made a point of rubbing his finger against my hand and I know it was on purpose because he's done it before, and I swear a chill went through my entire body.

As soon as I got inside my apartment I gulped down a beer then started another, tore open the chips and sunk onto my couch, which I got from the street, leather and really nice except for a few stains and a tear on one of the back pillows and on one arm which I fixed with Scotch Magic Tape and you can hardly see it now, I'm handy that way. Then I skimmed through my new book and read all the titles making sure I was not moving my lips even though no one was around because one of my girlfriends, Susie, I think her name was, made fun of me for doing that.

I was sorry I hadn't asked the white-haired guy or the English lady which were the best tales, as they were called, because there were so many, so I just went by the titles, like I do the names of the horses when I put a few dollars down at OTB, though I usually don't win.

The first tale I chose was about a gold bug that bites a guy, I think, I wasn't sure because it was really hard to read with too many words and sentences that went on so long that I had to reread them and I finally stopped and might have given up and been really annoyed that I'd wasted seven dollars if I hadn't started another tale which grabbed me right away about a nervous guy who gets pretty crazy as the story goes on because this old guy's eye is driving him nuts. It was pretty funny and got me thinking about the guy in the deli downstairs and his pinky, which is arched up away from his hand as if it's been yanked out of the socket and put back in all wrong with no nail at the end, just a stump. I always end up staring at it, you know how that is, and then it stays in my mind. Sometimes I avoid going into the store for weeks so I won't have to see it but when I need something quick it just makes sense to go there and then I see it again and it's all I can think about for days.

I didn't want to think about the finger so I read another tale about some guy named Roderick and his friend who bury Roderick's twin sister, only she isn't dead, which reminded me of the time I found an injured bird on the sidewalk outside my apartment building when I was a kid. I think it flew into the side of the building; it was alive but couldn't fly. I put it in a shoe box and fed it birdseed and gave it water with an eye-dropper but it just got weaker and I knew it was going to die which is exactly what Roderick and his friend thought about Roderick's sister but I couldn't kill it outright so I buried the box in an empty lot on the corner and marked the spot with a brick. A week later I dug it up but it was gone and I was never sure if someone else dug it up or if the brick got moved or what happened so I tried again with a mouse that I caught in one of those glue traps.

I didn't wait so long this time, just a day, but when I dug the mouse up he was dead. Mice are easy to catch, so I used more, burying one for like a half day or so, dead when I dug him up, another for like a third of a day, also dead, so I decided I had to make it more methodical. Like I said my mind works best when I'm methodical which is why I was good in the post of-fice and would still have that job if I hadn't gotten into that fight with a co-worker, which wasn't my fault.

I buried the next mouse for exactly eight hours, dead, then one for seven, also dead, and so on subtracting an hour until one finally lived. Two mice lived for five hours after being buried alive. It was awesome, you know, to open the box and see this little creature panting for breath but alive. But then I had to see if they could live for six hours and they both died.

I did that, buried animals and such, on and off for the next few years till we moved away from the corner lot and I sort of stopped thinking about it; well not really but I hadn't thought about actually doing it again until I read the story because Roderick's sister who doesn't die but comes back at the end, like a zombie, and falls onto her brother and they both die and the friend races out. I couldn't blame him for that, and when he looks back the house is cracking apart and crashing down and my heart was beating like the heart under the floorboard in the first tale but I kept reading and the next tale was about the same thing like the writer was speaking just to me all about being buried alive, and worse because the guy who told this tale had this like sick fear of being buried alive and in the end he wakes up and he is buried alive, at least he thinks so, really he's in a boat or something, which was a cheat, but it got me all caught up again in the idea of being buried alive, well not me, but something, someone.

I couldn't get the idea out of my mind. It was all I thought about for days while everyone else was thinking about Christmas.

Now they're saying it was premeditated, and it's true I thought about it, a lot, I even dreamed about it, but I still say, and I told this to my court-appointed lawyer—a woman who looks at me with a blank stare and wears the same suit every time I see her, gray stripes with a different blouse so she thinks it looks different but it doesn't   that it was the book, the tales that were the premeditation part, not me. You see what I'm saying? But she says that's no defense, which makes me think she's a lousy lawyer.

I've been here for seven months now and have read all seventy-three tales, some more than once, and a lot of the poems, which were okay, and they inspired me to write my own tale especially since there have been lots of stories written about me, one by a reporter who came to interview me but still got it wrong, so I decided to write my story, my own tale of what really happened and why. It was the hardest thing I ever did.

I let my lawyer read it and she says I should destroy it because it will *seal my fate*, but like I said I don't think she's a very good lawyer because I think I did a really good job of explaining my feelings and my motive, if you want to call it that, but you be the judge.

The Tale of the Man & the Construction Site

First of all I am not nervous. I am sensitive. Very, very, dredfully sensitive, but not so dredful that it is a bad thing. I eschew that people are saying I am crazy—mad as they use to say in the olden days but I am not. How could I be mad and get away with what I did and I would have gotten away with it, I could have if I wanted to. That is the unequivocal point!

I was careful and filled with dissimulation for days before I did it and I was methodical which is how my mind works and a little melancoly mainley because I live alone and there is a veil of gloom draping over my apartment and I was all-absorbed with this fancy of being buried alive which is like the shadow between life and death and I had to know where one ended and the other begins.

It vexed me for days but methought I could not do it I mean you cannot exactly bury yourself and even if I could get someone to help me like Larry who laboured beside me at the post office how could I keep track of the time and unearth the grave and see if I lived, right? Impossible!

So I needed a volunteer! I wasn't sure who but once I had the idea I was inflamed with intense excitement and bought the trunk which was not made well just a mockery of cardbord painted to look like lether which I could scrap off with my fingernail but I thought it would work singularly well for my endeavor!

There was a construction site right next to my apartment and I went thereupon at night feeling torrents of blood beating in my heart and dug the grave way in the back where they were not building yet. It took me 3 nights but fineally I was ready and with slight quivering I went down to the deli and there he was! Giving me the evil eye like always and I looked upon that hideous bent finger of his and my blood ran cold and I had a bottel of chloroform and a rag with me but there was a customer a woman buying laundery detergent so I went into the back near the frozen food and my nerves were very unstrung and I waited and he could not see me but I could see him and his finger!

I waited a customary duration for the woman to leave then I seezed upon a package of Oreos and delivered them to the counter and I could see the guy was vexed to see me because he made a little grunt which I heard because my hearing is acute and like I told you I am sensitive. For a moment I did not think I would be able to do it but then his hideous finger brushed against my hand and I shivered all the way to my soul and I got the rag over his nose and he fought me but he was not very strong and even when he made a low mowning cry I had an impetuous fury that kept me going and I did not stop until he grew tremulous and slumped down and fell on the floor.

I felt intense paroxysms and went back upstairs in haste to bring the trunk down and closed the deli door behind me and put the closed sign in the window and endeavored to get the guy into the trunk. Not easy! I had to be careful not to touch that gruesome hideous finger! It took like an eternal period but I fineally got him in and then the top would not close! I was vexed and inflamed but found some duck tape which worked to keep it shut tight in case he tried to get out.

It was all blackness and absolute night when I dragged the trunk outside and my heart was vacillating and no doubt I grew very pale but I had made solem promises to do what I was doing so I dragged the trunk around the corner and into the construction sight and back to the grave I had dug and pushed the trunk in vehemently and piled dirt over it so it was very entombed. Then I found formidable rocks and put them on top the whole time sweating and my heart pounding but it was thrilling!

After that I went back to the deli and my limbs were trembeling but I fetched two bags of potato chips and a six-pack of beer and a Snickers and went upstairs to my apartment where I was consumed by a burning thirst and drank the beer and devoured the chips and Snickers and my heart stopped pounding and I was feeling less vexed and I counted off the hours because I needed to know how long the guy was entombed. My plan was to keep him buried over night. I did not wish him any ill harm! I wanted him to live! I had good intentions! It was not a crime! It was an experament!

But then I realized with trepidation that I could not unentomb him in the morning because there would be a throng of construction workers and all my cunning and resolve would be ruined!

The next thing I knew it had dawned morning. I had fallen into a deep slumber from the beer and hard work and I was feeling unwell because all I had eaten was the 2 bags of chips and the Snickers bar but when I pictured the guy encoffined in the trunk and how by now the chloroform must be worn off and he could be awake and filled with a terrible dread I felt better and I read my favourite story again the one that inspired me to such fancy and I made a methodical decizion to wait another day and night because one night was not much of a test for a premature burial and so I resolved that he should stay buried for 2 nights!

I was again filed with a hunger so I went down to the deli which still had the closed sign in the window to keep people out and got some Kraft American cheese and Wonder bread and mayo and a giant-size bag of chips and 2 bottels of Yoo-Hoo and went back upstairs and made cheese sanwiches and watched TV til I fell asleep and the next day dawned. Then I watched DVDs of old movies to pass the duration even though I could hardly sit still thinking about the man and what must be going thru his mind in that underground box and that kept me stirring until I started thinking that if my experament worked and the guy lived it would be no good if I was the only one who knew about it and I got tumultuous and started pacing and I did not know how many hours passed but it was starting to darken again and then it came to me who I could tell and it made perfect sense so I raced downstairs in haste and ran 5 blocks feeling like I was in a gossamer dream and went right in and saw all the books and decorations that reminded me it was Xmas and the English lady was there and she looked surprized and discordant to see me and I asked if the white-haired guy was around and she said you must mean Otto and I said yes if that is his name and she went to fetch him and he came out of the back room and I told them both *how they must hasten to come with me that I had something awesome to show them and I guess they could see how aroused I was because Otto told the young guy with all the tatoos who was at the desk near the door to watch the store and then they followed me into the gloomy night.*

Otto kept telling me to calm down but I could not and when we got to the construction site Otto said to the English lady Sally to wait on the street but I said no she had to come to see what I had done and she said ok and Otto held her hand because the ground had much irregularity and depression from all the construction.

Then we were there and my heart was thumping in my chest and I took the rocks off and started scrapping the dirt away with my shaking hands and Otto asked what are you doing? but I just kept going and then you could see the trunk and I got really aroused and had to rip the tape asunder to get it off but once I did I stopped because it was a rapturous moment and I remembered the line I had memorized and bespoke it

Arise! Did I not bid they arise?

Otto and Sally stared at me with discordant looks and then I did it! I took the top off! and there was the wretched guy! Groaning and filed with agony! and whiter than the sheet of paper upon which I write these words but alive!

Otto and Sally looked truly vexed and impetuous but Otto helped the Korean man out of the box. He was trembeling and pitiful looking and Otto tried to calm him down and I saw Sally was getting her cel phone out but it was ok because I had made a discovery! A man could be entombed for 2 nights and live so the world should know and praize my endeavor and when the police came I did not put up a fight I just went into the car with them.

The End

I sent my story to the one person I was sure would like it, the white-haired guy Otto and he wrote back asking if he could publish it in this book he did every year about true crime. He said he was going to use the magazine article written by the guy who interviewed me and would publish my story along with it, which was awesome because that way people would get to hear my side. Otto said there would be about twenty stories in the book and I'd have my name on mine but he couldn't pay me because it was illegal to make money from a crime, though I still say it wasn't like a real crime but that was okay because the idea of having my tale in a book with twenty others was awesome and Otto promised I could have ten copies to give my friends though the only person I could think of was Larry and maybe the man from the deli so that he would understand what I was trying to do. It gets pretty boring in here so I'm looking forward to the book and reading my tale and the others too. I hope there will be some good ones that will appeal to my sensitive nature and maybe even inspire me.

What's in a Name?

By Mary Higgins Clark

It is December 18th, a cold, blustery day but signs of the holiday season are everywhere including within The Mysterious Bookshop. Just inside the door a life-sized Santa Claus is sprawled in an armchair. I'll be surprised if someone doesn't trip over his glistening boots before the afternoon is over.

I am Lexey Smith: single, thirty-two, a former trapeze artist who decided a couple of years ago that flying through the air might one day hurtle me to a forced landing so I decided to quit while I was ahead. I am average height, have blue eyes, even features and natural blonde hair. I am considered attractive. My friends point out that I have one serious fault. Because of grabbing my partner's hands as we met in mid-air hundreds of feet above the stage, I have a strong handshake; in fact, it's been called bone-crushing. I am trying to remedy that shortcoming.

Two years ago I was hired to coach the superstar Amanda Mays for her role in a movie about trapeze artists. We became great friends and she talked about me during her publicity tour and how I wrote funny stories about our collaboration on my website.

Bless Amanda. Thanks to her, my website has become very popular. Every day I write an article on any subject at all. I never thought of myself as a writer but love being one and have picked up some very good sponsors.

Except for my reason for being here, none of these personal details has anything to do with the events I am about to share with you. However, I have learned that most readers like to have at least a brief sense of the appearance and background of the narrator.

The Mysterious Bookshop is located in Tribeca, the section of lower Manhattan which is a mecca for celebrities and would-be celebrities. Always an avid mystery reader, since I moved into the neighborhood I have become a regular customer of the shop and therefore something of a friend to the proprietor, Otto Penzler, who today is bustling about with a broad grin on a face framed by a shock of thick white hair.

As I have come to observe in these past months, Otto is not always smiling, but one of the sights that will give him the look of a four-year-old on Christmas morning is having a best-selling author within the premises and the cash register jingling as eager fans rush to buy his or her latest book and get it autographed.

Today's event is really special. It began at noon and has been going on for three solid hours. I know because I've been here ever since Alvirah Meehan, the author, followed by her husband Willy, got out of her limo and greeted her cheering and clapping admirers.

Surely you have heard about Alvirah Meehan, the cleaning woman who won forty million dollars in the lottery five years ago, then became a columnist for the *New York Globe* and turned her attention to solving crimes. As an amateur sleuth she has no peer. She also heads an organization which helps lottery winners to avoid the pitfalls of instant wealth—which happens to too many of them. The examples are legion: The guy who bought a white elephant hotel in Maine, the one who went to jail because he forgot to pay income tax on his winnings, the dozens who got swept up in Ponzi schemes.

Now Alvirah has another feather in her cap. Her new book, *From Pots to Plots*, is a national bestseller, even having hit number one on the *New York Sunday Times* list, which is no mean feat, if you ask me. Otto Penzler is her old friend and he asked her to do a signing today because he said her book would make a great Christmas gift, which indeed I am very sure is the case. She had already signed it here in the spring when it first came out.

I admit I've been feeling really down and even the prospect of being with Alvirah hasn't helped. My beloved grandmother, Nana, died three months ago and, since my mother now lives in Chicago, the dreary task of clearing out the house in the east Bronx where she lived for the last sixty of her eighty years fell entirely to me. I've been at it for the last ten days.

Nana was interested in everything and in particular she loved animals, birds, and fish. She was loaded with allergies and never could have a live-in pet but was passionate about anything that flew, walked, swam or crawled. As a result, over the years, her small two-bedroom house became crammed, stacked, bursting—you choose the word—with magazines and books and pictures of any and all of the above. When I started throwing out the magazines and books I was surprised at how many of them had tabs on pages where she'd circled a paragraph or two. God only knows why.

Nana bought stuffed versions of her current favorite creatures and kept them all. For example, she had four Lassie dogs in various sizes, one of which cost me two stitches on my forehead when I was ten. I hadn't realized it was in the bathtub when I turned on the faucets. When I got in the tub I realized I was bathing with what appeared to be a hairy bloated monster. Shrieking, I jumped up, dove to safety, and cut my head on the toilet seat.

But it is definitely thanks to Nana I became a mystery buff. Nana loved to read and especially adored mysteries. When other grandmothers were reading *Winnie the Pooh* to their little darlings, Nana was introducing me to Nancy Drew and Edgar Allan Poe.

It was about twenty years ago, after she retired, that Nana decided that she could write better suspense novels than most

of the ones she was reading and that, with her crime background, she would be a bestselling author in no time. Did I
mention that for forty-two years Nana worked in the Bronx
County courthouse? Her job was escorting prisoners back and
forth from the holding cell to the courtroom.

She attacked her new goal with single-minded dedication
and, as often as not when I phoned, the message on the answering machine was: "Writer at work. Sorry to miss you. Will
return call when possible."

To keep an eye on her, my mother and I visited regularly. In-
evitably we'd find her in the second bedroom, now converted
to her writing office, clattering away on her typewriter. Yes, I
said typewriter. A huge Webster's dictionary was on one side
of her feet, a thesaurus and books of quotations on the other.
Behind her, boxes of apparently discarded pages were piled
haphazardly. Dresser drawers, too stuffed to close, were
loaded with hundreds of typed pages held together by rubber
bands. Brimming file folders competed for space with thick
manila envelopes on top of Nana's old-fashioned vanity.

About ten years ago, to our consternation, we saw a growing pile of bulky self-addressed, stamped packages begin to
pile up on the floor of the closet. It was obvious to us that
Nana was submitting to agents or publishers regularly and
being just as regularly rejected. I swear—I think with few exceptions her only outings in those last years were her trips to
the post office to mail her new effort.

Despite our pleading, she never let my mother or me read a
word of anything she wrote. When we hinted how discourag-
ing it must be for her to work so hard without any success,
she briskly assured us that no one with her knowledge of the
court system would go unnoticed forever and, besides, she had
a brilliant concept that someday some editor would have the
brains to appreciate.

My tentative suggestion that, as a mystery buff myself, I
might help her in some way was turned down flat. She was
going to become famous on her own and that was that and
when she became famous we would share in her glory. She

also made us swear that, if she didn't become successful before her death, we were to load every single sheet of paper, whether loose or in files or packages, into garbage bags without reading a single word of them and throw them all out.

Yesterday the Goodwill van arrived to collect whatever was worth giving away. I'd already moved her treasured hutch with her own grandmother's set of china to my apartment as well, of course, as family photographs and other small memorabilia. By then I'd gotten rid of everything in the house except for the products of Nana's creativity. Today is trash pick-up day on her block so this morning, before I came here, I went back to her house for the last time.

I scooped everything she'd ever written into eight of those big black garbage bags, even closing my eyes sometimes to avoid reading a word of type. However, I couldn't avoid noticing the titles on some of the manuscripts or the fact that she'd been using noms de plume. When I realized how she'd chosen those names I laughed out loud. It was so like her.

Then I dragged the trash bags and put them out on the curb. I was crying when I did it.

Back to the present. I've already read Alvirah's book and it is very entertaining. Each chapter tells the story of a crime she solved, starting with the episode in a spa where someone tried to kill her because he knew she was beginning to suspect he was a serial killer.

In a funny way Alivirah reminds me of Nana. She has such a kind face. She's a little plump, just the way Nana was, and has red hair which she joked about because she said when she used to dye it herself the result was bright orange. Nana dyed her own hair coal black which we could never convince her that at eighty was a bit much.

I don't think I told you that before Alvirah began signing, Otto asked her to say a few words to her fans. She spoke for about ten minutes, telling a little about her early life as a cleaning woman and then winning the lottery and becoming a columnist and how much she enjoyed helping to solve crimes. Then people in the audience asked her questions about her writing schedule, and if she ever got writer's block, and how much editing she did before she turned in a manuscript.

I have to tell you that sitting there listening to Alvirah's answers, I had tears in my eyes. I could just see Nana answering those questions if she'd been a successful author.

Then Otto said, cheerfully, that they had time for just one more question. "There's a   long   line   so   we'd   better   get started." He looked around from side to side. "You," he said, pointing to a timid-looking middle-aged man who had been taking copious notes of every word Alvirah uttered.

The man looked thrilled that he had been called on. Wide-eyed, he cleared his throat. "Mrs. Meehan, is there *any* unsolved crime that you would love to solve?" he asked.

"You bet there is," Alvirah said, "and Otto certainly would like someone to solve it. Right, Otto?"

The smile disappeared from Otto's face. He shook his head sadly. "Just in case somebody hasn't heard, you tell what happened, Alvirah.," he said. "It still upsets me too much to talk about it."

"It was nine years ago, right here in The Mysterious Bookshop," Alvirah began. . . "It was a major event. Rufus Barbanacle, the only living writer even approaching the genius of Edgar Allan Poe, was here on this very spot signing the newly published classic edition of his first book. He had not written one in five years. But that day, to the delight and shock of his admirers, and of course particularly Otto, he held up a manila envelope and announced that after he finished the signing, he was going to deliver the manuscript of his new book to his publisher.

"I was here," Alvirah continued, shaking her head at the memory. "Even before we struck it rich, I loved to read mysteries and in particular I was devoted to anything Rufus Barbanackle wrote. Well, when Rufus opened the envelope and held up the first few handwritten pages everybody began to cheer. It has taken these five years to tell this story,' he said. 'It is my finest piece of writing. It is my masterpiece.'"

I gulped. Oh, Nana, I thought. If only people thought of you as having written a masterpiece.

"Otto, you tell the rest of the story," Alvirah encouraged.

His voice heavy with emotion, Otto said, "It is not unusual at autographing events that would-be authors try to persuade a celebrity author to read their own unpublished manuscripts. When that happens, most authors graciously explain that they cannot read unpublished material because someone might later accuse them of stealing ideas. However Rufus Bar- banackle, brilliant though he was, was notoriously rude and brusque when that kind of request was made."

Otto was unable to go on. "Alvirah," he said, "I can't talk about it. I get too choked up."

"Otto, just try," Alvirah encouraged. "I had already left when you realized what had happened."

"I'll try." In a husky voice Otto told the rest of the story. "When the signing was over, Rufus left to meet his editor. An hour later, he and his editor, Madge Marshall, who inciden- tally is also Alvirah's editor, arrived back here, both in a state of hysteria and shock. Rufus was carrying a manila envelope, a duplicate of the one which contained his final book. But his handwritten masterpiece was not there and he had never made a copy of it. . Instead there was a typed novel that to quote Madge, "after reading two pages I can categorically state that this is the worst drivel I've ever read in my thirty- five years of editing."

"I always try to spot anyone trying to give a manuscript to my celebrity author," Otto continued, defensively, "but the line was so long, I had to go outside and ask the people on it not to block the intersection."

"Well, surely, whoever wrote it left an address or phone number," the timid man protested.

"There was a note from the author stating that she knew Rufus Barbanacle's editor was Madge Marshall and she'd call her the next week to discuss her novel. Our guess is that she was smart enough to know that was the one way she might get Madge to even look at her manuscript. She never did call and if she took Rufus's manuscript by mistake, she never returned it. All efforts to locate her came to nothing. She, and the manuscript, vanished into thin air."

By now it was clear to me that Otto would never recover from his guilt that the priceless manuscript had been lost under his nose.

"And that is the mystery I'd like to solve," Alvirah concluded. "Now we had better get to the signing. The people waiting outside will be freezing."

And so for these three hours I sat listening to how much people loved Alvirah's book. Many of them had already read it but bought multiple other copies for their friends for holiday presents. One woman said she'd been feeling so down because in this economy her husband had lost his job, but reading Alvirah's memoir made her brighten up and realize that things can change in a heartbeat.

All the while I kept thinking if only Nana had had a day like this with everyone telling her how much they enjoyed her work. Finally the last book had been signed. While his assistants took care of any customers who drifted in, Otto pulled up chairs around the autograph table and opened a bottle of champagne.

Otto, Alvirah's husband Willy (who is the image of Tip O'Neil, the late Speaker of the House and one of the nicest men I've ever met) and I toasted Alvirah. "We not only sold every one of your books we had in stock but took orders for more," Otto announced happily. Clearly he'd put the loss of the Rufus Barbanacle manuscript out of his mind.

"Alvirah's signings are all like this," Willy announced. "I'm so proud of her."

As we began to sip the champagne, Alvirah, who is that friendly kind of person who is interested in everyone said, "It's nice of you to write about me for your website, Lexey. Since we made this date I've been checking the website every day and you are a talented storyteller. Does anyone else in your family write?"

When Alvirah asks a question, you really get the feeling that she wants to know the answer. Before I knew it, I was telling her how Nana decided that she could be a successful writer and spent twenty years writing novels and enduring rejection slips all that time and yet she never gave up.

"The number of unpublished writers is beyond belief," Otto commented, "but publishing is a tough field and then, once in a while, an unknown gets sprinkled with star dust."

"Where did your grandmother live?" Willy asked.

"In the Bronx. She loved it there. She got so mad at people who made fun of it."

"They make fun of Queens, too, and that's where Alvirah and I grew up," Willy said. "What kind of books did she write?"

"Mysteries. Always mysteries." And then I explained that she never, ever, let my mother or me read them and that just today I had fulfilled my final promise to her, that I would throw out all of them without reading a single word.

"Some of them were still in manila envelopes," I said. "My guess is that she didn't feel they were ready to submit. Others were in the usual self-addressed stamped envelopes. God knows how many times she sent them out, or maybe it was only once. We don't know."

"What was your grandmother's name?" Alvirah asked.

"Her name was Annie Dowling." Then I laughed, the kind of laugh you give when it would be easier to cry. "I think she must have heard that when agents or editors see a name that they recognize as someone who isn't saleable, they don't even open the package or read the first page. From the dates on the returned envelopes, it looks to me as though, eight or nine years ago, Nana began using noms de plume."

"A lot of them try that," Otto said. "Sometimes it works."

"Nana had a vivid imagination," I said. "When I was putting all of them in the garbage bags this morning, I realized that she was mixing up the first and last names of famous writers as her pen names."

I felt the atmosphere around the table suddenly change. It was like Alvirah and Otto had been hit by lightening. What's the matter with them? I wondered nervously.

"Do you remember any of the names?" Alvirah asked quickly.

I felt as though something was terribly wrong. I could hardly think.

"Let's see," I stammered. "One of them was Daphne Collins. I figure she was combining Daphne du Maurier and Wilkie Collins. One was Stephen M. H. Clark and my guess is that was a combination of Stephen King and Mary Higgins Clark. Another one. . . ."

I stopped. Otto's breath was labored. Alvirah was staring at him. "Otto," she said. "The name on the manuscript that was substituted for Barbanacel"

They said it together. "Daphne Bronte."

"Did you see a manuscript with that name on it?" Otto shouted as he jumped up knocking over his glass of champagne. It broke on the table and spattered all over his jacket but he didn't seem to notice.

"No," I stammered again, trying to remember, "but I did see one by Bronte Poe so maybe…" Then I became defensive. "My Nana never stole anything in her life. If Rufus Barbanackle had been insulting about her manuscript, and she picked up the wrong one by mistake, I know she probably was so hurt she just put it aside with the rejected ones."

"I'm sure that's true," Alvirah said, "but Lexey, if she did accidentally take it, you said you threw out all your Nana's manuscripts this morning. Where did you throw them?"

I was so upset I could hardly form the words. "In the trash," I whispered.

"What time is pick-up in Nana's neighborhood?" Otto's voice was hoarse and trembling even more than mine.

"They get to Nana's block pretty late," I said. Oh, my God, I thought, did poor Nana take Rufus Barbanacle's manuscript by mistake and, if so, was it now on its way to a landfill?

"Let's go," Otto shouted.

The limo Alvirah's publisher had provided was waiting outside. Seconds later the four of us, Alvirah, Willy, Otto and myself, were diving into it. Otto jumped in the front seat with the driver.

"Going out to dinner, Mrs. Meehan?" the driver asked amiably.

"No!" Otto screamed. "We're going to the Bronx."

Seated in the back, Alvirah, Willy and I didn't say a word. I'm sure that, like me, they were praying that if what we suspected was true, we wouldn't be too late.

Otto, on the other hand, kept frantically urging the driver to step on the gas as, battling holiday traffic, we crawled up the West Side Highway, inched our way along the Henry Hudson Parkway then, beyond frustration, limped along the Cross Bronx Expressway. "Do you enjoy being parked?" he barked. "Try that lane. Don't let that guy cut in front of you. Where did you learn to drive, or did you?"

Along the way Alvirah got the idea of phoning the Sanitation Department to see if someone there could make contact with the truck in Nana's neighborhood and, if it wasn't too late, instruct them to leave her garbage intact. She never did make contact with any living person. "Press One for. . .Press Two for. . .press three for. . ."You know how that works, especially if you want to report trouble with your phone or television. Alvirah finally gave up.

It was six-thirty and it started to snow just as we turned off Morris Park

Avenue onto Lurting Avenue. Even though it was dark I knew her house would be the only one on the block that wouldn't have a wreath on the door or a Christmas tree showing through the living room window.

She had lived in the last house of the long block. The driver didn't need Otto's instructions to "floor it." We could all see the outline of a huge garbage truck parked near the corner. "They're at Nana's house," I screamed and grabbed the door handle. It was dark but because of all the lighted Christmas trees on the nearby lawns I could make out that there was a man dragging heavy black garbage bags down the driveway. Then I saw another guy standing behind the truck and hoisting a bag to throw into its grinding mouth.

I used to fly through the air with the greatest of ease but I never moved faster than I did at that moment. I leaped out of the limo as it screeched to a halt and sailed across the driveway. As the sanitation worker lifted the bag over his head I lunged for it and caught it in midair. That crushing handshake my friends complain about were the reason I was able to hang onto the bag inches from certain destruction. The weight of the bag was so great that I lost my balance and went sprawling on the curb.

"Lady, are you nuts?" the sanitation guy demanded as he stood over me. By then, Otto, Alvirah, and Willy were on the scene. As Willy helped me up, Otto demanded to know if any of the bags had been thrown in the truck.

"No, this was the first. Do you want to play catch with the rest of them?" the worker asked and, without waiting for an answer, climbed into the cab of the truck and it rumbled off.

"Lexey, have you got the key to your grandmother's house?" Otto asked. "We can dump all this stuff out and just take the Barbanacle manuscript if it's here."

"I have the key," I said, "but the electricity was turned off today."

"That means we'll have to go through these bags somewhere else," Alvirah said practically. "I've got an idea. I know Madge was planning to work late, then go to the office Christmas party. When I tell her that we may have Rufus's manuscript, I'm sure she'd let us bring all these bags down to her big conference room and go through them there."

As I think you will remember, Madge Mitchell, who is Alvirah's editor, also represents Rufus Barbanacle.

Alvirah dialed Madge and when she answered began, "Madge, I know you're probably on your way to your office but. . ."

When she said that Barbanacle's manuscript may have been found, we could hear Madge screeching through the phone. "Forget the party. I'll have a bunch of people here to help hunt through the bags and—do you realize what this means to the company if it turns out to be true that we've located a massive bestseller?"

Otto, Alvirah, Willy, the limo driver and I quickly loaded the bags into the limo. Two of them didn't fit in the trunk, so Otto had one on his lap in the front and Willy, Alvirah and I kept our feet dangling over another one in the back seat.

An hour later we were in Madge Mitchell's conference room on East 56th Street. True to her word, she had four other people waiting to help with the search. They dumped one bag at a time on each end of the table, rapidly tossing aside pages on the floor.

I felt sadder and sadder as I watched them. It seemed like a desecration of Nana's years of work, but at the same time I was scared they wouldn't find the Barbanacle manuscript because I knew they were sure Nana had been the one to take it.

Every once in a while, someone would read the pen name Nana had used, like "Rendell James"—short, as one of them pointed out, for Ruth Rendell and P.D. James. Even in their haste, they all got a chuckle out of that.

We were all pretty nervous by the time the seventh bag was opened and the lost manuscript still hadn't been found. Then Otto grabbed the last trash bag and turned it upside down. A jumble of manila envelopes both unmarked and self-addressed fell out. Otto began ripping them open to see the contents and then suddenly pulled some handwritten pages out of one of them and let out a victory cry that resonated, I'm sure, through all of Manhattan.

"It's here," he shouted gleefully. "It's here! We've found it! It's here!" He held up the pages for everyone to see, then kissed them.

Everyone began clapping and jumping up and down. Madge rushed to the phone to call Rufus Barbanacle, then remembered he never answered his phone after six p.m., but left him a delirious message which, I'm sure, absolutely made his day when he finally heard it.

I realized how tired I was and how seeing again all the products of Nana's years of hard work had really broken my heart. But there was one thing I was sure of. I had made a promise to Nana to throw out her novels and I had kept my promise. But fate hadn't intended them to be thrown out and I was going to store them in the big closet of my apartment even if I kept my promise to never read them.

I looked at Madge Mitchell. "Before we go, I'd like to have all my grandmother's things put back in these bags and, if you don't mind cluttering up your conference room until tomorrow, I'll come by with some friends to collect them."

I could tell from her expression that she thought I was crazy but she was very nice about it. "Absolutely." She opened one of the trash bags and began to fill it herself.

"Something else," I said. "Do you still have the manuscript my grandmother left by mistake, the one I think you said was drivel?"

I will say Madge looked uncomfortable. "Yes, I do. Of course I didn't know where to send it and besides we hoped that somehow we'd still be able to trace the author and see if she had the Barbanacle manuscript. It's in a file in my office."

She darted into her office and came right back with it. As I suspected, it was in exactly the same size manila envelope as the Barbanacle one and neither one was marked on the outside. I pointed that out to everyone. "I'll take this one with me," I said. "Sorry my grandmother caused so much trouble."

Alvirah stopped me at the door and reached out her hand. "Lexey, would you mind if I read it?" she asked. "From everything you've told me, your grandmother had a marvelous imagination."

I was going to refuse but, looking into Alvirah's face and the kind interest in her eyes, I knew I wanted her to see it. And I swear it was as though I could hear Nana saying, "Give it to her, Lexey. Go ahead. Give it to her."

So I did.

The Mysterious Bookshop—One Year Later

Once again I am sitting in The Mysterious Bookshop. This time I'm the one doing the signing. Alvirah is sitting next to me because she's going to write a column about me for her newspaper.

It turned out that when Alvirah took Nana's manuscript home, she sat up all night reading it and absolutely loved it. First thing the next morning she called Madge and asked her how much of the book she had actually read because the story was so wonderful.

"Alvirah, it starts with a woman cop in a Bronx courthouse discussing her problems with a talking fish," Madge protested.

"But that's the fun of it. Between them they solve the crime," Alvirah said.

On Alvirah's say-so, Madge read Nana's book and enjoyed it. Then she decided to take a chance and publish it. The initial printing of two thousand copies came out in June. I was so proud for Nana but get this! Her book is now in its twentieth printing and has sold over one million copies.

Of course, Madge then read every other word we found in those trash bags. It's just incredible but Nana had completed twenty-two other novels. In each one of them, her main character, Daisy, the courtroom cop, has a different talking pet who works with Daisy to solve a crime. Sometimes, like the first one, it's a fish. Other times, it may be an animal or a bird or even an insect.

The other novels will be published, one every six months. This is the second time I've signed her first book in The Mysterious Bookshop but Otto was right when he said it would make a great Christmas present. The line is long and he is very happy.

I am too. I feel as though Nana is sitting here beside me glowing in all the wonderful things people are saying about her book. Incidentally, half the money my mother and I receive from Nana's royalties will go to places like the Animal Rescue League and zoos and aquariums and bird sanctuaries. She'd like that.

A final note. Rufus Barbanackle's last book, his so-called masterpiece, was a dud. Nobody liked it. He'd have been better off if it had stayed lost. It's so mean of me but I can't help being delighted about that.

And now you know all about what's been happening lately in The Mysterious Bookshop. Merry Christmas to each and every one of you from Nana and me.